girl

flees

circus

LYNN AND LYNDA MILLER SOUTHWEST FICTION SERIES
LYNN C. MILLER AND LYNDA MILLER, SERIES EDITORS

This series showcases novels, novellas, and story collections
that focus on the Southwestern experience. Often underrepresented
in American literature, Southwestern voices provide unique and
diverse perspectives to readers exploring the region's varied landscapes
and communities. Works in the series range from traditional
to experimental, with an emphasis on how the landscapes and cultures
of this distinct region shape stories and situations and
influence the ways in which they are told.

GIRL FLEES CIRCUS

a novel

C. W. SMITH

University of New Mexico Press   Albuquerque

ISBN 978-0-8263-6407-4 (paper)
ISBN 978-0-8263-6408-1 (electronic)

LIBRARY OF CONGRESS CONTROL NUMBER: 2022936833

Founded in 1889, the University of New Mexico sits on the traditional home-
lands of the Pueblo of Sandia. The original peoples of New Mexico—Pueblo,
Navajo, and Apache—since time immemorial have deep connections to the
land and have made significant contributions to the broader community state-
wide. We honor the land itself and those who remain stewards of this land
throughout the generations and also acknowledge our committed relationship
to Indigenous peoples. We gratefully recognize our history.

COVER ILLUSTRATION Gabrielle Hill
DESIGNED BY Mindy Basinger Hill
COMPOSED IN 11/14.5 pt Adobe Jenson Pro,
Fonseca Regular, and Mina Regular

CONTENTS

arrival

1

THE AVIATRIX'S BRAND-NEW MONIKER WAS SKIPPY BAKER. She'd dropped it on a farmer whose field she'd landed in last evening, but she'd considered others—Marvella Gold, Harriet Harley, say, or Betty, uh, Armhart? The name had to shine like a screen star's billing but not sound made up. Tinkering with names was a pleasant pastime while she piloted the Travel Air through a clear, mild morning over stretches of West Texas. She'd never seen such open country lidded by that vast a sky, and the craft ate it up. With the railroad map spread on her lap and the twin shining rails two thousand feet below guiding her as sure as a compass, she sailed past Abilene just after noon, pleased to gain confidence in the airplane, getting to know its in-flight quirks. She knew the specs by heart—where some girls might scribe the name of a crush in diaries over and over, she sketched views of the fuselage from all angles. She admired the aircraft beyond all reason, and on this third day out the vibrations of the Wright Whirlwind 9-cylinder radial coursed through her veins like whiskey shots. Soon you'll be a crackerjack pilot, claimed Curly, and she could remember his grin and the two thumbs up when she'd done her first solo. (All before squeezing her heart like a marshmallow in his fist.)

But those railroad tracks ran out on both the map and earth. All on the compass now. The day went hot, the air boisterous and rowdy, and the craft turned from a bird into a butterfly—no more straight ahead, steady-as-she-goes, but up and down and sideways, a leap over here and another over there like a drunken dancer, then a wave upending her nose into a stall like a boxer taking an uppercut to the chin. A sudden elevatored downdraft drop put her stomach in her throat and a fist of fear clutched her heartbeats.

And what had begun as a smudge like a bruise on the horizon now pushed rudely at her as she fought to keep the aircraft on a heading.

Uh-oh. Curly, regaling compañeros about these big burly storms out here. Like an ugly dirty iceberg in the sky, and you've lost your gee-dee paddle and the current's rushing you right into it—you can't go over 'cause it's just too darn tall some of them 40,000 feet, and too damned pardon my French honey wide to go around, so's yer lookin at how the bottom of that black mass seems nice and level and flat at about seven eight thousand or so and you're figgerin on just sort of gliding under it, but what you don't know is the updraft on those monsters can suck your little crate right up into its dark black heart and zoom you up like a scrap a paper in a whirlwind and spit you out way over whatever ceiling the specs on your craft might claim, air too darned thin to fly in or to breathe and next thing you know you're blacking out and the little coffin that's wrapped around you's headed straight down, and if you're lucky you'll wake up soon enough to pull out and keep the nose from digging a twenty-foot hole in Mother Earth.

Taking quick glimpses of the map she tried to pair something on the paper with its like below, but instead of landmarks, nameless gullies and miles and miles of cruelly featureless plain. No hills, mountains, highways, railroads, rivers, or lakes, only the seemingly endless and threatening sky looming ahead.

She'd never encountered a storm this huge—the ugly dark strato-cewm-you-loahs like Himalayan peaks shooting up to she couldn't guess the elevation, impossible to top them—the craft officially had a ceiling of 16,000 feet, and just like Curly said the air there was far too thin to breathe, and besides, oxygen hadn't made the list of things snatched up in her hasty departure. Oh, this son-of-a-biscuit-eating storm—was it a tornado?? It might tear the ship apart, and she didn't know whether to try for a forced wild landing on unknown ground and wreck or get herself ripped to shreds aloft. *Oh, why oh why!! You stupid little crud knuckle! You thought you could do this? What would Curly say or do? Hang on?*

Her hands might've shaken had they not been welded tight to the stick. Then the headwind came hard at her and not even that big J5 could do much more than suspend the ship as it shoved against the front, marking time mid-air, rain pelted her windscreen and drenched her, the airplane shook and shuddered, dipped and see-sawed side to side, and it was only by the keychain Curly had hung from a knob on the panel that she knew she was right-side up. It was crucial to keep the wings level and the craft from turning without her knowing, but lost inside the horrendous rain without horizon or ground to judge by, she had to trust the turn indicator and her altimeter to stay aloft and true. Curly said he knew a pilot strapped a half-full pint of whisky to the panel as a level and when sloshing turned it useless, he drank it. *Watch your tach and air speed—if the speed goes down but the engine revs up, you're likely heading uphill, if your tach backs off and your air speed jumps, you're probably in a dive. If the wind in the struts start to whine and sing, you need to pull her up or look for a hole in the cloud floor to dive into.*

The blithering snot-booger rain turned into stinging flecks of hail—would it tear holes in the wings and elevator? Would she go down like a tattered kite? The upper wing shielded her a bit, but the prop wash peppered her with pellets of ice, and she was shivering terribly in her coveralls.

Holy malarkey, oh my dear Heavenly Father! Please let me live through this! If you do, I'll . . . turn myself in!

The storm pummeled her on and on, she wrestled it like busting a bronc, and when at last she spied a glimmer in the west she figured she'd fought her way to the backside. Within minutes the air was sweet and calm and clear, cooler now from the rain, water on the wings and the windscreen glistening. Her breathing slowed, though she still trembled, and she banked right and left a bit to prove she was master now. Soon the air was friendly enough that she took big sloppy slugs from her water jug and ate an apple the farmer had blessed her with this morning. Then she unleashed her harness, wriggled free of her bottoms, and jammed her pee-pot underneath her.

Resettled, she squared her shoulders. The storm was all behind her. She sighed, deep, swiped her goggles with her sleeve, settled back into her pilot's posture. She was drenched but knew the warming air would dry her. Her compass showed that despite the tumbling and pitching, she still roughly hewed a southwesterly line. All seemed if not well at least a lot better. In fact, darned if she didn't feel a little bit, well, *proud* now! A story she could tell in the hanger lounge. Beat a big storm and lived to tell about it!

As for the promise in the prayer—well, all the danger wasn't over, right? And so didn't her contract with the Lord include safety clear to Los Angeles? If you promise if I live through "this," who's to say what the length or breadth or depth of "this" is?

She looked down to read the map.

Gone! Flat blew out of her lap!

A frisson of fear zapped her nerves, but she slapped it back. That railroad map wouldn't be much help now, anyway. The flat terrain still lay as featureless as before—just a big brown table studded here and there with stunted trees. The dash clock showed she'd been aloft a little over six hours. The ship boasted a range of 650 miles on 67 gallons, but that depended upon cruising constantly at 103, and though she'd pushed the craft along earlier, having bucked the head wind through the storm made it impossible to calculate how far she'd gone and how far she had to go before her next check point, Pecos, Texas.

The fuel gauge needle was tickling the Empty bar.

Also, she was running out of afternoon. In all that trackless waste a half mile beneath her wheels, could she spot a stretch suitable for putting down? But then what? She might as well set down in the Amazon, where the last thing the natives might offer would be a barrel of high-test gasoline. Here, unless someone saw her alight (or crash), she'd have no notion of which way to walk or how far. Cowboys might one day ride up on her desiccated corpse. Headline in the paper: GIRL FLEES CIRCUS! And below—*Bones Found in Desert.*

It wasn't like her to take the gloomy prospect when a sunny one lay handy. But that native cheerful outlook got sorely chafed as the miles rolled on without any sign of habitation; meanwhile, that needle got tired of tickling the Empty bar and just laid its head down on it like a pillow.

Just when hope became a frayed rope about to part, she spotted a thin, meandering road hardly wider than a wagon trail going south, so she banked low to follow it. She took heart that the ruts were well-worn and clean of weeds She sailed over a truck trundling north against her flow, and the dust plume off the wheels scurried sideways and showed the wind was westerly. Within minutes, just as the engine hiccupped once, on the horizon up popped several buildings lined beside the road, and a bit to the west, what looked to be a wooden oil derrick. That might mean fuel! Guess the Lord had no quarrel with her quibbling about the terms!

She chanced one quick low pass over the settlement to check for obstacles in the only street—it was empty—and she read the plume of exhaust from the drilling rig's engine like a wind sock: she'd be landing with a cross wind, a stiff one maybe, and she'd have to sideslip the craft to keep it on that narrow line, all the harder when the sputtering engine would be little help. She banked and turned and came in from the south. Her luck had held! Not just a place to safely land but also maybe she'd get fuel, supper, and a bed—she was suddenly bone-tired and utterly drained, and she eagerly anticipated rolling to a stop and climbing down to stretch and . . .

Damnation! A Model T rolled out into the street and wheeled right into her path. She yanked the stick back and hoped she had speed enough to hop the thing without stalling—

2

MABEL WAS SORELY SHAMED HER AUTO CAUSED THE ACCIDENT with the airplane. Her father had bought her the Ford Model T "Tin Lizzy" back in '24 never dreaming she'd use it to move herself all the way from Cincinnati to somewhere way out West. Her mother feared she'd wind up with a cowpoke and never come back. Besides, everything there must be so *primitive.* Lying, she assured them she had electricity and didn't mention that a lack of plumbing meant she had to do her business in an outhouse behind the church/school along with her students and whatever town folk found themselves beyond reach of their own privies.

She'd claimed this post would only be a year. She didn't tell them it was on the way to farther west. (When she'd heard Al Jolson sing "California, Here I Come" something swoony crept over her like a cozy blanket. Palm trees, oranges big as softballs, and ocean waves—lots of ocean waves—swarmed behind her eyelids.)

And yet now she was about to start her third school year. The Golden State's beckoning call had faded, and less often she insisted to herself that she wasn't marking time or just saving up to go. That first year was rough, though. The "school board"—a dozen ranchers, farmers, and merchants who'd pooled their money for her salary—had put her up in what they hilariously called "a cottage" but was hardly more than a lean-to attached to the hip of the settlement's lone café. But even when some said pity she had to live in "a rebuilt pig pen," somebody pointed out that she'd turned down Arabella Bohanan's offer to lodge in her handsome Spanish hacienda.

When the board begged her to stay, they enticed her with a ream of outlandish compliments, higher pay, and better digs: everybody pitched in to knock up a cozy cabin alongside what was called "the church" due to a structure on its roof that might be a steeple or a miniature oil derrick. A service did take place first Sunday of every month when a preacher of any denomination would circuit by. Usually, though, pews were shoved against the walls to accommodate the dozen school desks or when folks had a yen to put on a rowdy hootenanny with a motley trio who played wash-tub bass, a "gittar," and a "fiddle," all three of whom distressed Mabel greatly with their nasal yodeling and habit of drooling "baccy" spit onto the wooden floors of her school room.

With a brilliant older brother and a gorgeous younger sister, she'd been the invisible middle child, the one least talked about and from whom the least was expected. She'd gone off to Stephens for two years without hardly a soul missing her. On Mabel's first visit back to Cincinnati after a year of teaching out West, her sister, recently debutante-ified, had badgered Mable to bob her hair and buy step-ins and an Empire-waist dress in an effort to slim down her bust and hips to comply with the current boyish fashions. Felicity also scolded her about being out in the sun so much—Mable's skin looked "like leather."

Out here, no hair stylist existed to maintain that fashionable bob; it grew into unruly bangs and page-boy curls then just a long mess draping over her shoulders that she dealt with the way women here did: pinned up in a bun, swirled into what might look like a cow patty atop her head, and tucked under a hat, or tied back with a comely ribbon. When they felt a need, the women cut their own or each other's hair with sewing scissors.

Surprises had held her here. One—she was far from invisible. She taught a dozen or so students ages eight to fifteen, and she was respected by almost all and even adored by a few. Her opinion on matters big and small was valued—she was an ambassador of a larger world, someone who'd been to college, had lived in an eastern city, owned books, could recite poetry by heart, practiced pretty penmanship, and by default inherited the traditional "schoolmarm" virtues of a superior moral sensibility and judgment, so people often sought her opinion.

Living here, she'd grown confident, felt her dormant self swell to fill the new, expanded borders of her life.

Why are you going back? Her baffled folks had asked that first visit home.

Sky. How do you talk about sky? And does it sound moonstruck daffy to even bring it up?? Illustrated-Bible sunrises and sunsets! Ohio had sky, of course, but it was like the ceiling of your parlor: imminently useful and ever-present but hardly ever noticed. Out here the sky was everywhere, and you lived in it as if a fish in an ocean of air. The settlement had but one building over one story, so nothing manmade obstructed your view of the heavens day or night. It had a hundred colors—from the deep lavender just after sunset and the later inky charcoal to the blistering white on a summer noon that peeled your eyeballs back. And at night—at night! Here on the plains deep after the sun lay down to sleep the sky asserted itself with a magnificent and admirable arrogance, strewing buckets of stars on an overhead screen, everything adazzle and alive. Make you gasp, reel, and brace yourself against the nearest solid object. It seduced her into studying—of all things! Who'd have thought?—astronomy.

And then the daytime sky had myriad moods, many weathers posted on the compass points of this great expanse—you'd note a thunderstorm on the far horizon marked by curtains of surly gray rain, while turn a tad to the north or south, and the horizon looked as serene as a preacher's wife.

Below the sky the terra was humble, scrub oak and sandy hillocks, mesquite thickets, native grasses—never an actual tree unless one had been planted—and the earth itself ruddy in the banks of arroyos where the water plumed and spumed, tumbling boulders when a rain did finally come.

And you could spook your back-home folks right good with tales of rattlers and tarantulas (*What's that? Well, a spider big as a* BASEBALL!), as well as coyotes, though they were as skittish as whipped dogs.

She'd considered learning to ride a horse but hadn't gotten to it. (Ditto hoist a firearm.) People didn't find that strange, anyway, since she owned and operated a motor vehicle. Her Lizzie was one of a half-dozen vehicles in the settlement, and she was generous about taking somebody to a doctor in Loving or the train station in Seagraves (and more than once a goat, a sheep, or a calf). Leonard had begged her to teach him to drive, and she'd been pleased to do that, though she'd foreseen the next step—his wanting to borrow it. (He argued he could make a trip for her, save her time and effort.)

Of course, folks back home were curious about her prospects. She kept mum because speaking of Leonard might raise eyebrows. To this point in her life, she'd never had a fellow fall be-smitten under her supposed spell. He had what they called a "crush," and that was endearing and flattering. Of course, he was too young at eighteen and too much like an eager puppy, but he was good-looking and sturdy, well-intentioned and full of curiosity. Pity Mabel was one of only a half-dozen unattached females of marrying age around. Cruel indeed how they called him "Lonesome Lennie" behind his back. His adoration and attention were hers to enjoy, even at the expense of a nagging guilt.

Normally she'd not be behind the wheel of her automobile on a late Saturday afternoon such as this, putting herself and that poor pilot in such mortal danger. But Louise Larsen had been upstairs above the Owl Café where Wally Jackson had finished reupholstering the seat of her one good parlor chair, and Louise had hinted to Mabel that it would be "lovely" to have Mabel come to supper, only she had to pick up her chair from Wally first. Louise was a dandy cook and Mabel wasn't, so giving Louise and her chair a ride home was a very fair exchange.

She'd heard a sputtering motor before she'd pulled out into the street, but she'd just presumed it came from that drilling contraption behind Roy Bentley's corral. She saw Otis step off the porch of the Owl to peer up the street, wide-eyed. She straightened the wheel and suddenly an aircraft hardly three feet off the ground was zooming right at her windscreen, looming like a threshing machine a giant had flung at her, and all she could do was shriek, slap her hands to her face, and turtle her head into her shoulders. She heard the wind in the wings as it swooped up to avoid a crash, the motor coughing, and luckily her own engine died else the auto would've driven itself right into the cafe's front door.

When she sat up, Leonard was wheeling past fast on his Hawthorne DeLuxe Streamline, chasing after the aircraft as it jittered on.

3

THE OLD SAW THAT IN A SMALL TOWN EVERYBODY KNOWS your business got a rigorous test in the West, where a contrary frontier law holds that nobody *asks* your business. Case in point was Otis Jefferson and Mildred ("Wally") Jackson. They ran the Owl Café—he cooked, she cleaned up, managed the cash and the provisions. Nobody knew if they were married, but their spacious upstairs abode was one long room stretched to the footprint of the building, and it had only one bed. Other useful furniture took up space, but just the bed figured into people's speculations.

Supposedly, he'd been a Buffalo Soldier in the US Cavalry in Texas after the Civil War and had been born a slave—they figured his age at sixty-something, but nobody could say he'd claimed that. Aside from cooking, he had a garage out back where he kept smithy's tools to shoe a horse or rim a wagon wheel. He owned an old GMC platform truck, new in 1915, and he made runs to Loving for gasoline that he sold to the hamlet's other motorists at a slim profit all considered fair. Lately, he'd done welding for the driller, brazing the seams of the casing as it was pounded into the ground, and he'd made one overnight trip to the train station in Seagraves to get cable for the job.

Wally was white and somewhat younger, thin-lipped and thin-hipped, with one eye that detoured on its way to seeing something (hence the nickname), and when she talked, you heard remnants of a long-gone accent that people couldn't place. Whether from temperament or their particular circumstance, they gripped their cards bosom-tight, and though Wally was talkative, she was never personal. Like almost all the women, she made many of her own clothes, though she seemed better at it than most and did odd jobs for others, such as putting new upholstery on Louise Larsen's parlor chair. Their community service included keeping the town's only public telephone. It was posted on the cafe's rear wall, and a side table stood there with a big pickle jar for honors-system users to drop coins into. Two other telephones were in the homes of outlying ranching families.

Now and then, Otis had "moods" whose arrivals and duration no one could account for. Sometimes, inexplicably, he might mutter, "Dark days, dark days," shaking his head. People suspected that his trips to Loving included a secret stop for a Mason jar of illegal hootch, but since he never howled at the moon or even raised his voice, it didn't matter, and he wasn't alone in sneaking a slug behind closed doors. The only lawman around was the sheriff at the county seat in Loving, who wouldn't rouse himself over such a trifle.

The Owl always closed after lunch, though lately they'd held off shutting down until that driller, Ralph Johnston, or his helper came to get sandwiches.

Otis had just taken off his apron and stepped out onto the porch to sit and smoke his pipe when the aircraft's engine caught his ear; he stepped into the street to locate it coming in low from the south, engine sputtering, and it had all the appearance of preparing to land on the one unpaved thoroughfare, but suddenly up popped Mabel's Lizzy square in its path. He gawked, cringing, but then the craft swooped up and over it—the word BEECH-NUT emblazoned in yellow on its silver flank—and toddled on north; he trotted farther into the road to watch it stagger away on the cross wind, slipping sideways, the engine sneezing it sounded like, emitting oily puffs of exhaust. Looked likely to crash.

4

LOUISE LARSEN WAS THE CLOSEST THING IN THE SETTLEMENT to a doctor. She'd grown up in Kansas City on the Kansas side near a veterinary office, and as an adolescent she'd hung about asking questions. The vet had taken such a shine he brought her on his calls to assist birthing calves and foals and lambs. Soon as the Big War broke out, an upswell of patriotism pushed her to enroll at the Illinois Nurses Training School attached to the new Cook County Hospital. Then she was a trainee at the Fort Sheridan Hospital #28 just as the first wave of injured from France arrived in 1919. Howard was a shellshock and mustard gas patient; she was by his side for two weeks and felt such pity that when he asked her to marry him, she had.

Then he revealed he was a widower whose wife had died of the Spanish flu while he was overseas and that his twelve-year-old daughter, Isabel (Izzy), then living with his sister in Indianapolis, would be joining their new family as they moved to New Mexico where the good clean air would help his lungs and the absence of threatening noises offered a peace that might soothe his tortured nerves.

That news stunned her. Aside from how he'd kept it from her (anything else?), that already half-grown daughter seriously scarred her dormant dreams about children of her own. How to jockey around this new development? She worked herself up to asking Howard had he thought of having more children. He chuckled nervously, vaguely waved a hand over his torso, and said, "One thing at a time, darling."

Did that mean getting well or raising Izzy?

Try as she might, Louise could not make Izzy like her—definitely not as a step- or surrogate mother, and Louise's efforts to be friend, big sister, aunt, or mentor were met with a rejection so dedicated it seemed inspired. Izzy only begrudgingly accepted Howard's authority. She had the worst disposition of any child Louise had ever met—a virtuoso saucebox, a world-class whiner, she hated *everything* about living out here. Louise was once tempted to sneer at Howard, *Are you sure your other wife is dead?* but flogged herself for such uncharitable thoughts. After all, the girl *had* indeed lost her mother and a home in a civilized place, etc.

Louise had farm wives' chores—they kept cows, a flock of laying hens, a couple of hogs and horses, a dog, and a sizeable patch of alfalfa, grain sorghum, and cotton, plus a kitchen garden. But she was also expected to school the girl. Before Mabel Cross was hired, people taught their children at home, or, if they had the money, sent them off to boarding school (especially the girls). The Larsen budget could never stretch that far, so it was up to them. Louise had hoped to pass along her rudimentary skills for nursing and veterinary care, at least, but the child was far too squeamish; she was fond of "dressing up" in an old nurse's hat, though, and forcing their indulgent canine into playing the role of "wounded soldier," inventing tragic love scenarios with melodramatic dialogue clearly gleaned from the moving pictures.

She'd turned fifteen three years ago. For about five minutes, it looked as if she might strike up an interest in horses—more as an equestrienne than a caretaker, for sure—but that was related to wanting to curry favor with the Binkleys' more affluent daughter. Next thing they knew she was spending too much time with a young rep of an Abilene hardware firm scouting locations for an outpost. Howard balked, protested, tried to rein her in, but the result was a note laid on her unmade bed that claimed she loved her father but *yearned* to be out in the world. She promised to write.

That was three years ago. One postcard from Santa Monica,

California, several months after she left. Louise kept the thought *Good riddance!* to herself, and since Howard wasn't one to share his own, she believed he was relieved. But when she heard him stifling his sobs in the barn one day, a wave of guilt just floored her. Then she had to ask—did I do enough? Was it because of me? Does he blame me for this? What can I give him to make up for it? Does he want another child now? Do I want one at this point? Would we be good parents? All this while she'd been careful to monitor her cycle out of respect for that *one thing at a time*, but also trusted her luck to the device she kept in the washroom drawer.

She'd heard the aircraft's engine but just thought the sound came from a motor car. She was up in Wally's place inspecting the newly up-holstered chair seat. Wally had made coffee, and Louise had bummed two cigarettes and smoked them on the spot. (Howard was dead set against women smoking, but Otis had no beef about it.) She'd brought her copy of *The American* and *Liberty* magazines to trade with Wally for *Time* and *The Woman's Home Companion*. A half dozen women were in the trading circle, and the magazines arrived at their "post office," an apple crate in George Purvis's sort-of general store.

Wally said, "You want this?" *The Farm Journal.*

"No thanks. I already know too much."

"I'll offer it to Mabel, then."

They laughed. Mabel's tastes ran to the likes of *McClure's*.

Then Wally had to move aside a pair of overalls she was patching for Leonard, and that set off another round of tsk-tsking about what are they going to do about that poor boy? At eighteen, he was still everybody's pet but was wasting his potential. Odd-jobber—well, he was *good* at fixing things, Otis had taught him that, and it was always handy to call him when you needed an extra body on the farm. But the boy is *smart*, ought to be studying something like electricity some-where. Worry about him living in that Indian teepee, though in truth his Uncle George's one-room place behind that store isn't a whole lot more civilized. Wally had gone back there to bring a shirt of Otis's that she'd remade for Leonard and, my, you would not tolerate that sort of dirty mess for two seconds.

"He's getting better-looking all the time," said Wally. Since Leonard was the same age as the runaway Izzy, Louise had once imagined them as a pair, then had snatched the thought back. Wouldn't wish that on poor Leonard. She considered Wally's comment. Yes, he was handsome, especially when his face was at rest. Tumbling blonde curls, grey eyes, square jaw—his mother must've been a Swede.

But he was so rambunctious, tripping over his own feet, and way too talkative—a happy chatterer more like a twelve-year-old than a man—so that diminished his appeal. He was fun, very good-natured, you *liked* him, though his stories about, say, the trouble he had fixing a flat on his bicycle tire or helping his uncle pluck and dress a turkey left no detail undescribed.

"It's such a shame Mabel thinks she's too good for him."

"Oh, I don't think it's *that*," said Louise. "He's just . . . too young."

"Won't always be."

Wally lit another cigarette and Louise was tempted to ask for a third but didn't. "You know that boy is strong as an ox. Otis had him lift up one end of a wagon yesterday while he slipped a wheel on, and it was full of stuff."

Wally had a mental list of Leonard's attributes, and she often trotted them out one by one. Louise didn't need to be convinced of Leonard's eligibility as a bachelor in want of a wife. But Wally bore a stronger maternal impulse, maybe because, thought Louise, she hadn't had children or hadn't had to endure living with one who hates your guts night and day.

About then Otis was hollering up the stairs, "Louise, you better come down! There's been a wreck up the Carlsbad road."

5

—THE CRAFT DID LEAPFROG THE AUTO STOPPED DEAD IN THE street, but when Katie flew down the other side of the mountain you could say it was like skiing on new snow fast and slippery, fighting the wind to stay on a line, hoping the engine had a few sips of gas left. But suddenly the airplane dipped back to the road, and her right wheel hit something, and she went alley-oop, a ground loop left, digging the left-wing tips into the turf, swinging up up up, then down and coming to rest half hiked up on a fence, her hanging almost upside down in the harness. She unclipped fast in a panic and tumbled to the dirt.

Her left wrist smarted. A big rip high on that sleeve showed a bloody gash on her shoulder. She clasped her hand over it and, panting, stood looking at the damaged airplane. Like being a babysitter and you turn your back and the kid you're supposed to keep safe has fallen down a well.

She bent over to the side and puked.

Two kids stood watching her. They wore matching denim overalls and looked like twins, but one had hair in pig tails. It dawned on her that she'd hit something while landing. Her heart thonked in her chest.

"What happened? Is everybody all right? Is anyone hurt?"

"Kilt are pig," said the boy.

She followed his gaze up the road to where sure enough a pig lay.

"Aw, Jiminy Christmas, I am so sorry!"

"He wasn't no pet," offered the girl.

"He run off when Pa got out the butcher knife."

"*Fugitive,*" the girl said. She smiled at herself.

"Pa called him Bacon," the boy said.

They walked to the porcine corpse and peered at it. Her legs were shaky. Her wrist was throbbing now. She felt nauseated and light-headed, the sort of woozy dizzy you got from an all-nighter on too much coffee. White noise in her brain cavity, a hissing. She turned to look back at the aircraft. The tip of the lower left wing had carved an arc in the hard red sand of the road, and the lower right jammed up against a fence post. Dimly she remembered that for an instant the ship had cocked up vertical after the impact and that had crushed and ripped the tip of the upper wing, and the elephant-ear aileron. The airplane's unnatural posture all at once disturbed her immensely—it was like a scream *you did this!* and she was desperate to right it, as if restoring its proper stance could undo the damage.

Ignoring her aching wrist and the bleeding gash, she scurried to where the lower wing was jammed against the post, tried to lift it up and away but failed, then scrambled to the fuselage near the tail assembly and heaved with all her might to back the machine away from the fence.

Someone appeared beside her, shoving, grunting, straining mightily, and together they managed to free the wing, and the plane settled into its normal horizontal position but cock-eyed in the road. But when her helper backed away from their task, he stumbled, and in an effort to catch his balance planted a boot right through the skin of the elevator. She winced and groaned.

"Oh, golly, sir!" He went to all fours, scrabbled under the elevator, and cradled the torn surface in his lap, head hanging over the ragged boot hole. "I can fix it, I promise! I'm . . ." He kept shaking his head. He was a young fellow, likely her age. He'd ridden up on a bicycle that now lay nearby, the back wheel slowly turning, as if dying; her dazzled gaze flicked to where that dead pig had lain only to see it running down the road with the two kids chasing it. Everything was happening too fast and all at once.

"Oh my gosh, sir, you're bleeding!" The fellow looked horrified. He was standing beside her now, over her.

She shoved back the tattered ears of the fabric's tear, and they inspected the cut. She felt herself sliding away from her body while her self levitated into the cockpit. She couldn't tell whether the cut was serious, but her wrist ached like crazy. Maybe broken?

"Thanks for the help." He looked confused. She realized her voice had boggled his misperception of her gender. She tugged her goggles onto the top of her helmet so that he could see her eyes, her face.

By then, the accident had drawn a crowd that included three women in a Model T. One was apparently a nurse who insisted that she be taken home to have her injury seen to.

the guest

1

AFTER HIS HUMILIATING FIASCO AS A RESCUER OF THE INJURED pilot, Leonard slinked back to his teepee and brooded with gusto. His innards churned; his heart took a lengthy tour of the underworld. Just one awful blunder after another. Called her sir, to begin with, and, sure, it wasn't his fault that in a washtub full of pilots, wouldn't be but one or two females, maybe, but for Pete's sake, she was itsy-bitsy maybe a hundred pounds soaking wet, so tiny fellows on racehorses flashed through his mind while he heaved beside her.

Then he had to stomp a size 10 hole in that tail part that made her darn near faint with dismay.

On top of that!

On top of that she slid her goggles up onto her head. Looked him right in the eyes. Sprigs of reddish blonde curls peeked cutely around the helmet's rim, and across her adorable little nose and flushed cheeks lay a bountiful spread of golden flecks, and then—her brows and lashes—molasses! Molasses lashes!—framed two big brown orbs that when his own bumbling gaze met their regard, they telescoped to the bottom of his soul. It was all he could do to stay upright. KO'd. Snatched his breath, juggled his heartbeats.

Right before they took the pilot off to tend to her injuries, Louise had pulled him aside to say likely they'd have supper for the aviatrix, and she'd love to have him at the table to reward him for his help.

Aviatrix.

That sounded like the name of an exotic species of bird and failed to capture the *wonder* of her miraculous appearance. Goddess-like. Angel, kind of, though you wouldn't expect one to wear an aviator's outfit.

Maybe he had the guts to show up at Louise's. And maybe not. Sure spoil the pretty pilot's appetite. If she saw him in the Larsens' pasture herding cows, she'd probably think he was a "cow poke," as an Easterner might say. But truth was, he didn't like cows much and deeply distrusted horses, and last on his list of aspirations would be tender of any kind of livestock.

Leonard was a very forward-looking fellow. He had an innate belief in creating better outcomes for all endeavors, so it was only natural to consider how to make amends and to mend the damage he'd done. Could that rip in the airplane's skin be sewn? Then taped? Then painted? What thread would that require? How could you sew the rip once you couldn't get your hand inside the cavity? Wasn't there a curved needle? Would Wally know? Was the paint specially made for aircraft, or would plain old shellac do in a pinch? In lieu of tape, how about strips of linen glued in layers over the suture? Then the paint?

Cross fingers whatever's wrong can be repaired. He believed most things could. Machines were a closed system, and once you learned how the parts worked in harmony, you could eventually solve the puzzle of why they didn't. He preferred his new Hawthorne DeLuxe Streamline bicycle to any horseflesh, no matter how fancy. (It had taken him a couple months to save for it, had pasted the torn-out page from the Monkey Ward catalog into his scrapbook: *This Motobike represents the highest example of bicycle design and construction . . . Attractive, lustrous cherry red, with cream ornamental head . . . and Always dependable New Departure Coaster Brake . . .*).

When the drilling rig had rumbled into town, he hung around the site asking too many questions. He and Otis and another fellow were hired to erect the wooden derrick. It was a "cable tool" or "percussion drilling" rig, he was told. Simply put, the engine lifted and dropped a heavy, bullet-shaped tong that pounded the earth over and over, and the motor that heaved the cable to raise it ran on kerosene. One-lung, they called them. To his ear, it was music—the engine went *POP pop pop pop pop Pop POP* in time to the *ker-CHUNK* of the bit as it punched the ground.

So, aside from the pilot's gender, the arrival of the biplane at his doorstep seemed fitting. For a moment, he'd linked the aircraft to the drilling rig. He'd felt all along that he was arriving into adulthood on the breast of a coming wave. The future held undiscovered marvels, and he was eager to encounter them.

He'd been the first here to know of Lindberg's transatlantic triumph last year in *The Spirit of St. Louis*. He'd read about crystal set radios in a newspaper article and had ordered Circular #120 from the Department of Commerce titled "Construction and Operating of a Simple Home-made Radio Receiving Outfit." He used (again) Wally's Montgomery Ward catalog next for these: Standard Galena Detector ($1.45), Murdock #55 headset ($4.50) and connecting block ($2.75), 500' copper antenna wire #12 gauge ($5.50), and a two-slide tuning coil ($3.50).

At Leonard's uncle's store you could buy a clutch of nails and a can of beans, but the inventory was skimpy—Uncle George didn't stock more than one of anything at a time, and he wouldn't order an item unless more than two or three customers had bought it recently. If you wanted something others always went for, he'd be out of it. If you wanted something few had sought, he'd never stocked it. But if you were looking for something really common but also not in demand, Purvis Mercantile was your store. Result was—most folks put off buying until they had to go to Loving.

Uncle George poorly paid Leonard to do almost everything but own the place. Stock the shelves, deliver, clean, sort, inventory, run the register, bookkeep. But since there was little business, Leonard was free to shop his muscles and his talent around the settlement. He was top-of-the-list for handyman tasks, and from Otis he'd learned what makes an automobile go, so he'd kept Mabel's Model T in top tune. If your butter churn hit a hitch on a turn of the handle, if your apple peeler wouldn't peel or your gramophone table stopped turning, you called Leonard. He had a knack. But since electricity hadn't arrived here, he had yet to learn the secrets of devices powered by dynamos. Loving was the closest distance to any electric light, and a few citizens there owned big Magnavox radios in mahogany cases with glowing faces that picked up stations from Denver, Albuquerque, Fort Worth, and beyond.

One by one the parts for the crystal radio arrived by mail, and within a day he'd built it on the base of an apple crate end. He strung the antenna up one of the lodge poles of his teepee and through the top. Then it went fifty feet or so to his uncle's building, ran back the way it came and down to the block. Supposedly, this arrangement would bring in stations within three hundred miles.

He knew radio signals traveled much farther at night. So, after dark, he slipped the headphones on and "tickled" the crystal with the feeler, gently ooching the slider along the tuning coil. A lot of static, crackling. He swept across the cylinder of copper coils with a sinking heart, but then, suddenly—music! An orchestra jiving on a happy ragtime number! He jumped up and shouted and would've danced if the wires to the headset hadn't yanked him back.

"Hey, it's music on the radio!"

Mabel! She'd love to hear this, he bet. Wally and Otis! He had wanted to run into the streets, wake people up, lasso them into his teepee to hear the marvelous music, free to whoever wished to listen in. It was wonderful to think of music floating out there all the time, soaring like flocks of notes in migration, and he had a memory of characters in a Shakespeare play Mabel had the older kids read—characters wandering lost in a wood at night, hearing music and not knowing where it came from, marveling at it, putting it down to the work of nymphs or sprites.

The night of May the 21st just last year, his radio brought him the news of Lindberg's solitary Atlantic crossing, and Leonard proudly trotted about like a town crier the next morning to repeat it.

So, the appearance of this aircraft today scarcely a year later was like a prophecy fulfilled, the arrival of a moving outer boundary of the future, the way water spreads across a floor.

But that pretty pilot? How did she fit the picture? Her face—those eyes and generous, mulberry-colored lips—aroused him deeply and made him tremble with a nameless fear. Like trying to walk the rafter of a barn, teetering, flapping your arms like a bird, you're racing across praying you'll reach the other side before you fall.

His one-room digs had one good chair, an old, upholstered wingback a rancher's wife had bartered for his labor, and he was perched on it now with his elbows on his knees and his palms cupping his chin. Going to supper at Louise's was the last and the first thing he wanted to do. His one good Sunday shirt was currently at Wally's awaiting being laundered. More than one female had remarked upon his table manners and not to praise them. He had a thousand questions for the pretty pilot but couldn't ask them unless he had the guts to put himself within range of her attention.

2

YOU DON'T LIVE ON A FARM YOU DON'T HAVE TWENTY THINGS to do at once. Louise was used to that, so soon as she'd told Howard to build a fire under the wash pot in the yard, she steered the injured aviatrix into the kitchen. Mabel dogged her heels expecting to be given tasks, but it was easier to do things herself than to coach another woman. Louise sat the pilot at the table, fetched a bottle of alcohol and a clean cloth.

"Honey, you mind shedding your uppers?"

The pilot was clad in a canvas two-piece overall set, and without hesitation, she unbuttoned and shrugged free of the top. Under it was a filthy cotton blouse that might've been red in the last century, and beneath that a dingy white linen camisole hugged her small breasts. She seemed dazed, passive. Shock?

"Honey, how about that hat?"

The pilot tugged the helmet up from her head, undamming a waterfall of strawberry blonde coils. Cleaned up, the kid would be cute as a bug. Louise would guess eighteen, maybe a tad older.

Mabel hovered. "Mabel, would you look in the pantry? There's a basket of eggs I gathered this morning. Maybe you could get a bowl and scramble them? There's bacon in the ice box too, and we'll hash a couple potatoes. We can toast the butts of bread loaves I'll scare up. Howard likes breakfast for supper, and it's always easy."

Mabel said, "Should I salt and pepper the eggs when I mix them or wait? You want me to keep the skins on the potatoes or peel and mash them?"

Louise endured a current of irritation. She'd forgotten that Mabel lived mostly on canned goods. What Louise needed right now was a woman who knew her way around a kitchen.

"Just beat the eggs with a fork. I'll take care of the rest."

"How many eggs?"

"I think there are about a dozen."

All this time, Louise had the cloth in one hand and the bottle of alcohol in the other, her hands poised over the girl's bared shoulder. The cut was no longer bleeding, but the coagulant residue streaked down to her inner elbow.

She smiled into the girl's harried upturned face.

"My, you're a mess! Hang on, this may smart."

"What's your name?" asked Mabel. Louise supposed that was meant to distract her. The pilot said, "Skip—py Baker," just as the damp cloth swept across her cut, and she winced.

"I'm Mabel, and your nurse there is Louise."

"Thank you," said the pilot. "Mind telling me where I am? I lost my map. Is this still Texas?"

"No, New Mexico," said Louise.

"Noname," offered Mabel.

"There's no name?" The girl looked puzzled.

"Yes. I mean no. Noname. That's the name."

"No Name's the name?" She seemed troubled, as if they were poking fun at her.

"You got it." Louise grinned. "Some people want to say No-NAH-may so it sounds like an Indian chief, though."

"Or NO-nah-may."

"Or Non AHmee, like Bon Ami."

"If you say it real fast it sounds like Nonum."

The girl shook her head as if shooing gnats.

Mabel, who enjoyed the novelty of it and always offered this snippet to folks back East, said, "Some people say when this burg got noticed by the map-maker for the new state government, he asked somebody around here and they told him it didn't have a name. So, he wrote down *Noname* on the map—made it look like one word, poor cursive skills, you know—and that just stuck."

Louise kept dabbing the cut with the cloth until she was down to the raw, clean flesh and her cloth was pink. With each swipe a grimace rippled across the girl's brow. The cut oozed and seeped. Louise was pleased to prescribe further treatment.

"Skippy, looks to me like you'll live! But I think you need a couple of stitches. Do you mind?"

"No, ma'am. Thank you."

Mabel had been opening the cabinet doors one by one without choosing a vessel, as if she was looking for one labeled "for scrambling one dozen eggs," so Louise said, "Top row. The blue one."

Louise retrieved her surgical needle and thread from a drawer in the kitchen counter. She sterilized the needle with the alcohol. To her surprise, the pilot bent her head to watch as she prodded the lips of the cut and sent her needle through. The girl's jaw muscles beat in time with the poking, and her lips pressed tight.

Louise put a dressing on the cut, smoothed it with her palm, patted it. "There, now! All done!" she said, as if having just put the finishing touches on a new hairdo. The pilot peered at the bandage. She burst into sobs. She bent forward in the chair and planted her face in her palms, her shoulders heaving. Louise and Mabel exchanged looks of alarm and curiosity, then Mabel slipped into a chair beside the girl and curled her arm around her shoulders.

"There, there," she cooed. "Is it hurting?"

Violent shake of her head. She gasped, sniffled. But when Mabel drew her closer, she exploded again and planted her face in Mabel's chest. Howard had come into the mud room carrying a bucket of warm water and had advanced across the threshold before the ensuing drama smacked him in the face. Louise saw him reel backward and retreat into the yard.

Louise and Mabel waited patiently, miming to one another over the girl's trembling form. Mabel could feel a peculiar smile threatening to creep over her face. It seemed inappropriate, this smile, but dimly she tried to cast it as a sign of pity (*poor thing!*). The girl's heat, her damp cheeks against her breast, the unruly curls smelling of dust and maybe petrol billowing up around Mabel's chin—the contact overwhelmed her with feelings of . . . being a mother? Big sister? Friend?—and aroused an indefinable and shocking pleasure. She didn't often hug or get hugged out here. It'd been so long she'd apparently forgotten to miss it.

The girl pulled herself away, blew and wiped her nose on a sleeve of her undershirt, mildly shocking them.

"I'm okay now, really, I'm sorry."

"No need to be!"

"It's okay, honey. What's upsetting you?"

Both women's attention leaned forward; both believed it might be a "who" and not a "what" sparking her misery.

She sighed. "Last thing I ever wanted was to wreck that ship."

Looked as if she might break down again, but she ferociously sucked in air, then whooshed it out through ballooning cheeks.

"It was my fault," said Mabel.

The girl's brows hiked up with astonishment.

"My automobile. In the street, when you were . . ." She waved one hand as if imitating a bird.

"Oh, no! It was the pig in the road that made me ground loop. Hit my right strut. Is it okay, you think? Where it is, I mean? I was so rattled after it happened that I didn't even think to check all the damage, but I guess when I ground-looped, the elephant ear probly got smashed on that side . . ." She started weeping quietly, eyes squinched, then she swiped at them with the hem of her undershirt. That is one unhygienic garment, thought Louise.

"There's folks here good at fixing things," Mabel said brightly.

"You think it's okay there in the road?"

"Hardly anybody comes that way past sundown," said Louise, "and there's room to pass. Don't worry, hon."

"After you've had a chance to rest and eat, we'll go take a look!" Mabel offered. "Make sure."

"Oh, thanks! I don't want to be any trouble."

"Well, whatever trouble you might be we're inclined to call excitement," said Louise.

Mabel went to breaking eggs one by one over the blue bowl without keeping shards of shell from falling into the mix, but Louise ignored that. She needed to get the rest of supper in order. The girl had fallen into a brood that twisted her lips and knotted her brow.

"You have a hotel here?"

"Gosh, no," said Louise. "But you needn't worry. There's plenty of room right here." She gestured toward the hallway.

"Me, too," Mabel said meekly. "Besides, I could stand the company."

"Aw, gee, thanks so much! You've both been so kind!"

"Nice of you to say," said Louise. "And believe me, it's nice to have your efforts appreciated." She was on the verge of adding *for once* but bit her tongue. She went into the mud room and picked up the bucket of warm water.

"Hon, why don't we go clean you up and let you rest?" In part to keep Mabel from following her, she said, "Mabel, would you set the table, please? There's silver in the sideboard in the dining room."

"How many places?"

"Well, four. Five if Leonard shows up."

The pilot followed Louise into what had been Izzy's room, and, to judge by the décor and furnishings, might still belong to her. The pilot sat on the bench at the marble-topped vanity; she was massaging her left wrist with her right hand and clenching her jaw. Louise poured water into the porcelain wash basin with the rose pattern. She opened a drawer in the vanity, drew out a washcloth and towel, and handed the stacked pair to the girl.

The girl had carried her coverall top wadded under her right arm; Louise took it from her and, though she recoiled a bit to do it, set the garment on the pristine pink coverlet on Izzy's bed. Then something turned over in her.

29

"I know you'd probably like something fresh to wear once you've washed your face and such—I know I do." She went into Izzy's closet and drew out a linen blouse with a sailor collar and blue piping. She held it up. "Our . . . daughter, she's a tad bigger than you, but I think this might do."

"Oh, it's too pretty and clean."

"Don't be silly." Louise heard both *I'm not worthy* and *Don't like snobby stuff* in equal parts.

At the washstand she scrubbed her face, arms, and neck, using mostly her right hand. Louise watched from the corner of her eye. Maybe another injury? "Don't mind me." It nagged at Louise not to violate her privacy but reminded herself she had innkeeper's rights. Seeing her at Izzy's vanity pricked at her mysteriously. It violated some rule that she suddenly wanted to flout.

"I'll just . . ." She futzed about, slapping at the bed covers and tugging at a curtain hem. The hangered blouse lay on the bed, confronting her as if occupied by its surly owner. It prodded her memory—this garment was a favorite not of Izzy's but of Howard's. Seeing the pilot in it—what effect would it have? Good or ill? Had she picked it for that reason? Should she substitute something *unfreighted*?

The pilot forked her curls back from her face with the tined fingers of her right hand. Her skin was flushed, a rosy sheen on her damp cheeks. Young. She caught Louise's gaze in the mirror.

"Hon, you can use those combs and brushes. Whatever's there." *Open the drawers. Use what you find.*

Take what you want.

"My hair's so dirty."

"It bet it's beautiful after a wash. We can give you a good scrubbing tomorrow. If you like, I mean."

"Aw, that'd be swell." She gingerly picked up a silver-backed hairbrush. "I hope your daughter doesn't mind." She gestured to the vanity, the porcelain basin, the four-poster bed.

"No, she doesn't mind," Louise said tightly. "She's . . . away."

3

HOWARD WAS STRUGGLING TO OBSERVE THE PILOT WITHOUT
laying eyes on her. Light from the kerosene lamp on the table gilded the
women's features; the young pilot stayed face down over her plate as she
wolfed her supper, so her bushel of unruly hair flamed like a burning
shrub to his eye. He could hardly eat. Louise and Mabel chattered as
if the interloper were deaf and blind, nervous trivial nattering, who
went to Loving yesterday, this or that magazine article, and it was all he
could do to keep from screaming at Louise, *What right do you have??!*

More bacon, Howard?

No, he did not want more bacon. He did not want more of anything.
He wanted less of everything.

Whatever possessed Louise to dress her in that special blouse?
Out of everything and anything in his dear daughter's closet, this
was the garment the woman who supposedly cared about him had
chosen for this urchin to parade about in? Surely, she realized that Izzy
had stopped wearing it because it was "childish"—the very reason to
cherish it. He'd bought it for her in St. Louis. She went from loving
it to loathing it almost overnight. And even if she'd outgrown it, she
didn't have to say she hated it.

Was Louise being spiteful or only thoughtless?

What a choice.

His face was glum as a pewter plate, no doubt, but he couldn't seem
to rise to the role of the host who puts his guest at ease, so Louise and
Mabel had double duty. They tried to include him by asides ("We had
a hard winter, right, Howard?") and while he grunted, they'd quickly
move on, their skittering glimpses snatched back as if to address him
too directly might be to poke a rattler. Clearly the girl was intimidated
by his ill humor so fell mute unless questioned. That normally would
deserve his pity, require it, but he was in far too truculent a stew to
surrender. One-two punch, a cruel confluence—first the noise of
that horrendous airplane gouging at the oozing bruise of one horrific

wartime memory followed by the aviatrix dressed as his vanished Izzy to shunt him into another terrible time. Bad enough to have that infernal drilling machine banging away all day long.

And Louise—rubbing it in? Sure, she'd argue that her nursing skills had been on call, he could credit that, but there'd been no need to troop her through Izzy's room, her things. She'd managed to splint the driller's finger when he broke it without inviting him to dinner. Plenty of other folks around to give the girl bed and board.

Mabel Cross could've easily driven off with her after Louise had tended to her injury. The whole damned town was in an uproar and any one of a dozen local matrons would rush to whip up casseroles. The girl did not have to be at his table. Did not have to be wearing his daughter's clothes, tramping around in his daughter's room.

And the bawling he'd stumbled onto—Good Lord! He'd already heard enough mewling and wailing and moaning there in his kitchen to last a lifetime. Izzy could even *screech* . . .

He quietly took a long deep breath and stayed observant. Mabel was always a dainty eater, though you'd not judge so by her generous form; Louise ate more when she was upset, and he noted that despite her chipper demeanor and gratuitous giggles, she'd gone through her portions and had started in on what he'd not taken from the platter. The pilot seemed ravenous. Now and then, she chanced a glance his way, and, apparently scalded by his uninviting regard, shot her eyes back to her plate. A sliver of guilt shimmered up his spine. Not her fault. And of the foursome there, he and she did have in common a passionate desire that the other not be present. The other two were hard pressed to keep the awful lead blanket suspended over their heads from dropping to smother them, while he and the girl were refusing to help by even moral support.

"Where are you coming from?" He'd interrupted Mabel's description of her worst pupil, and his abrupt masculine thunder startled them. He'd meant to sound curious, even sympathetic, but heard in the echo of his outburst the demand that she account for her whereabouts.

"Uh, North Carolina." She let a fork full of egg rest on her plate.

She waited, head up, swinging her gaze left to right as if everyone had asked the question.

"Like the Wright brothers!" offered Mabel.

"They were really in Ohio," the girl said quietly. "Dayton. I think Mr. Orville still lives there."

"Do you know him?" asked Louise.

"Oh, gosh no. He's—"she hiked her hand above her head—"you know, in my world . . ."

She waited, and when nothing more was asked, cautiously went back to her happy task of finishing off her third helping of potatoes and eggs. The bacon and toast were gone. There'd be nothing for the hogs or dog.

To save himself—and maybe them—he finally muttered, "Best check on things" and left the table.

"Got chess pie left from last night!" Louise cried much too merrily at his retreating back, but he waved her off. Least she could be honest—she'd breathe easier with him gone.

On Howard's way to the barn, Pal roused himself from his hollow under the stoop and jogged after him.

"I apologize that I've got no treat for you except the dubious pleasure of my company," he told the mutt. Though he never said so to the dog, he'd once told Izzy that Pal was the ugliest canine in twenty counties. When God told Noah to pair up the animals, Howard reckoned a sheep had wound up holding hands with a bulldog, with the result that their progeny such as Pal looked like a broad-shouldered woolly jackal.

But Howard prized the beast as he did all the creatures under his stewardship, because the one thing you could count on in an animal was that it would never upset you in ways that might make you want to shoot yourself. Or someone else.

The barn was dark and quiet as a church, the rich olfactory mélange of straw, dust, and manure settling his nerves like an imbibed tonic. He dipped a bucket into a bin and toted it to Mildred's stall, roused her interest by pouring the grain into her trough. Chores helped, too.

Never any lack of those—if anything, with only he and Louise, and Leonard when he could, the upkeep on the acres of cotton, alfalfa, and grain sorghum, the pastures with his cattle, the chickens and hogs—it could overwhelm you, though when he laid his head on his pillow, exhaustion was both a reward and a balm.

Like most folks, they had a large garden plot for corn, potatoes, cow peas, black-eyed peas, and "salad crops"—lettuce, radish, onion, and the like. Louise tended that, and she also took charge of the chickens. Howard was considered successful, smart, and progressive. (Prior to his wartime service, he'd finished two years at Vanderbilt.) He'd been the first to bring in a motor from a wrecked Ford truck, mount it on a platform, and use it to pump water from his well—it irrigated the garden and the cotton. He'd also piped it to a tank on stilts outside the kitchen window and the adjacent bathroom, so they had running water, even though only cold. Out in his pasture was another well and a concrete tank kept full by a windmill. Generally, fellows out here did dry-farming, and though the soil could be productive, the rainfall was fitful, and when he'd begun irrigating his cotton, he started producing about a bale per acre. Unlike some, he didn't resist the county extension agent's advice, though he shunned the suggestion to kill the prairie dogs with sorghum laced with poison.

At the garden, he noted its greenery looked parched. On the western horizon the last pink and violet layers of a calm and unperturbed sunset reminded him, again, of the peace to be had from the land where the sky was free to command obeisance so seductively. A half-moon already silvered the graying atmosphere. Soon the stars would begin their welcomed pinpoint inoculations of light.

The evening air was cool as always at this elevation even in the summer, and the dark shapes of bull bats flickered overhead as they began their nightly feeding on insects drawn to the crops. At the pumping platform, he surveyed his kingdom. He breathed deeply in and out. Pal stood waiting for orders, then, lacking them, collapsed with a grunt to his belly, chin on forepaws.

For every foot he'd walked from the house, his blood pressure had sunk a notch or two. He hated to spoil the peace, but necessity urged him crank the engine to life. The motor coughed and rumbled on. He let it run for several minutes, watching the outtake gush into the trenches and scurry to their heads, then he shut it down. In the silence, Mabel's Ford started up. He watched as the pilot climbed in on the passenger side, then the car waggled out of the yard and down the road.

Good riddance!

Light within the barn was visible as he approached. So, she had something to say. Possibly an apology?

"Mabel took the pilot out to check on her airplane." She stood in the breezeway holding up the lantern. Didn't come for a lengthy chat, then.

"I saw them go out." And though it was rare for him to confront her or anyone this directly, he asked, "Why did you give her *Izzy's blouse* to wear?"

"She said she'd like something fresh to put on." She shrugged as if the answer were that simple. He stared to show her it was insufficient then moved to the tack room door. He had let her know how it upset him, hadn't he? And she'd more or less replied, *Who cares.*

To his back, she said, "She asked about a hotel. I said we didn't have one."

"So, I suppose you invited her to stay?"

"Yes," she said after a moment.

"In Izzy's room."

"Yes."

"Don't you think you should've talked to me about it?" His voice soared up a scale, and his hands were trembling.

"Well, I am."

"No, you're telling me."

"I believed it was a hostess prerogative."

They faced off a moment.

"Well, it's a damn shame you weren't always so . . . *hospitable.*"

Before she could reply, he stepped into the tack room and shut the door behind him.

35

4

MABEL WAS GIDDY TO HAVE THE AVIATRIX TO HERSELF. SHE was sailing merrily on a wave of gratifying experiences—the excitement of the girl's arrival, for one, and having a meal with a family was always a pleasure, even given Howard's inexplicably cold behavior, and she didn't often have the chance (or take the chance) to drive her Lizzy in the dark. Everything seemed wonderfully transformed by the big round lights posted on her fenders; familiar mesquite thickets turned mysterious by the play of shadow and electric light, the ordinary showing its back side as it were like the dark half of the moon. Grasshoppers and mayflies, swarms of gnats, lit up like Fourth of July sparklers in the white lamp light.

"Louise and Howard are *such* nice folks!" gushed Mabel. "You know their daughter Isabel ran off three years ago." It pleased her to be the bearer of her hosts' history—like a Noname docent. She riffled through her mental dossier on Izzy to decide how much to tell, what was pure gossip and what was known.

"How come?"

"Izzy never liked it here, and I'm told that when a fellow showed up to say come away with me, she did."

After nibbling, the girl took the bait. "Gee whillikers, I'm not running away!"

"Oh, I never . . . Well, sure, of course you're not!"

"I'm supposed to deliver the ship to this yahoo in California who owns it!"

'Oh! Well—"

"And now I've gone and wrecked it!"

"Maybe things aren't as bad as they seem."

The aviatrix sighed. "I sure hope so. Generally speaking, I'm a glass half full kind of person."

"Gosh! Me, too."

They'd reached Noname's clusters of buildings, and Mabel noted that Wally and Otis's windows on the upper story of The Owl had a soft back glow.

"Fellow who lives up there—" She lifted a hand to point. "He's a crackerjack blacksmith. I bet he can fix it up."

The girl peered up at the windows, but her silence spoke her doubt. Mabel continued her investigation.

"I don't mean to be nosey, but it's not every day an airplane piloted by such as yourself lands right on our one main street, so you can guess you've stirred up a whole lot of curiosity. Actually, it's not *any* day it happens."

"Sure, I understand. I'm kinda used to it."

Mabel took that to mean fire away. "Is Skippy your given or your nickname?"

"Well, it's my show name."

"Show name?"

"Yeah, I'm with an outfit does air shows at county fairs and the like. A flying circus. I do barrel loops, falling leaves, and Immelmanns and things. Take rubes up for rides. But not with the Travel Air—it's special—I have an old Jenny I perform with. I've crashed that crate thousands of times."

"No kidding! How thrilling! A flying circus!"

"My real name's Katherine. My friends call me Kate or Katie."

"Well, Katie, I'm mighty pleased to meet you!"

Mabel let a lull ease the way for a renewed probe.

"Are your folks performers as well?"

The girl took her time with this one. "My mom's a wing-walker," she offered finally.

"A wing-walker! My word! I saw that once in a news reel! It looks horribly dangerous!"

"Only if you fall off."

Mabel felt a chuckle bubble up but stifled it. The question *Did she?* rang like a gong in her skull.

After a silence suitable to memorialize the girl's mother (if dead),

Mabel said, "Well, of course we don't know how long you might be stuck here, but I'm wondering if maybe tomorrow or the next day you'd be willing to give a little talk about your wonderful vocation? I know my students would be excited beyond all measure even though they're still on summer vacation—I'm the only teacher here, by the way—and their parents as well?"

"Jeepers! I'm not much on public speaking!"

"Not a lecture," Mabel hastened to add. "Just talking, you know, answering the questions people might have. We could have it in my schoolroom or we could gather around your airplane if that would make you more comfortable."

Even in this dim light Mabel saw those heavy amber brows dip into a V.

"Well, just think about it, okay?"

"Sure. I'm just hoping that my ship's air-worthy really soon."

By now they were on the Carlsbad road, and Mabel slowed and swerved to and fro to avoid the pits in the hardened sand. Ahead, in the cone of bleached light, figures emerged out of the darkness, three adults and three children, walking toward them. Mabel squinted and soon recognized four Baxters and a brace of Higgenbotham kids, Clarence and Marjorie. Clyde Baxter was carrying an electric torch.

"Looks like you've had sightseers."

The girl reared up and groaned, lunged her head toward the windscreen, but Mabel rushed to add, "Don't worry. Folks here respect other people's things, and I know they wouldn't touch anything without permission."

She slowed as the strollers came alongside, gave them a friendly beep as they rolled on by. Soon Mabel made out shiny parts of the machine glinting as her headlights hit them. The girl seemed to hold her breath.

"Everything looks dandy so far!" Mabel was eager to vouch for her neighbors, but soon as she had, the girl—Skippy, Katie, whatever her name—burst out with, "What's *he* doing there!?"

Leonard was sitting cross-legged under the wing, and as they arrived, he rose and stepped out from under it.

"Oh, it's Leonard. I know him!" urged Mabel. "It's the young fellow who helped—"

"And stuck his blasted boot right through my elevator!"

"He always has the best intentions."

Leonard strode to Mabel's window. Without seeing the pilot, he asked, "Is she all right?"

Then he saw the girl frantically pawing at the passenger door to find the handle, then seconds later scurrying toward the airplane.

"Oh, hey, listen!" he called out. "I just thought it'd be a good idea for somebody—"

She whirled on him. "Did you go into the cockpit?"

"On, golly no! Kids out here wanted to, but I was standing guard."

The pilot vanished in the shadows. Under the wing lay a patch of cardboard and rolled-up blankets.

"Leonard, were you planning to spend all night here?"

"Swear to God I didn't do nothing."

"Anything."

"Anything."

They waited in the oddly comforting thrum of her idling motor, then the pilot appeared on the wing as if coming onto a stage and hopped off the trailing edge of it carrying a small brown valise. As she strode past Leonard, she held it up to brandish it at him.

"Better not be nothing missing from this!"

"Anything?" ventured Leonard.

"WHAT??!!"

"Uh . . . nothing," he muttered.

Leonard stood helplessly in the headlight glare while the pilot clambered back into the automobile, silently fuming. The girl had been inexcusably rude to poor Lenny, and tendrils of guilt and sympathy crept about Mabel's heart.

"Katie. . . . If this were my airplane, I'd be happy to have him watching it. I think he was planning to spend the night."

"Aw, geez." The girl sighed. "I think I'm mostly upset and hopping mad at myself for tearing it up."

Mabel set the hand brake and, leaving the engine running, climbed down from the driver's seat, and stepped in front of the radiator. He was full in the light and his face looked like a sad clown caricature, it was that pitiful. To her own astonishment, she leaned and drew him into a hug. It was their first such physical contact, and his shock vibrated through her breast and loins. He smelled of rank boy-sweat and bad bacon maybe, but under that a piquant sweetness sparked a mysterious interest in her blood. It was a day for hugging. He was too surprised to react and froze like a palace guard tormented by a tourist.

When she released him, she patted his cheek. She wondered if she'd put on this show for the pilot.

"There, there. Lenny, our aviatrix regrets her behavior and deeply appreciates that you're willing to help."

"No kidding?"

Happily, he waved toward the vehicle's windscreen and grinned.

By the time they had returned to Louise's, the girl had fallen asleep with her cheek resting on arms crossed over the valise in her lap.

5

NOW KATIE WAS WIDE AWAKE. YOU'D THINK THAT GIVEN how she'd spent the previous night catnapping in the cockpit, she'd be far too worn out to keep awake. Then, too, taking into account the nonstop adrenaline rush from fighting the storm and crash-landing, then having to talk to strangers and answer endless questions, then worrying about the damage to the Travel Air . . .

Plenty enough to floor a normal person. But Katie had more zip, pep, vigor, and spunk than most folks who start their day running on a pot of coffee. Never a still moment as a baby or a tyke, a countdown ticking off in her bloodstream, and if you made Katie sit still to untangle her wiry copper mop, toes would tap and nails would drum, and you had the feeling if somebody goosed her good, she'd shoot off like a rocket.

She lay in the dark in the strange girl's four-poster bed between sheets that smelled of talcum and rose water. Being sleepless let her relish the luxury of wallowing in a bona fide bed in a room by herself. This was her fourth night out; first night was a farmer's back porch; second night a barn, and though last night's farmer offered a bed inside, a glint in his eye and the news his wife was away put her slumped in her cockpit. In her frantic first departure, she hadn't considered that airfields with hangers and gas pumps and the friendly aid of fellow pilots would be off-limits.

Spending a night in someone else's bed tugged at her imagination. She'd heard arguing right after her hostess settled her here, and she suspected it might be about her but hoped not. The lives of grown women her mother's age who've chosen the path of ordinary home and hearth didn't interest her much. But that the girl whose bed she was lying in had run away did pique her curiosity. To Katie, the runaway Izzy had lived like a princess—this private room, with the marble-topped vanity and three-paneled mirror, an array of powders and spritzers, a book shelf, a five-drawer chest, the upholstered wing chair in which sat the most adorable huge stuffed teddy bear you could imagine, the bed with its bounteous soft linens and pink flounce bordering the "roof," and a closet of fresh, clean, pretty clothes—holy baloney! It was everything you'd ever want, no?

Ran off with a fellow? Well, that was easy to believe. Maybe since then she'd had that baby and kept it, and maybe that fellow was a sticker or just a roller and a cad. Maybe the girl's living high off the hog or hunkered in a squalid tenement with a snot-nosed toddler hanging on her apron. Maybe she and her mother had argued night and day about the daughter's future, maybe that ugly dad had tried a thing or two—or, if not that, he'd beat her blue one too many times.

However you look at it, at least when she was in *her room*, she darn sure had it good.

Moonbeams lit up the bear's bright eyes. Pick me up, he said. Come on, won't hurt nothing. He had a white torso, black legs and ears, a black head with a white face, button eyes and nose, a cute red tongue protruding from his lips, as if he'd just polished off some toffee. She eased from under the covers, got up, and lifted the furry fellow into her arms like a toddler with his legs straddling her hipbone. The bear was big as a five-year-old! Had Izzy given him a name? Were his shoulders soaked in Izzy's tears?

"If you could talk, what would you tell?" she whispered.

Under the bed covers, she cuddled the bear. His fur smelled dusty; it was stiff and scratchy to her cheek, but soon as he'd absorbed her heat, he seemed to give it back, and his soft chest pillowed her head. Her blood grew sluggish, her lids relaxed. Now she was tired at last. Never had she flown so many days in a row and or so many hours in a day, and never had she made so many landings where no airplane had set down. She longed to report her experiences, what she'd learned, to Curly, but that was impossible for so many reasons.

But even given how scared she'd been, it was hard to say which had been more troublesome—the flying, or the lying.

repairs begin

WALLY WAS FIXING BREAKFAST WHEN LEONARD BURST IN the back door, so she doubled her flapjack batter. She'd missed the uproar yesterday, so Leonard eagerly caught her up.

"The pilot, she's what they call an aviatrix!"

While she watched the cakes bubble and brown, he recounted how he'd helped her move the airplane and that he'd spent the night fending off sightseers while she was at Louise and Howard's. She was really tee-nine-sy and red-headed with freckles, and it was hard to picture her flying that aircraft all the way from wherever she'd come. She really has . . . pluck, he said, smiling dreamily.

"Be careful, Lenny."

"Huh?"

"Don't put too much into somebody who won't stay long."

"Aw!" he snorted. "She just thinks I'm a country bumbledy-turd."

"Well, I'm not talking about what she might think of you. Anyway, how long's she staying?"

"I dunno. I just talked to Otis. We're gonna take the truck out to the Larsens and pick her up and go out to the airplane, so I'm thinking we can see about fixing it." He added, "I mean, *if* that's okay with her."

"What's she like?"

Leonard laughed. "Kind of like a hummingbird with a stinger."

Otis came in from the shop wiping his hands on a rag, then they ate the flapjacks and bacon while Leonard shot questions to Otis: what could they do if the wing was bent or the propeller busted or if the engine wouldn't start—it was a radial piston engine, never seen one in person but read about them—or how about the hole in the tail?

Otis said, "Have to see, son."

When they'd finished eating, Otis said, "Go crank up the truck. I'll be out in a minute."

Leonard shot up and hurried out the door. Otis sipped contentedly from his coffee cup. He chuckled.

"Boy is determined to play the Galahad."

Wally frowned. "He better watch out."

The visitation by the airplane had thrown their schedule off—normally, Otis spent his mornings cooking for lunch, so they'd worked out a menu that Wally could easily handle on her own. He'd cooked a pot of collard greens and ham hocks last night, so she could mash potatoes and fry pork chops. She usually made the cornbread, anyway, since she believed hers was better. He put sugar in his batter, so she often joked that he made cake, not cornbread. A dozen to fifteen customers would be a normal service, but with gawkers coming in as word got around, the crowd might swell to twenty. People in Noname sometimes whined that the only café should be open for breakfast and dinner, too, to which Wally often said, "Please feel free to open your own place! I'll be your first customer!"

She was peeling spuds when someone tapped on the glass front door. Through the side window she spotted the big cream-over-burgundy sedan that Otis had told her was a brand-new Chrysler Imperial, so she knew who it was.

"Hello, Wallace!"

Apparently, Arabella Bohanan had never realized that "Wally" was a nickname and presumed it was a diminutive, and Wally hadn't corrected her because she relished the irritation the mistake aroused in her. Never once had the woman deigned to eat at the Owl. A breeze wafting through the opened door proved a nip in the air but not a chill sufficient to justify the coat, Wally considered. An unidentified dead rodent curled around the collar.

"Howdy, Arabella. What a surprise."

"Well, I was just driving by. I heard about the visitor with the airplane and wanted to know where she might be staying."

While Arabella hovered in the threshold, Wally still had her hand on the doorknob. She was supposed to say *Please, won't you come have some coffee?* Would saying that make her a sap? Would not saying it be rude? Or teach Arabella you can't push Wally and Otis around, by God. Which makes her the bigger person?

Well, it must've cost Arabella to reveal she believed Wally knew things Arabella didn't. Wally would enjoy using up Arabella's time with no result.

"Come on in."

Wally left the door open and strode toward the back. "Would you like some coffee?"

Arabella stepped inside but hung back from the early morning murk of the room.

"Thanks, but I better not tarry. I want to put on a luncheon for the aviatrix."

"How generous of you! I'm sure she'd be pleased. I got no idea where she might be, but my Otis has gone to check on her airplane, and I've told him to invite her for lunch here today. And dinner tonight."

"Oh, well, that's nice. Of course, I was thinking of tomorrow or the next day. I'd want time to prepare something special."

My God, thought Wally, *she is so good at this.* "If I see her before you do, I'll be sure to tell her." Lots of things.

"That'd be kind!"

Wally watched the two-toned sedan drive off. She hated how exchanges with Arabella upset her so. Like the business about the "luncheon." That would mean a meal at her home at the area's largest ranch attended by guests who wouldn't include Wally and Otis. A "luncheon" would happen when the Owl was serving lunch, so they'd not attend even if invited. No attempt to smooth over what might've been an awkward moment if Arabella had been aware of the insult. It wouldn't occur to Arabella to invite them or that it could offend them to be left out. Seemed to be a silent pact they abided by. At times she felt that she and Otis weren't considered full-fledged tradespeople but just the house maid and the cook who'd left the "Mastah's" big house and had gone out on their own with dubious permission.

She always thought it odd—and admirable—that things like this never dug under Otis's black skin. He'd just shrug. White folks. And she wished she could be as . . . what? Resigned? Indifferent? Bigger somehow? She always bit the bait and wound up humiliated.

Great example would be the ridiculous lie about having the aviatrix for lunch and dinner today! Good honk! Just plain pitiful.

2

OTIS LET LEONARD DRIVE THE TRUCK OUT TO THE LARSENS. He'd taught Leonard to change an engine's oil, clean spark plugs, flush a radiator, change a tire, how to set the timing and clean a carburetor. He'd taught him how to make a forge fire, use a hammer on the anvil. The boy's uncle either didn't know things or didn't care to pass anything along, so Otis filled gaps in his understanding. Taught him to butcher a chicken, but Leonard's attention wandered in the kitchen. Taught him to solder and use an oxyfuel cutting and brazing torch, use a crosscut saw, an awl, a plane, compass, and a whetstone. He'd taught Leonard that a curse word is like a mud puddle—no need to step in it if you can walk around. All things he'd been taught by a father, things he'd long ago told a son now absent from his life.

Leonard normally fell mute while driving, too intent on getting everything right—a good reason to put him behind the wheel. They passed the spot where he'd seen the aircraft hop Mabel's Model T.

"She run out of gas or what?"

"Uh. Oh! I dunno. I guess. When she went over me that motor was coughing like a one-lung geezer with a cheap cigar. But she wasn't in no mood to explain herself to me."

Otis felt duty-bound, though not eager, to take up Wally's worry. "She hard to get along with?"

"She bit *my* head off sure enough."

"Well, don't you be taking it to heart, hear me?"

"Yessir."

Leonard drove into the Larsens' barnyard. The fire under the wash pot was smoldering. Howard and a girl Otis took to be the aviatrix stood in the barn's big opening. That ugly dog sat on its haunches between them, the girl scratching its head as they watched the truck pull to a stop. Otis noted the extra little spring in Leonard's step as he bounded from the cab, pleased to have been seen behind the wheel, though the girl moved away toward the corral as they approached.

Otis greeted Howard with a shake, and they stood jawing about the weather, the crops, the day's tasks. The two men enjoyed a low-keyed mutual respect for one another's abilities and often found themselves aligned in local disputes, though they'd gotten at cross purposes about that drilling operation. Howard resisted change that came sudden and couldn't be controlled, but to Otis it might mean reliable income. Some folks said if oil was struck, they'd sure want a rig on their farm, while others warned of fire and getting overrun by hordes of riffraff from the boom. They all hated the noise, and Arabella Bohanan said she'd do her best to see it was curbed after sundown.

But Otis and Howard shared the same quiet style of presenting their opinions. The Larsens' garden often supplied the Owl's vegetables, and Otis was on call for a spot of welding and the like.

Otis nodded toward the girl.

"That our pilot?"

Howard said, "Mmm."

You'd never guess it to look at her. Khaki trousers, rumpled white blouse half-tucked in. She had a lot of red hair tied back with a thick green ribbon like a horse tail. Her back was to them, but she apparently spoke to Leonard because he visibly flinched.

"You seen her airplane?" asked Otis.

"No. Seen more than enough to last a lifetime."

Otis described how he'd been on the porch of the Owl when it came sailing along and leap-frogged Mabel's automobile, thinking it might draw out Howard's own account, but none came. Louise stuck her head out the back door and called to him—she had cabbages to take to Wally.

He let himself into the mudroom and on to the kitchen. Three cabbage heads sat in a dish drainer over the sink.

"Won't you sit a minute?" He had a passing thought that she meant to be polite, but then she took a chair at the table. He pulled out another and sat opposite.

"Coffee's gone but there's tea if you like."

"I'm all right, thanks. Filled up already."

Louise craned her head to peer outside, checking apparently for eavesdroppers.

"Listen. Would you do me a favor?"

"Always."

"That girl spent the night here because it only made sense after I'd doctored her and all, but it's got Howard all twisted up because she's in Izzy's room, and, you know—" She waved helplessly. "Worst part was I didn't say word one to Howard about it until it was already done."

Otis shifted his feet under the table. Wasn't his favorite thing, getting between folks, especially white ones, in their squabbles. Or even aside them. Ten-foot pole time.

"She a lot of trouble?"

"Oh, my word no! You never saw anybody more grateful to get a hot bath and a homecooked meal. When I went in to wake her up—" She looked away, and he caught a glint of moisture rim her eye. "She was sleeping with her arms around Izzy's teddy bear, for God's sake. About broke my heart. I'd have given her the damn thing on the spot if Howard wouldn't leave me over it."

Otis felt confused. Seemed to him that hearing this was Wally's job.

"Anyway, it's brought everything up again. He thinks I meant to hurt him by having the girl stay here."

"Oh, now. We all know you wouldn't do that."

"He won't talk to me about it."

Otis steeled himself. He looked through the door into the barnyard. The pilot and Leonard were talking. He'd as soon eat a tub of horse hockey as speak to Howard about this. And, sure enough—

"I thought maybe another man . . . One he respects."

He felt at an absolute loss—what in God's green Earth might he say to Howard?

"Well, I'll do what I can, but it ain't the sort of business I'm worth a hoot at."

Louise beamed. "Oh, thanks! If I thought Wally, you know . . ."

"No, I understand."

To Otis's great relief, Howard had already gone to service his windmill when Otis left carrying the cabbages in a paper bag.

3

WHEN KATIE WOKE, HER FLYING TOGS WERE GONE. SHE'D slept in step-ins and a camisole she'd taken from the chest. She did a quick search, rifling through her valise thinking maybe she'd stuffed them there before she'd gone to bed, searched under it and on the big stuffed chair where the bear had sat. Panicky, she yanked her sole pair of trousers from the valise and one of the two reserve blouses, scrambled into them and went looking for her hostess.

"I can't find my clothes!"

The woman—Louise—stood at the sink washing a head of cabbage.

"Oh, hon, I hope you don't mind. They sure looked like they could use a wash. I scrubbed them and hung them on the line early this morning."

Because her face must've registered her distress, the woman added, "I should've asked, but I didn't want to wake you. Our air's really dry, takes no time, really."

"I'm hoping to leave today," Katie said helplessly, though even as she said it, she realized this wasn't likely. She felt . . . trapped. And now that she was fully awake, the aircraft, crippled, loomed up. "There was something in the pocket of the bottoms."

"This?" Louise stepped to the table, picked up and handed the pewter-colored disc to her. Katie gripped it in her palm, squeezed it.

"Oh, gosh. Thanks! It's my good luck charm."

"Well, I know you sure wouldn't want to lose that considering all the risks you have to take up there."

"I got it—" she began but stumbled. *At a carnival from one of those machines that stamps your name around the edges. Curly bought it for me.* "A long time ago."

The woman offered her coffee and toast with jam. Katie sat watching her wash two other heads of cabbage, place them in a dish drainer, then move to the bread box. Her head felt clear this morning after that good bed sleep and her senses had slowed their interior churn to allow her a calmer assessment of her surroundings. Her hostess—she realized now—was a beauty. Brunette, large brown eyes and heavy brows, high cheek bones, and a big bow mouth with cushiony lips, Indian princess–looking. The daughter whose framed photograph stood on the chest didn't favor her—she had the father's long face and thin lips. To have your mother be that good-looking and you not so much . . .

"I'm cooking up a batch of hot water." Louise pointed to the wood stove. "And there's a wash pot full heating in the yard about ready, too. I did promise you a hot bath. If you like, I mean."

Hansel and Gretel. Still, though, to sink herself into a tub of hot water seemed as irresistible as chocolate cake.

"That'd be really swell. If it's not trouble."

"No more than it'd be for any of us."

In the bathroom stood a big claw-footed tub. Louise gave her a towel, and when she left to get the water, Katie stripped and wrapped it around her. Though her left wrist had ached yesterday, it seemed less sore now, so she told herself it was only a sprain and not a break. She stood by while her hostess lugged a huge bucket to the rim of the tub and poured out steaming water, sloshing some onto the linoleum floor. When she held the bucket over the tub, her biceps strained the half sleeves of her housedress.

"I'll get a couple more."

No point in asking if she could help—she was wearing only a towel.

Louise brought in two more buckets, dumped them.

"The tap on the tub will run cold if you need it. Howard pumps water into the tank that's outside. That ought to get you started. I'll bring more in a bit. It gets tepid pretty quick."

Katie lowered herself into the steaming water, hoping it was so hot it would sting a bit at first, and so it did. But she wouldn't temper it with cold. She lay back, let it lap her ribs, her hips, over her navel, her breasts, up her neck, her chin. She had a passing thought about the bandage on her shoulder, but she couldn't resist the water's warm blanket. She inhaled steam, feeling the sweat creep through her scalp, onto her forehead, and into her eyes. She dabbed at the sting with her wet fingers. Tension slid away. She pushed her hair up the tub's incline behind her to keep it dry and let her head slide down until the water licked her ears then covered them. She could hear her breath come and go as if in a cave. Her mind seemed to evaporate, and she was just a melting body.

A tap on the bathroom door brought her knees up into her torso, and she leaned up and into her thighs. Louise cracked the door open, stuck her head through.

"I've got a warm clean rinse here."

She stood over Katie, tilted the bucket, and let the water splash over her shoulders and down her spine, slowly, moving the rim back and forth.

"There! You got your dressing a little damp, but it needs changing, anyway."

Katie pressed the bandage gently and winced. Pink water trickled out from under the bandage.

"What about that hair? Should we give it a once-over?"

"Aw, no. It takes too long to dry."

"Well, you got a lot. I'm surprised you can get it tucked into that flying hat."

"I know. Last time I thought about it, it was short, you know. I'm not partial to it being long. Just happened when I wasn't looking." She thought of the brushes and combs on the runaway girl's vanity.

Louise chuckled. "A girl with hair like this and she doesn't even look at it! Will wonders never cease!"

Though it was a gentle tease that contained an offhand compliment, Katie blushed. Was she being criticized? She wished Louise would leave. The water was still warm enough to enjoy.

"Did your mother wash your hair for you?"

"No."

The answer was so blunt that it served as intended—Louise tried a different probe.

"I have a friend—she runs the café here—and she's pretty darn good with her scissors. She cuts my hair. If you're interested . . ."

"Aw, thanks. Truth is, I'm kind of tight right now. And I know I owe you for fixing me up."

"Don't be silly! We're not gonna charge you. You're a guest."

Why are you so nice to me? "Well, thanks a lot. But like I said, though, I'm hoping I can leave real soon." Each little gesture of hospitality was a strand of a web woven over her form. Like one of those dreams where you're running from someone and you can feel their breath at your back, their fingertips claw your shoulders. She didn't want to be hosted, toasted, or detained, and acts of kindness tugged her deeper into these people's lives, though what they'd given was truly needed and appreciated.

In the runaway's room, Louise laid on a fresh bandage then left her alone to dress. Back to the khaki trousers and the blouse she'd chased her hostess down in. She set her valise on the bed, cocked the lid full open. Yesterday she'd been whisked away from the Travel Air without bringing it, and when she'd realized it, panic jolted her like an angry parent shaking her shoulders. The money she'd scraped up in a hurry was stuffed into an envelope and slid under her clothes, and though she'd checked many times since getting the valise back, she pushed things aside and tapped the white paper with her fingers. It came to her that she didn't used to be so distrustful. But she needed to stay on guard. No telling how much repairs would cost; maybe barter would be possible—once she got the ship aloft, she'd offer rides.

She went out the back door. The big black wash pot on a stand still let off wisps of steam, but the fire had gone to coals. The outhouse she used last night stood beside it. To the west lay an empty horizon, and to the south distant buildings shimmered in the early heat. How far was she from the ship? She could walk it but had no idea where to go, and once she got there, it was still out of gas and maybe unflyable. Hopeless.

She bit her lip, her eyes stung, she squeezed them shut. Gritted her teeth. She held her breath until her heart dropped from a gallop to a walk, let the air out through kissing lips.

The clothesline stood beyond the wash pot, three wires strung between T-frame pipes, very sturdy, she thought, the lines taut. Sheets, pillowcases, men's collared shirts and work trousers, and near one end hung the pieces of her flying suit and the two shirts she wore under the top. She squeezed the sleeves of the shirts—dry already, just as the woman promised. But the coveralls were canvas with a cotton lining, and they were coolly damp to the back of her hand. The woman had wisely turned them inside out to dry. Also, she'd mended the tears in both the flight suit top and the undershirt.

A clink caught her ear. At the barn a large woolly dog with a big square head sat upright in the door, one hind leg slapping at an ear and setting the collar a'jingle. He watched her with great interest as she ambled to him. She stroked his head. When she let up, he pushed against her palm for more. His eyes were a lively brown but sorrowful.

She went to her knees, slipped her arms around his chest, and put her cheek against his neck. He stunk. An urge to confide in him rushed up, but she checked it.

"Well, now *you're* a brave one!"

The husband—Howard, she recalled—had eased up behind her. He smiled on one side of his mouth.

"Does he bite?"

"Oh, no. Not even sure he knows how. But he does stink something awful. Rolled around in a dead coyote, and I haven't had time to scrub him down."

"He doesn't care." Katie rose to her feet but kept her palm on the dog's neck; he leaned into her knee. The farmer had a pair of leather work gloves bunched in one hand like a blunt brown bouquet. He seemed taller but thinner than he had sitting at the table and his face less like a dirty dinner plate with a cigarette stubbed in it. Calmer.

"Well, that's true enough. Did Louise get you all settled?"

"Yes, thanks." She wondered if this was an oblique apology, a reassurance that she'd been welcome.

"I guess she told you about my daughter, Isabelle."

"No, sir. Just that she wasn't here right now."

"One way to put it."

Katie's curiosity at this point weighed only one ounce against the fifty pounds of eagerness to get away.

"I saw her picture in her room. She looks really nice."

"Yes, yes. If and when people gave her half a chance."

She was about to ask where her aircraft lay in relation to the farm when Howard said, "Looks like word's got around," and pointed toward a dust plume moving slowly across the fields headed by a truck. Howard leaned and squinted. "That would be Otis."

The truck came to a stop in the barnyard, the dust skirt billowing out over them before collapsing. The young fellow, Leonard she knew now, jumped from the cab, and a black fellow in overalls stepped down from the passenger side. Leonard stood looking everywhere but at her, then turned his back, strolled to the corral, planted a boot on a rail and his elbows on another, as if expecting a rodeo to break out.

She eased up behind him. "Did you stay all night?"

He looked down at his resting boot. "Yes, ma'am."

"Is everything all right?"

"Yes, ma'am."

"Anybody there now?"

"Yes, ma'am." He half-turned to squint at her forehead. "I paid Ronnie Quigley a nickel to watch it. Their place is right there. You can trust him, I swear. I told him I'd blister his bottom if anything was out of place when we got back."

"What would his Mama say to that?" It was fun to tease someone as bashful as this fellow. It seemed she had a certain effect on him. Always gratifying, like discovering a little cash hidden in your dresser drawer.

He ventured a glance into her eyes. His were gray-blue, framed by hazel lashes and brows. He looked away.

"Aw, she knows me." He sounded hurt. "She knows I wouldn't do that."

"Just kidding. I owe you a nickel."

His lips twitched in a nervous smile.

"Hey, I appreciate what you did. Bet you didn't get much sleep."

"Aw, I like sleeping outdoors. I live in an Indian teepee."

"Really? How come?"

He blushed, as if realizing she might consider this peculiar. "I actually live with my Uncle George—he runs a mercantile across from the café. But he's only got one room in the back, and he snores something awful. Besides, I like it. I've got it fixed up." He swung his gaze up to her face. "I've got a radio!" he exclaimed, as if just discovering it. "A crystal set, anyway. I listen to WBAP in Fort Worth every night." He stuck out his hand. "My name's Leonard, by the way."

The hand was huge and warm but rough with callouses, and he seemed careful not to squeeze too hard.

"I'm . . . Katie." Might as well at this point. Cat's already out of the bag. "Is that your truck?"

"Naw. It's Otis's. But he lets me drive it. I help him."

Her ride to the Travel Air? Just as she was framing the question, Leonard said, "Thing is, see, we came to see if you wanted us to take you out to your airplane to check the damage. Me and Otis—maybe we can fix it."

"Oh, gosh! That's . . . *perfect!*"

"He's got tools of all kinds," Leonard gushed, as if he needed to sell her on their help. "We do a lot of different repairs around here—I work on people's automobiles, like Mabel's Lizzy, so if there's something wrong with your engine, me and Otis together we can probably figure it out even though I've never worked on a radial engine."

"It's a Wright Whirlwind J5. Nine cylinders. It's air-cooled, not like autos. 220 horsepower. It's the same engine Charles Lindbergh had in the Spirit of St. Louis! I've watched one like it be worked on a bunch, but it's not like the Curtiss OX-5 in my old Jenny—I know that engine like the back of my hand. Cur . . . My teacher had me take it down to where it was just hundreds of parts laid out on a tarp and then put it back together."

Leonard seemed to be sweating suddenly, his eyes widening.

"Guess what I'm saying is that if the problem's serious, there's not much we can do without the right part."

"We can try!"

"I like your can-do spirit," Katie said dryly. "I think the only thing wrong is—it's just plain old out of gas."

"We can sure fix that! Otis keeps a five-gallon can in the truck for everybody who needs it. We've only got a dozen autos around here."

Clearly, he was eager to get to work.

The man Leonard called Otis stepped off the back stoop carrying a paper bag. Introductions and explanations were made, and Katie said, "I really, really appreciate this." The fellow was maybe sixty or so, sturdy-looking, with skin so dark it looked almost purple in the sunlight. He carried himself with an easy grace and radiated a welcoming energy. He had a missing front tooth and one eyelid hung lower than the other, almost eclipsing the brown iris.

She told them she just needed to get her things. At the clothesline, she unpinned her garments, bunched them under her arm. The damp lining of the flying suit felt cool to her ribs.

"Miz Larsen?" Louise was at the table writing in what appeared to be a ledger. "I got a ride to my airplane. I'm hoping to get aloft later today, so . . ." She shrugged. "Thanks so much for everything."

"You're welcome, hon. I hope you have a safe journey."

"Thanks."

"I reckon those aren't quite dry yet."

"It's okay. Seems like I'm always flying into rain, anyway."

"I hope somebody's there to greet you where you go."

The woman turned large brown eyes up into Katie's face. Red-rimmed, puffy. Katie shuffled. What Louise said sounded like a traditional blessing, though the tearful look turned it more personal.

"Yeah, thanks. Me, too."

In the runaway's room, she flipped back her suitcase lid, folded the clothing as tight as she could. She usually wore the bulkiest item—the flying suit. The white envelope was safe, still. Though the bed had been made while she was outside, the bear lay there with its head on a pillow as if ready for another night of cuddling. Her hostess, sending a signal she guessed: you're welcome. Seeing it diverted her antsy obsession with the immediate future, tripped her, and in that sprawl, she saw a flicker of images from the past hours: the overheard arguing, the borrowed clothes, the angry father. She'd brought the runaway back, but for unknown reasons there'd been no joy in the homecoming. *I hope somebody's there to greet you where you go.*

The fellows were waiting. She latched the suitcase lid, paused on her way out to consider the photograph on the dresser. The girl there looked far too young to be out on her own or with a bounder, but the portrait was made years ago. No telling where or what she might be. So many things could happen to a girl between then and now.

"Maybe you should come back home," she said.

4

LEONARD FELT SHORT OF BREATH. WITH KATIE JAMMED UP against him in the cab, the contact along his left shoulder, hip, and thigh was agonizing, so he cringed and screwed himself up tiny as he could into the hard metal of the door handle and window crank. He stuck his head out the window like a dog to get air.

The girl's engineering bent floored him. *It's a Wright Whirlwind J5. Nine cylinders. It's air-cooled, not like autos. 220 horsepower. Curtiss OX-5 . . . I know that engine like the back of my hand . . . took it down to hundreds of parts laid out on a tarp then put it back together.*

Holy cow! She might as well have said, *I'm going to take off all my clothes and you can put your hands on me anywhere you want.*

Leonard's tongue was tied down tight as a roped calf. Otis never had a lot to say. The pilot held herself rigid, so Leonard felt all swoony with the tension; the rough road pitched them to and fro against one another, but at least the motor and the junk rattling in the bed made noise enough to smother his discomfort.

Before the truck had halted, Leonard bolted from the cab and ran up the road flapping his arms. "You kids stay away from there!" Children knotted under the wing scattered like quail, giggling. Ronnie Quigley hadn't done his job. His folks, Clifton and Lurleen, stood inside their own barbed-wire fence jawing with the Clymers and a clutch of folks he didn't know well but saw once a month at church. The geezer who brought the mail from Loving once a week was with them, his buggy parked in the road.

When Katie walked up to the plane, they all fell silent.

"You that pilot?" somebody hollered.

Katie flapped a hand as if shooing a gnat and tossed them a wan smile.

"You from Beech-Nut?" someone else yelled.

"You got gum?" came a child's voice.

Katie ignored them. She led Otis and Leonard under the nose, ducking beneath the propeller, where she hunched over the bent outrigger strut on the landing gear. Leonard was sweating profusely. August heat came on strong mid-morning, even with air dry enough to make shade comfortable. He eased under the wing. Should've worn his hat.

"I can't take off or land with this strut all buggered up. She won't travel true on the ground coming or going."

The onlookers edged closer and stood as if at the final green of a golf tournament.

Otis gripped the metal at its bend.

"Reckon that's fixable. A little heat and we can probably get it straight again."

"Once it's bent back, though, that spot's gonna need a brace," offered Leonard.

"Weld it," said Otis. "Good thinking, son."

They moved to the tail section.

"I've kicked myself a hunnerd times about that hole!" Leonard burst out. "I'm really, really sorry! Everybody's always warning me about watching where I put my feet, but I'm just doggone clumsy. But maybe Wally can sew it up and then we can glue the stitches with layers of cloth strips and paint it? It's gotta be strong and smooth so the wind won't catch on a loose bit like a hangnail and tear it open. You think?"

"Happens pretty often." Katie nodded to the rip in the elevator. "You hit a bird the wrong way or hail . . . Probably what you say will work."

"Whew! I was really worried!"

"I think the biggest problem's going to be the elephant ear."

Otis cocked his brows, Leonard his head. Katie led them to the port-side wings and stretched up to point at the tip of the upper wing: this model of Travel Air had an added L-shaped appendage to the ailerons they called an elephant ear. Her ground loop at knocked the airplane briefly vertical, and the port-side ear had been crunched, the fabric torn open.

Otis gingerly waggled the loose, dangling part. "Hmmm. I'd probably have to skin it altogether to see what can be done."

To move the ship, Otis said they could fuel it and drive to the shop, or they could tow it behind the truck.

Katie said, "Let's use the engine if we can."

Leonard retrieved the gasoline can from the truck bed. Katie showed him the fuel port on the nose. He hoisted the container head-high to pour into the receptacle. To Katie he looked solid and steady as he held those forty pounds that high for that long.

Katie seemed unaware of the spectators; though some were drifting away to attend to chores, but the remaining dozen or so traipsed around the wing and stood back while Katie led Otis and Leonard to the propeller.

"Here's what you do," she said to Otis. "First we rotate the prop a couple turns to get old air and oil out of the cylinders." She reached up on her toes to grip the two-bladed propeller and brought it down counterclockwise. "The mag's off now, so the engine won't start until I turn it on."

She reached up to crank the prop again, but Leonard asked, "Can I do it?"

She nodded and Leonard perfectly mimicked her action.

"Okay. I'm going up in the cockpit. You get over here," she moved to the righthand side, "grab the prop and do the same thing clockwise, okay? You gotta be ready to jump back, okay? Because the tank was bone dry, I might have to prime it, so it might not start first crank. Or stay started. Okay?"

"Roger! Don't worry!"

"When it starts, I'll let it warm up, and when I let up on the brakes, though, we'll start moving. You guys stay back at the tail and push it side to side to keep us going straight. I don't know how that bent strut's going to behave, you know."

Katie monkeyed up into the cockpit. Leonard turned to the on-lookers. "Y'all stay back!" He readied himself with his hands on the prop as if to chin himself.

Using the cockpit's hand pump, Katie sprayed fuel into the intake manifold, switched the mag on.

"Ready!"

Leonard heaved on the prop, nearly stumbling backward, and the engine coughed a billow of blue smoke, cleared its throat, spat a wad of oily phlegm, ululated, crowed, hopped out of bed, slid into slippers, and started its day. The onlookers cheered and clapped. Katie gave Leonard a thumb's up.

All they needed would've been a marching band to make the parade complete. The engine's throaty roar drew everyone within a mile, and by the time they'd tacked back and forth across the road to bring the ship into town, folks were lining the fences along the way, stepping out from the stores to watch, the daredevil kids racing along in front of the whirling propeller and ignoring warning shouts from grown-ups, men on horseback, the mailman from Loving following in his buggy, and at one point, Otis gave over his post at the aircraft's trail to Ronnie Quigley so he could retrieve his truck from the site.

By the time they'd maneuvered the aircraft into a space behind the Owl, it was noon, and Wally hurried out the back door to collar Otis: the café was swamped. He needed to get that apron on!

5

THE GIRL ATE LIKE A LUMBERJACK. HEAD DOWN, PLOWING on, as if against a gale. Maybe she thought she'd never cadge another meal until she got where she'd meant to go. Wally had served her two helpings of pork chops and gravy, mashed potatoes, a mess of collard greens, cornbread. Along with her usual customers, today she had the drop-ins who wanted a gawk at the aviatrix. Most were polite enough to order lunch while they took up space observing the feeding aviatrix as if at a zoo, but downside was she plain ran of chops and starting saving back for her regulars.

Among those not polite enough to order even a cup of joe was Arabella Bohanan, who brazenly plopped herself right at the girl's table and tried to interview her while slyly suggesting that the pilot was already mixing with the wrong crowd. Would the aviatrix be staying long? Arabella would be delighted to offer her lodging and meals for the duration of her visit—the ranch had a guest *house* with "modern conveniences," (meaning indoor toilet). To Wally's satisfaction, Arabella wasn't making headway, looked like. It was hard to compete with a full plate of hot food, one more reason for Wally to keep bringing side dishes that weren't on the menu—a bowl of black-eyed peas with bacon, steamed cabbage with likewise. The girl paid only slight heed to the patter Arabella served up as she ate, and, truthfully, if it had been anyone but Arabella, Wally would be tempted to say the girl was downright rude.

She didn't look like someone Arabella might favor with her attention. If you didn't know she'd flown that aircraft, you'd have placed her as a street urchin. A starving one at that. Dirty fingernails, hair all a'tangle. If you were the girl's mother, you wouldn't brag about her table manners, either, and she sure had not been taught to small talk and smile all the while like an idiot. She was polite enough to say thank you, but Wally'd bet a dollar to a doughnut she'd not learned to arrange a vase of flowers, play the piano, or recite poetry by the Brownings. Something rough and tumble about her.

Wally's kind of female, in other words.

Eventually, Arabella departed, but Wally couldn't say what agreement had been reached. When the pilot—Katie, she said—finished her chow down, she seemed dazed, stunned, though she stirred enough to shake hands with folks who dropped by the table to introduce themselves and welcome her.

When the last blue-plate special had been served, Wally took the seat that Arabella had vacated.

"Sorry there's no pie today."

The pilot grinned and rubbed her stomach. "Nowhere to put it, anyway. This was all really great. I was so hungry I forgot to even ask what it cost."

"You look way too pore to pay. You can work it off and we'll hold your machine in pawn."

Wally was known for her dry delivery; folks who didn't know her well often couldn't tell if she were kidding.

"I can't cook but I can wash dishes and scrub floors."

"That works."

Wally drew a pack of Camels from her apron pocket, tapped one halfway out, and pointed it across the table.

"Smoke?"

"Not yet, thanks."

"Wanna save it for later?"

"I meant not yet in my life."

Wally nodded. She lipped the cigarette and lit it with a kitchen match.

"Just wanted to let you know," she offered more earnestly. "There's a telephone in the hallway. Not many around here. Everybody uses it. It's on the house." She winked.

The Bohanans also had a telephone, and Wally didn't know if Arabella had included it in the inventory of amenities. She was dying to find out if Katie had succumbed to Arabella's wretched charm but was far too proud to ask.

Katie said, "Huh. Okay, thanks."

Mabel had slipped in the back door and ate a mug of peas and cabbage in the kitchen, then came out to greet Wally and the flyer. Wally left her in charge of the visitor and went to the kitchen to help Otis with the clean-up.

She scraped food from plates into the slop bucket.

"That Arabella Bohanan makes me so goddamn mad!"

"Aw, now."

"No kidding. I couldn't believe that cow would actually set foot inside our place just because we had that pilot, and she had the goddamn gall to sit there jawing at her and did not order a single blessed thing!"

"Aw, now."

"I mean it was just like her to try to monopolize her. She carried on like she was an ambassador to all the finer things of Noname and wanted to save that pilot from rubbing up against the wrong folks. I couldn't believe it! I wanted to slap her silly."

"Aw, now."

"I got a notion to call her on that goddamn telephone she's so proud of and tell her that if she shows up inside my place again, I will kick her hiney from here to Kingdom come!"

"Aw, you don't mean that."

"Like hell I don't! You watch me!"

Otis was standing at the counter dipping plates in a tub of rinse water; he shook off his hands, turned and drew Wally into his arms. Right now, being in his clutch made her half glad but also half mad.

"Simmer down. She's a piss ant."

"Well, I'm gonna squash her under my shoe, then. I say up your hole with a totem pole to the whole damn lot of them."

They stood embraced a moment, gently rocking.

"Bo's okay. We get along. Bo's given me a lot of work."

"He never *gave* you nothing! He pays you to do things he either can't or doesn't want to do."

"Aw, now."

After a moment, Wally said, "Sometimes I wish you'd get mad on my behalf."

He unwound his arms from around her back and turned toward the washtubs on the counter.

"I reckon you're always fired up enough for two."

Wally went back to her scraper and the dirty plates, but unsaid thoughts ruffled her efforts at calm. She believed that Arabella snubbed them because Otis was a Negro. Not one of those honey-colored fellows or one of those can't-really-tell-if-he-is-or-not Negroes that white folks warm up to quicker. No, Otis was a Bona Fide Black Man. Suspecting Arabella of that insult made Wally angry on Otis's behalf. But he should be the one stomping around the kitchen raving and ranting and she the one to coo and pet and sing a lullaby.

She was so proud of him. He'd been the first around here to order propane cylinders to fuel a gas cook stove, and, without that, having the Owl wouldn't be possible: too much labor, wood was scarce, and coal was costly and filthy. And that three-hundred-gallon water tank on stilts beside the Larsens' house—Otis's idea. He and Howard had helped one another with the installations both there and here.

Aside from her telephone, no telling what the Bohanans could boast of now. Arabella's telephone was private, but Wally took pride in offering theirs to anyone. She'd made a point of making sure the pilot knew the use was gratis. She thought the girl would be pleased and surprised. Instead, though, she'd seemed—well, indifferent. But polite. If Wally had crashed an aircraft alone way in the middle of East Jesus, she'd be antsy to find a telegraph office to send back news that she was safe and sound. Let loved ones know so they wouldn't worry. Not that Wally had any loved ones elsewhere now, but at the girl's age she had. Also, Mabel told her the girl had said she was delivering the airplane to its owner in California. Wouldn't *that* person want to know what happened?

"I told that girl she could use our telephone. No charge."

"Sure," Otis said.

"Kind of odd, though."

"What?" He'd lifted the rinse tub to carry it out to the garden and stood holding it, waiting. Her thoughts were too scattered and unsettled for a quick answer. She shrugged, stepped to the screen door, and held it open for him.

"Nothing."

6

LEONARD HELPED OTIS JACK THE AIRCRAFT ON BLOCKS TO free the right wheel off the ground. They were exploring how the strut assembly could be dismantled for repair. Katie stood by watching, and something suddenly occurred to Leonard.

"Say, I've been meaning to ask. How come the word BEECH-NUT is painted big on both sides of the . . . fuselage?" He was pleased to use this new word. "Is that the chewing gum company? Do they own the airplane, or are they your sponsors?"

"Uh . . ." She turned to peer at the flank of the aircraft as if noticing the lettering for the first time. "Uh, yeah. I mean, they *used* to be. Sort of. Not now. Not the owners, I mean." She stared at the letters for a bit, then she turned to Otis.

"Do you guys have any paint I could borrow?"

"Paint? Like *house* paint?"

"Any kind I guess."

"Fresh out," said Otis.

"We got some at my uncle George's. It was left over from when I did a corral fence. Does it matter what color?"

She pointed at the letters. "Whatever will cover that."

Leonard stifled his surprise. All along she'd seemed half-hydrophobic to flap her wings soon as she could, and now? If he hadn't asked about the letters, would she have thought to paint them over?

"I could do that while you guys . . ." She waved at the crippled landing gear.

"Okay. I'll go get it. It's just across the street."

He'd not gone a dozen steps when he heard her call, "Wait up. I'll come with," and she skipped up beside him. He thought his head would explode. People would see them together. He took a smaller stride to slow their pace. He wished he lived a mile away.

"Thing is, Lenny," she said. "I'm kinda short on funds, you know, I mean *emergency* money. I don't know how I can pay you guys. How much do you think Mr. Jefferson will want for fixing my ship?"

He blushed. *Lenny!* "Gosh, I dunno, but I sure as heck won't say word one to you about whatever I do, seeing as how I did half the damage!"

"See, what I'm thinking is that once it's fixed, I can give people rides. It's what we do at the county fairs. I wouldn't charge you guys, of course, but maybe there's enough rubes around willing to cough up bucks for a thrill like that, so I can pay Mr. Jefferson back and have pocket money to boot. What do you think?"

"Yeah, sure!"

"Somebody has to spread the word and everything."

"Hey, I'm your hawker!" He leapt and spun in the street, mimed having a megaphone. "Come one, come all! Step right up, see the amazing aviatrix! Ride in her flying machine and see your world just the way the eagles do! Zip and swoop and glide! Only five bucks a ride!"

Katie laughed. "Five, you think? Rubes are scared already to go up, so you don't wanna give them still another reason to balk."

"How about a bake sale? That's what they do around here."

"Aw, that's a sweet idea, Lenny. But that'd take forever to set up."

Her confidante now. He stepped more lightly, up on his toes. "You wanna see my radio? I'd like my uncle George to meet you, too."

"Sure. Ok."

A millisecond later, he realized he'd have to take her into the Comanche lodge. It suited him fine, that one circular room, and he even liked living the way they did, even if he didn't hunt buffalo. He'd overlaid leftover linoleum on the dirt for a floor, and some ladies had donated old throw rugs. His easy chair, his army cot, a student desk, a chest of drawers—it was all he needed. During the winter, he lugged in a cast iron stove from the store, set it right in the center of the room, and ran a flue up through the opening at the top of the teepee. Some folks thought his living here was childish or uncivilized, but the alternative was sharing one room with his uncle at the back of the store. He had freedom, his own space.

He pulled back the flap that covered the opening. "I have to warn you. It's kind of primitive."

He ducked inside; she followed. They stood looking about, Leonard struggling to see it with her eyes—or, rather, struggling to imagine that she saw it with his.

"There's my bed." The cot had a narrow mattress and a sleeping bag rumpled and bunched like a giant slumbering caterpillar. "That's my desk, and my chest of drawers. Hey!" He stepped to the dresser, raised his headphone set and waggled it. "My radio." He lifted the base to show it off. "I got all the parts from the Monkey Ward catalog. I wish I could get reception in the daytime so I could show you. But at night it's really great to hear music and news from WBAP in Fort Worth, and sometimes I get Denver."

She gave a little hop and fell backward into his easy chair. She patted the arms with her palms. She grinned.

"Sweet mother of Frances, Lenny! This is so flippin' neat!"

"You really think so?"

"Gosh, yes! You have it all to yourself!"

"Yeah. I kind of put it all together. I got the teepee from a rancher I dug a bunch of postholes for. I mean about a hunnerd of them."

"I like it because it's not fancy." She crooked her little finger to mime a socialite sipping tea.

He laughed. "You can say that again."

"I like it because it's not fancy."

They both laughed.

"Where do you hang your clothes?"

"I don't have much takes hanging. Those four drawers is about all I need, but there's an old suit of my Dad's in back of the store for when there's a funeral or a wedding. Usually a funeral," Leonard joked.

"Where's your dad?"

"He didn't come back from France."

"Aw, I'm sorry. Lots of good fellows got killed."

"I guess that's what happened. I was just a tyke when he went. To this day my Ma thinks he's still alive over there with a French gal."

"Where's she?"

"Arkansas."

"You got brothers and sisters?"

Leonard took a breath. His face tingled. "Yeah. Too many. It's why I'm here."

"Sorry to be so nosy!" She apparently read discomfort on his face. "It's just, well, everything seems so interesting when you go somewhere else, you know? I'm just a naturally curious person."

"It's okay. I don't tend to talk much about it." He chuckled. "People say I'm a chatterbox, but it's the one thing I just, you know . . . I guess I've never thought it was worth telling. Nobody asked. I got here when I was twelve, so it seems like a long time ago."

"Golly! We kind of have the same story!"

"Really?"

"Uh-huh." She sprang up from the chair. "But we better go find that paint!"

Leonard took her through the front door of the store. His uncle was cutting a swatch of cheese cloth with pinking shears for Phyllis Slater, and they turned to look as he and Katie came in.

Thrilling as it might be to meet the aviatrix, their excitement didn't last the length of Leonard's blow-by-blow of all that had passed since Katie landed yesterday, and Katie tugged on his sleeve to pull him back on track.

In the rear of the store, Leonard found three near-empty cans of white fence paint, which he determined could be combined and thinned with turpentine. He and Katie carried them back to Otis's shop. Otis in the meantime had heated and bent the strut back into shape and was rifling through his scrap metal bin for a brace to weld to it.

Leonard and Katie set about painting over the big bold yellow letters. Leonard was torn between his normal pride in doing things well and quickly and wanting to make the task last longer. Though it would make sense for each to take a side, he couldn't resist standing alongside her to work.

He felt compelled to ask, "How come we're doing this?"

She shrugged. After a moment, she said, "Keeps people from asking, you know, are you with the company? Or like you heard them out there asking if I had samples of gum to give out."

"You wouldn't wanna give people the wrong idea."

"Right."

7

"I HATE LIKE THE DICKENS TO ASK THIS, BUT COULD YOU TELL me where I could buy some, uh, you know, pads?"

"Pads?" asked Mabel.

"Uh, yeah. For when you . . ."

"Oh! Gosh. Sorry to be so dense. Well, over in Loving there's a drug store—they put a cigar box on the counter for you to put your money in, then you pick them up without having to talk to a clerk. But that's twenty miles. Are you . . .?"

"Yep. Last thing I want. Very last."

"Oh, I know!"

"Kind of a surprise, too. I had it worked out I'd be where I was headed before . . ."

"Oh, always at the worst time! I buy mine through the Wards catalog, a batch at a time. They come in a big brown box."

"Could I buy a couple from you?"

"Buy them? Sweetie! Of course not! ¡Mi casa es su casa! That's Spanish—it means my house is your house! I may have an old belt, too. The elastic's all worn out, but you could probably pin it up to fit you."

Mabel was chugging along at a walker's pace, swerving to miss the holes so as to make her passenger's ride as smooth as possible, though, on reflection, she supposed the pilot was accustomed to being tossed about. Twilight had faded, and Mabel was once again enjoying the novelty of driving her automobile with its headlights tossing jittering orbs of illumination across familiar shapes.

Earlier, she'd gone to see how repairs were proceeding. Leonard and Otis were struggling to reattach the wheel assembly to the aircraft. She was surprised that the BEECH-NUT insignia had been painted over. Katie was in the Owl talking to Wally, but she soon emerged carrying a workman's black tin lunch box.

"Miz Jefferson fixed me some supper for later!" she declared to Mabel, waggling the box as she strolled to Mabel's side. "We'll probably work until past sundown. Miz Jefferson's going to bring sewing stuff to fix the tear."

Mabel was tempted to correct Katie's presumption that Wally's surname was also Jefferson; it was Jackson. Why the pair had different surnames was a source of speculation, and since Mabel didn't know why, she left well enough alone.

"Everybody around here has been really super!"

"They're both on the top of my list."

Mabel chalked up the aviatrix's ebullience to her pleasure in the repairs. She noticed the valise standing upright in the bed of Otis's truck.

"You're not going back to the Larsens tonight?"

"Oh! Well, I hate to put people out. They're nice and all, but fish and guests . . ." She smiled hopefully at Mabel.

Stink after *three* days, thought Mabel. Not one night.

"I was thinking maybe there's a hotel."

"Well, no. We do need one for sure." Mabel remembered that Katie had asked about a hotel last night in Louise's kitchen, and Louise and she offered bed and board. Was her memory that bad? Probably she'd been shaken up by the accident, still, and the injury.

"You could certainly stay with me. I can't offer much in the way of comfort, but it keeps the rain off my head. I was thinking maybe the woman you met at lunch—Arabella?—might've offered, so that's why, you know, I didn't speak right up about it."

"Oh, thanks! She did, and it was kind of her, but I just . . ." She shrugged. "Sounded too fancy for me."

"My place won't be too fancy, I guarantee you."

"Oh, thanks! That'll be so super! Two single girls! Miz . . . Uh."

"Bohanan."

"Miz Bohanan—" She turned her palms up, helpless.

"I guess she had a lot of plans for you."

Katie guffawed. "Yeah. Sure enough."

Half-panicky, half-glowing with pleasure, Mabel had scurried to her "cottage" to make it presentable. *Two single girls.* That conjured a pleasurable tete-a-tete, two heads on a pillow, giggling, secrets shared. A friend! Good Lord—it had been a thousand years since she'd spent a night way past sleep time just talking, lying in the arms of a friend, feeling *understood. Understood completely!* She and Elizabeth were sixteen; they were scrapbook crazy—they had one for their friendship and their mutual passions—peonies and petunias, Emily Dickinson, *Uncle Tom's Cabin, Wuthering Heights, Little Women, Five Little Peppers.* What they most prized about each other, how they'd spend their old age sharing rooms in an Italian *pensione.* They were the same size—almost, anyway—and traded clothes. They had jazz records and danced the Charleston with one another in their bedrooms. Ragtime. They used each other's faces as palettes for experiments in makeup. Elizabeth introduced her to cologne and lipstick. Elizabeth went to France and England with her parents and sent a postcard every day. *I miss you so terribly, terribly. French boys!!*

But she was married by the next year, and by the time Mabel graduated high school, Elizabeth had a son and was only interested in socializing with young mothers. When Mabel wasn't invited to the child's first birthday party, it broke her heart.

Two single girls! It made her pulse race.

Well, she could at least tidy up, fill the pitcher on the vanity with water, and set out the fanciest washcloth and towels she never used. A fresh bar of soap. She'd offer the bedroom to Katie, and she'd take the sofa.

The "teacher's house," so the schoolboard called it, was a two-room cabin. Her bed, a dresser with mirror and porcelain pitcher and matching basin, a straight-back chair, and an armoire for clothes occupied one room, a sofa and two wing chairs the other, plus a counter with a sink whose drain piped out into the yard. She hand-pumped water from a well out back. She had knick-knack shelves with framed photos of family, carpets, oil lamps, pictures on the wall. A bookcase stuffed with books and magazines. A secretary stood in the corner whose lid dropped down for a desk. A small table with two ice-cream parlor chairs was wedged into a corner. Most people would probably judge it had too much furniture, but she found clutter and coziness reassuring. She avoided hosting parents of her students and preferred to visit their homes, in part because the prestige of her position always warranted a good meal.

She'd left an oil lamp burning on the table beside the sofa.

"Golly! This is really nice!"

"You think so? It's so much better than where they put me up the first year—it was an old chicken house or hog pen or something that they'd tried to doll up, but, oh, it was awful! I would've left if they hadn't built this just to keep me here. Or any teacher, not just me, I didn't mean to imply I was that important."

"Oh, I bet you are!"

Mabel blushed. She pointed to the lunchbox Katie held. "Just put your dinner on the hah-hah 'kitchen counter' there, and I'll show you the hah-hah 'boudoir.' You can sleep there."

In the bedroom, they jousted about who was to take the bed (*you, no **you**, no you!*), then Katie insisted on rock-paper-scissors. Mabel had witnessed this mode of resolution but had never used it, believing it to be exclusively for grade-school boys, and so Katie gave her a quick tutorial. But the thing went by so fast that Mabel kept replaying it later before going to sleep. She'd brought out scissors on the count of three, and Katie had shown paper? rock? then immediately declared, "You won!" and sort of disbanded her fingers from the field of play so fast it was hard to tell what, assembled, they'd formed.

"Just as well," Katie said. "I might have bedbugs in my stuff. Wouldn't want to spread them to that nice bed."

Spying Mabel's expression, Katie grinned. "Just kidding."

Mabel told her that the pads and the belt were in the bottom dresser drawer, and safety pins were on the vanity. The pitcher had water "if you want to freshen up. I set out the washcloth and towel for you—and, oh, the soap, too. Don't be shy about using it."

Katie laughed.

"Oh, no! I didn't mean you needed it especially! Just that because it hasn't been used, people might be, you know, reluctant to be the first. I'll leave you to it."

Blushing, she hurried out of the bedroom. Then she paced and fiddled with items on the shelves, straightening the antimacassars on the backs of the wing chairs, at a loss, marking time. What should she use as linens on the sofa? She had one extra sheet and a quilt Frances Mossman's mother had given her for tutoring—a nice one, really, a star pattern. Those should do. Though the late August days still waxed hot by midday, nights here cooled, and if you opened the windows, you could sleep comfortably in the dry, cooler air.

A shame to have her guest sleep on the sofa. She'd lain on it for cat naps and knew that the lumps and sags—and the narrowness—would be trying. Had Katie really lost the scissors-rock-paper match? She seemed so reluctant to take help—you had to push it on her. You could admire that in a person generally, but it could also be a nuisance. If you clearly saw the obvious need that someone had, it seemed to Mabel that you shouldn't have to struggle to make them take your help, right?

But you had to offer help, anyway, of course. *This is silly*, she might say. *That bed's plenty big enough for two single girls. My little sister used to climb in with me nights when she'd be scared—or just lonely. And I had a friend, Elizabeth . . .*

Her hands were sweating; the nape of her neck tingled. No reason this should be so hard!

Katie emerged from the bedroom. Though she hadn't changed her clothes, her face still bore the ruddy flush of a scrubbing.

"Everything work out ok?"

"Oh, yes! Thanks so much! You're a lifesaver!"

"Well, hardly."

"I'm starving! Let's see what Miz Jefferson packed for us."

"Well, I'm sure she didn't mean for me to butt in."

"Don't be crazy! Come on!"

Katie set the lunchbox atop the table in the corner near the window. She moved decisively, as if everything were familiar, as if she were in charge. Mabel eased up beside her; she could smell the soap now that its scent had been activated. Not too floral, more herbal, woody. Pleasant. The girl had such marvelous hair!

"Wow! Looks like a bacon-and-egg sandwich ... wait! Two of them! Perfect!" She pulled a packet from the box and unpeeled the waxed paper. "Oh, my mother of holy water! Huge piece of apple pie!" She whirled and beamed at Mabel. "Way too much for just me, I swear."

"Okay, I surrender. Hey, you know what? I think I have wine! Would you like some? Do you drink it?"

"H ... E ... double hockey sticks yes!"

"Thing is, you can't breathe a word of it to anybody. Taking a sip of anything but grape juice at communion could get me tossed out of my school zippity quick. Even if it were legal, it's sure not approved for schoolmarms."

"My lips are sealed."

The bottle lay hidden in her armoire behind a stack of primers. She retrieved it.

"Uh-oh! I guess it takes a special instrument to open it."

"Lemme see." Katie took the bottle. "You got a paring knife?"

Mabel rooted about in her utensils drawer, found one, passed it over. Katie removed the metal wrapping, started gouging into the cork. Mabel retrieved two jelly tumblers, set them on the table. Soon Katie'd extracted enough of the cork to push the remainder into the bottle.

"There! Had to tear the cork up, though. Guess we'll have to drink the whole thing."

"Mmm. I've never had more than one glass at a time in my life."

"Always a first."

Katie poured the two tumblers almost to the brim. She held hers

76

up. "To clear skies." She tossed back half of her glass. "Aw, Geez. This is so much better than the hootch the pilots I know cook up."

"To new friends," said Mabel. She took a sip. It was red, anyway, tasted both sweet and sour. Maybe an acquired taste. All the wine she'd ever had tasted like grape syrup.

"Do you know anything about wine?"

"It has alcohol," said Katie.

"Me, neither."

Katie finished off her draw, poured herself another. "Come on, now. Keep up." She grinned.

Mabel squinted her eyes shut, swallowed a mouthful of wine. It seemed a bit less acrid now.

"There's a story about this wine."

"Yeah?"

Having overtured the account, Mabel felt a rush of doubt, hesitated, then obligation to the promise prodded her on. "I was running errands over in Loving. This would be, I don't know, over a year ago. I was in the post office, and his handsome fellow—I mean a *really handsome* fellow—helped me load some packages that I was bringing back here for folks. He was a drummer for a mercantile out of Dallas. Really handsome and friendly. He said he was looking for somebody to eat lunch with, he hated eating alone. It's not every day somebody like this fellow gives me a second look—"

"I dunno why not!"

"Because I . . . oh, anyway, I told myself what the heck. Lunch. So what? I didn't tell him I was a teacher—it just puts some people on edge, you know, they start watching their p's and q's, I mean literally. We chatted about all manner of things. When we finished, he said he wanted to give me something in return for my excellent company. He was driving a vehicle belonged to his firm, and he had a whole box of this hidden under a tarp. Maybe he was selling it on the sly or something . . . Anyway, he said he hoped I wouldn't be offended if he offered it to me, seeing as how it was illegal and all. If I was a teetotaler, why then I could just pass it along. Or even turn it over to the sheriff so long as I didn't let on where it came from. I said I hadn't had much experience with it, but I was grateful for the gift. Actually, it was kind of exciting, that we were both indulging in something, well, illicit. I'd become a bootlegger! He was *so* handsome, took my breath away. And truth be told I'd have been thrilled even if he'd just picked a button up out of the dirt and gave it to me. He said Noname wasn't exactly in his territory but if he had spare time before he had to go back to Dallas, he'd love to drive over and have me show him around. And I said I would be delighted. And then I thought about him all the way home. I thought maybe he'd come to Noname and we'd open the bottle and drink some together. I pictured all the places I could take him—not that there are many, here—but I know a place where the sunsets are, well, inspirational. Only hill we got in a ten-mile radius. I wondered what it might be like to be married to such a man, and I could be standing there in the threshold when he came back from his trips. Bringing me trinkets, and me giving him . . . kisses in return." She blushed, surprised at herself. She'd been sitting on this hurt all this time and never told a soul. And hadn't perceived before lighting into it just how pathetic it made her. "Such silly girlish dreams."

"What a romantic story."

"Well, it would be if he'd ever showed up."

"Aw, what a son of a . . . motherless goat!" Katie sipped a bit and licked her lips. "There's another way to look at that story."

"What's that?"

Katie shrugged. "You're little wifey standing in the door while he comes home after catting around all over the countryside, drinking wine with beautiful single gals."

"Well, there's that, too, I guess."

Katie waggled the top of the bottle. "Anyway, I feel favored."

"Had to open it sooner or later. Might as well be when there's somebody to drink it with. And that sure wouldn't be anybody I know here."

"Sorry I'm not handsome."

"You'll do in a pinch."

They clinked and drank again. Already warmth was spreading across her shoulders like a light shawl.

"Let's eat," said Katie.

They plowed through the sandwiches and split the pie. Mabel got two more glasses and poured water for them out of her stoneware crock. She noted that they'd managed to down half the wine, though Katie'd gone after it with relish and was probably three to Mabel's two on the glass count.

"Listen." Mabel merely leaned across the table toward the pilot, though inwardly it felt like a lunge. "I've been thinking. It's really bad manners for me to make you sleep on that damned sofa. It's a torture rack."

"Aw, heck, I'm used to—"

"No, listen! I got that bed from this married couple who were moving. Plenty big enough for, you know, two single girls. My sister used to sleep with me all the time after she stopped wetting her bed—"

"Better safe than sorry!"

"Uh, yeah. And I had this really dear friend, Elizabeth, we used to have the most wonderful times . . . You ever go to a *slumber party?*"

Katie shook her head. "What is it?"

"Well, it's when you and a friend or friends you stay up all night at somebody's house just . . . I dunno, just being together. Talking and the like. Maybe you sleep and maybe not. Elizabeth and I did that all the time. It was the most fun." She couldn't bring herself to finish *I ever had in my life.*

"I never got to have one."

"Aw, poor baby."

"Are you gonna cry for me?"

"Only if you want me to."

Katie tossed down another half glass of wine. Her capacity and zest for the stuff was an alarming surprise. "Sure. I'd love that. I deserve it, don't ya think?"

"I do. Indeed, I do."

Katie had trouble pouring from the bottle because chunks of floating cork stopped it up. Mabel suggested sticking the paring knife in the mouth to hold it back, and that successful solution resulted in two more full glasses and another toast.

"Here's to hootch."

"May it be legal again someday," said Mabel.

"Amen."

After a moment, Mabel asked, "Do you know any card games?"

"Yeah. Old Maid."

"I haven't got the deck for it. Besides, that name cuts too close to the bone."

"I know poker, too. I watched pilots play it in the hanger."

"I don't know that."

"I could teach you."

"Do you play for money?"

"Don't have to. You can use beans or matches."

"Okay. But first I have to pee-pee."

"Pee-pee?" Katie giggled. "You mean 'tinkle' or 'wee-wee'?"

"Oh, well, paw-don me, madam! I fear I have a need to micturate."

"Micturate!? Well, no, you must paw-don ME, madam, for I am feeling the urge to your-in-ate."

They started laughing, then the laughter of each fed off the other until they were gasping; Mabel clutched her belly and bent over the table, and a huge fart boomed out from under her. Katie exploded anew, and Mabel tried to say "Excuse me" but was laughing too hard to get it out.

When they'd regained their breath, Katie said, "This pilot I know— he always says he needs to drain his lizard."

"How elegant!"

Only rarely did Mabel use the outdoor privy at night: she had a chamber pot under her bed. The thought flitted through her mind to use it and to offer it, but a squeamish modesty held it back.

"Follow me. Let us go drain our lizards."

A hurricane lamp hung by a peg near the rear door; she lighted it, then went into the "yard"—a weed-strewn lot that Leonard was kind enough to scythe to cut a path to the privy. As always, the nearby buildings were dark, and only a dim glow showed in the Owl's upper story. She stopped, gazed up. The high black sky was sequined with a thousand visible stars, and the moon was dancing among them. Or wobbling, anyway. Or maybe it was just she wobbling. She felt dizzy but oddly elated.

"This is one reason I stayed."

"There's no sky where you come from?"

"Not like this. You ever fly at night? I bet the sky's spectacular up there."

"Never as a pilot, just as a passenger. Thing is, you're up there after dark it's really hard to get back down without breaking your neck. You've got to really know what you're doing."

She let Katie take the lantern inside the privy. Waiting, she stood surveying her surroundings—so mysterious at night! Something simple and banal as a privy trip's a thrilling adventure when you've got a pal and you're both half-lit! That was the thing about a friendship—it didn't matter doodly-squat what you did, where you went. It was the together part that turned it magical. So many things about Katie had surprised her, like the ease they had with each other, the rapport. Of course, since Katie was not a tax-paying citizen of the county, Mabel had no worries that anything she said or did would bring reproach. It was odd how you could be yourself with a stranger, feel free to show a weakness, confess to a silly pitiful experience, say, such as dreaming about a handsome drummer who'd paid you the mild compliment of his passing attention.

After the poker lesson in which Mabel had trouble remembering the hierarchy of winning hands, Katie yawned, and Mabel took the hint, though she was less sleepy than maybe she'd ever been her whole life, she estimated.

Katie's valise held her flying suit and only a few day-wear garments, so Mabel gave her a set of flannelette pajamas; they might've been dressed like twins had Katie not had to roll up the sleeves and cuffs.

They lay side by side in the dark, Mabel trying to calm her heart. The woody herbal fragrance of the guest soap wafted across the space between them. She could hear Katie breathing, feel currents of warmth easing their way toward her. It dazzled her, how having another human presence beside her in these intimate circumstances jazzed up her awareness, her self-consciousness, how every iota of her senses was devoted exclusively to gauging, detecting, and assessing the slightest motions of Katie's human form. It had been so . . . very . . . long. The darkness was a very warm blanket of comfort, oddly facilitating their mutual awareness yet also allowing for something hidden. Desire trickled like a rivulet through her body, though desire for what she didn't know.

"Are we having our slumber party now?"

"Are you sleepy?"

"I was," said Katie. "But I don't want to miss anything. Are you?"

"Not in the least. Not one ounce."

To her own surprise, Mabel began weeping.

"Oh, Mabel! Don't cry!"

"But I WANT TO!"

"Okay. Feel free."

She exploded into sobs, then she went at the enterprise with considerable gusto, boo-hooing to beat the band, and after a while she caught her breath, sat up, jerked open a nightstand drawer, yanked out a handkerchief and blew her nose like a bugle.

"There!"

"Is that what you do at a slumber party?"

"Sometimes. Elizabeth and I . . ."

"You don't have to talk about it if you don't want to."

"Oh, no! See, it's a *happy* memory! This takes me back. We'd talk and talk and talk and talk!"

"What about?"

"Anything and everything."

"Bet it was about boys."

"Oh, my word, yes! Endlessly!" She chuckled. "Pointlessly! Fruit-lessly!"

"Did you have a beau?"

"Oh, sure. We got valentines, they walked us home from school, soda shop, moving picture show, went to cotillions and the like. Boys that age, they're not the least particular."

"Cotillions?"

"Fancy dances."

"But nobody ever serious, right?"

"Right. Elizabeth got married, though, even before we graduated."

"Was she as pretty as you?"

"Oh, come on, Katie!"

"No, really. You have beautiful eyes. Sort of hazel, sort of green, always changing, like the ocean. Makes you mysterious."

"Well, my eyes are nothing compared to your truly spectacular hair!"

"Oh, my sweet mother of pearl! You can have it! 'Hey, carrot top!' 'Hey, you got a burning bush up there! Better call the fire department!' 'Hey, everybody, slam on your brakes, there's a red light ahead!' Swear by all that's holy next fellow who calls me 'Red' is gonna get smacked in the kisser. I HATE my hair! And the complexion that goes with it."

After a moment, Mabel said, "In college I had a terrible crush on one of my professors."

"My, oh my, do tell!"

"You're teasing me now."

"Yes."

"Do I seem . . . *innocent* to you?"

Katie sighed. "Not exactly. Just *normal*."

That stung a little. She'd like to be considered exceptional. Her rejoinder would be *at least I'm not feral*.

"What about here?"

Mabel laughed. "Well, look around."

"What about Lenny?"

"Leonard? Oh, Lord!"

"He's really good looking. Those blue eyes kind of make your jaw drop."

"Yes, there's a Swede somewhere in his line, for sure. But you know what's really interesting? Leonard has no earthly idea of how handsome he is. I don't believe he even owns a mirror."

"I didn't see one."

"You—hmm. He showed you his Indian tee-pee?"

"Yeah, we were just getting some paint."

Something unsettling about that picture—Katie in his quarters, where she herself had never been.

"He has many good qualities. There's not an ounce of guile in that boy. You could trust him from here to Eternity. And he's very smart, very curious. Always eager to please, eager to help. Hard-working. I think he needs a bigger sphere to develop in, though. I feel—well, I am fond of him. He'll make some lucky girl a really good husband and father someday. And I admit that he's had a crush on me for a good while. At least until you showed up."

"I saw you hug him last night in the road when we went to the Travel Air."

Was she being accused of something? "That was to reward him for standing out there all night guarding *your* aircraft," she snapped. "It should've been you."

After a moment, Katie said, "Yeah, you're right. I promise I'll hug him tomorrow."

"Don't get him too excited."

"I try to be very careful about that kind of thing now."

"That's wise. Okay, so how about you?"

"How about me what?"

"Beaus."

"Aw, geez." Mabel listened in the silence that followed—a hitch in the breath, a twitch in a toe? Was Katie concocting a story or screwing up her courage? She groaned, sighed, turned over onto her back.

"Okay, well, in the first place, I didn't have any kind of regular upbringing. No cotillions or slumber parties, for sure. No boys sending me Valentines or any of the other stuff. I went to a bunch of different schools and sometimes not at all. Sometimes I think I missed a lot but other times I think it was something special. I was with grownups most of the time."

"Well, yes—you're an aviatrix!" Mabel wanted to be encouraging.

"My Pop flew Jennys during the war, and when he came back, he and my mom hooked up with a flying circus. We didn't really live anywhere but we went everywhere. I told you she was a wing-walker. I'm their only kid but they didn't stay married long. They worked the same circus, though, then he went off with one outfit and she went with another, and I got flipped back and forth between them whenever one got tired of being in charge of a kid."

A lull fell. Mabel didn't know whether to coax her or simply wait her out in silence. Katie sighed, shifted back onto her side facing Mabel.

"I got tired of that and when I was about fifteen, I told them I'd just go where I wanted and with who I wanted, so there wasn't any point in trying to argue with each other about who was supposed to be the parent. I stuck with my mom's outfit because there was a pilot I'd begged to teach me to fly. He'd flown in France, too, but he'd lied about his age, so he was still young—well, right now he's only twenty-seven. Really scared of nothing, I mean *nothing!* He's like a lot of these guys, just living day to day hoping for a chance to get aloft. But he is—was—different, too. Kind of like a father or an uncle or a big brother, always looking out for me and stuff. He was really kind and patient, not like those guys who just don't want to see a girl up there in the cockpit no matter how good she is and are always looking to undermine you. He had faith in me, you know? He stuck up for me. And I believed I was something special to him."

Her voice cracked, and she broke to weep. Mabel's heart was sagging; she could see where the story was heading.

"So, he was your mentor."

"My what?"

"Teacher, guide."

"He taught me almost everything I know about aeronautics and mechanics, and about weather, a lot of math and geography." After a moment, she added, teeth clenched, "And—*let's don't forget biology!*"

In the lull, Mabel heard sniffling.

"Katie, honey, go ahead and cry. You'll feel so much better."

"But I'm sick to death of it! I'm wore out with it!"

Mabel tracked the sniffling, the choked-off sobs, the muffled keening, then another lapse.

"If you'd like to talk about it, I'm here with a sympathetic ear."

"I don't want to talk about it."

"Whatever you like."

"Thing is," Katie said, after a moment, "He *lied* to me!"

Mabel waited for Katie to go on, but as the minutes lapsed in silence, she fine-tuned her hearing to detect Katie's shallow breathing slow and deepen into a rhythm that meant sleep; soon enough, her own attention drifted like a dinghy with an untied painter away from a dock and into a gently flowing stream.

She awoke during the night with the girl's bony knees poking the backs of her thighs. Katie had spooned her, apparently in her sleep, as the muted purr of a gentle snore wafted against the nape of Mabel's neck. The contact alarmed her, startled her awake, and she lay in a state of electrified paralysis for a long moment of indecision. Then she surrendered to the posture Katie had bent them in and spent the next good while weeping delicious tears.

Knocking on her door startled her awake. Groggy, headachy, she struggled up, recalling suddenly her guest who, at that moment, was absent from the bed. She slipped on her robe, fairly staggered through her front room, eased the door open a bit, blinded suddenly by the sunlight. A figure was backlit in the frame.

"Miss Cross? Please forgive me for my intrusion, but I'm Wylie Thompson from the *Loving Leader?* We heard there was an airplane made an emergency landing here day before yesterday, and I was hoping to talk to the pilot—I understand she's a woman. Pretty big news for these parts, as you might guess."

Mabel absorbed the information in bits until she'd slowly pieced together what was required of her.

"Oh. Uh. Mr. Thomas?"

"Thompson."

"She was here last night." She was on the verge of uttering *Maybe she's in the privy*, then realized the indelicacy of the revelation. "She seems to have gone out. I'll be happy to convey your message if I see her before you do."

"Thank you. Just by the way, do you have any knowledge of where the aircraft might've come from?"

The sharpness of the question jolted her more awake. Without knowing why, she felt an unexpected and inexplicable urge to be protective.

"No, not really. You'll have to ask her."

the salon

1

LOUISE WAS TORN BETWEEN DEFIANCE AND GUILT. THEIR tacit agreement about labor charged her with the household but clearing out Izzy's room might set off a riot. It would show she didn't believe Izzy was coming back, but Howard always hoped.

Planting the pilot in that room without consulting Howard had been risky. She didn't believe that she owed Howard prior approval, but this had been a special case. Deep down, she knew it would disturb him. Deep down, she'd hoped it would.

She was tired of mourning the loss of a child who had no regard for their feelings. Well, maybe Louise deserved that indifference, but it enraged her on Howard's behalf that Izzy's refusal to stay in touch kept him eternally anxious.

Before he left to check on their cows after breakfast, she said, "I haven't given that spare room a good scouring in a while, and I need to do that this morning."

"Izzy's room? Did the girl leave a mess?"

"Oh, no! She was a very thoughtful guest. She made the bed, though I'll have to wash the sheets and pillowcases, anyway."

"Did she get her airplane fixed?"

"I suppose not. Arabella came by while you were in the barn to invite me to a tea she's giving for the pilot this afternoon, and she twisted the poor girl's arm to talk about her life as an aviatrix."

"She's far too young to have had much of one."

"She got herself here, didn't she?"

"True." He sipped from his coffee. "Didn't strike me as a person who'd be fond of public speaking."

Louise quietly rallied to hear this. She knew the subtext. Shyness in women was a plus for Howard, so Louise could mark this assessment as a plus. Izzy was unfailingly brazen.

"Didn't you find her admirable? I did! I mean, how many young women would have the fortitude to strike out on their own that way? And not the least bit keen on blowing her own horn."

Howard smiled slightly. "Well, I gotta give her this. Pal rolled in a dead coyote and in spite of it she gave him a greeting that an honorable dog might deserve."

Louise laughed. For Izzy, livestock were proof of her inferior status as a farmer's daughter. Louise was tempted to build on this show of good will to say she planned to invite the pilot back to stay tonight. Or pose it as a question. It was tricky to declare your plans without provoking unwanted resistance while at the same time appear to seek permission—especially when you weren't.

Besides, offering the aviatrix room and board wasn't the ultimate plan.

First thing, she stripped the bed. She inspected linens as if expecting to ferret out something like the souvenir disc in the pilot's pocket. The medallion said Durham County Fair 1926 Katie Burke. Image of a sheep on one side, a sheath of wheat on the other. Another name—Curly Knowles—on the reverse. The girl had said she'd had it a long time, but 1926 was only two years back. Maybe it seemed forever because the person who gave it meant a lot to her. Izzy had never revealed anything to Louise, and Louise's questions were soon regarded as interrogations. It wouldn't be that way with a daughter or son of her own.

What could she put away or throw out? Howard wasn't keen on clutter, so that helped. *So much stuff just gathering dust! I tried to tidy it all up.* Not likely he'd even look in the closet. She'd leave a few special items such as the sailor blouse that caused such an uproar, box up the rest, and go with Mabel to Loving to put it in the poor box at the Baptist church. Keeping those clothes was downright silly—even if Izzy came back, they wouldn't suit her, and no doubt she'd find them childish and not in fashion.

She'd tell him the flounces off the four-poster needed to be washed and ironed, then just don't put them back. Though he treated this room like a shrine, he hardly ever entered, probably wouldn't notice what's missing. Clear her old perfume bottles, her face powder, her lipsticks (Good Lord, the girl had more face-paint than Louise had!), her talc, her brushes and combs and barrettes, put them in a drawer in case he asks. A scrapbook filled with the covers of motion-picture magazines hogged space atop the dresser. Louise leafed through for anything personal that might be wedged into the pages, although Howard had torn this room apart down to the floorboards looking for clues to where she might be or evidence that she'd not gone on her own free will.

Here and there, a clue to a girlish bent: Blanche Mehaffey on the cover of *Motion Picture Classic* with bobbed hair—Izzy scribbling in the margin *O, I do so love this do!!!*—arrow pointing at the coiffure.

Louise sighed. A cousin in Indianapolis mailed Izzy the magazines. In her best moments, Louise could pity Izzy—Izzy had precious little chance to see a motion picture way out here in exile. Louise missed it, too. The nurses at Fort Sheridan often went together to Chicago. Lillian Gish in *Broken Blossoms*. Douglas Fairbanks, Fatty Arbuckle. Mary Pickford, *At the Old Stage Door*. But the pleasure was also in being with pals. Once here, Izzy (and Louise!) lost any chance to enjoy Chautauqua lectures, concerts, or theatrical productions. The gentle balm of entertainment was absent from their lives unless you counted chatting with Wally and Mabel and others about the reading matter they passed around. Oh, and Mercedes Cunningham taught piano at her home and her pupils put on an annual recital, which was as dreary an occasion as you could imagine. The men had to be practically drugged and beaten to get them there.

Truth was, if she'd been dragged out here at Izzy's age and not as a new wife, she'd have looked for an escape route, too.

She set the album on the bed, an interim stop on the way out of the house. She couldn't burn it in the trash pit without drawing Howard's attention—maybe Wally could take it.

A while later, the bed was piled with a heap of clothing, old magazines, childhood books favored by most girls but of little interest to Izzy (*Emily of New Moon, The Story of Doctor Doolittle, The Bobbsey Twins*), the bundled flounces from the four-poster.

A hinged triptych of frames held a studio portrait of Izzy at age twelve, one of Howard taken the same time, and a third of Izzy's mother, Ida. She was passably pretty, with a sweet round face and chubby cheeks that made her eyes a tad squinty. Louise had no idea what sort of person she'd been because Howard never talked about her. She folded up the triptych and laid it on the bed. The photos could be strategically placed in the parlor. *I just wanted to put them where they'd be seen more often.*

The big stuffed bear was a bear of a problem. Couldn't he just sit in that chair for the next decade? She pulled the bear up, sat, settled the bear in her lap like a toddler. *Why do I feel a need to toss you out?*

Because I'm the thing she loved most that she brought with her from her old life.

Any chance Izzy might call to make amends and say she had children of her own and hoped her bear could be sent to be enjoyed by her progeny?

On the other hand, Louise knew she wanted to neuter the room. The next occupant could be a boy. It was still possible.

She was lost in thought holding the bear when Howard suddenly opened the door and stuck his head in, startling her. She blushed as if he'd caught her at something shameful.

"Cows broke through the fence out near Billings' place. I'll be out for a bit." Then his brain caught up with his gaze as he scanned the room. He frowned.

Louise set the bear on the floor and rose. Her heart was pounding.

"I was thinking we should put these photographs in a more prominent place," she offered quickly, picking up the hinged frames and opening them. "Don't you think?" She handed them over, and he held them in his palms like a hymnal.

"Yes, that'd be nice."

"Thing is, I'm having to take everything out of here to get it really clean." She pointed to the bed piled with the potential discards. "There's stuff here too that I think other people might need more than we do, you know?"

"What things?"

"Oh, just some ancient magazines and nightgowns and the like." She shrugged, smiled. "Odds and ends."

"Okay, I guess."

He kept staring at the heap on the bed and frowning. Oh, he *must* know what we're really talking about! A wave of rage swept over her, and she shoved it back, took a deep breath.

"Howard, how old am I?"

He blinked with surprise. "Thirty . . . two. Why?"

"How long have we been married?"

He thought it over. "Right around eight years, I estimate." He looked puzzled, then he chuckled. "Aw, I get it. This is one of those woman things, right?"

She stared him down, refusing to surrender to the joke.

"You betcha it is."

2

WHEN OTIS WENT OUT TO THE PRIVY JUST AFTER DAWN, THE girl was already working on the aircraft. Yesterday she and Wally sutured up L-shaped rips in the tail. Now she was tearing muslin strips to glue in layers over the stitches.

"Child, you sure at it early."

She looked rested, though not calm: you could feel her engine churning under that peachy skin.

"I'm happiest when I'm up there." Finger poked skyward.

"Everybody got their happy place."

"Where's yours?"

He grinned, tapped his forehead.

She laid another strip over the repaired tear.

"How long's it take this glue to dry?"

"I'd give it a day."

"Is it waterproof?"

"I wouldn't count on it. Y'all need to shellac it once it's dry."

"Aw, jeez. I know that's slow-curing."

He shrugged. "You want it done so's it'll shed the rain."

"Yeah. Definitely."

She dipped a paint brush in a pot of glue and basted the strip over the threads.

"Hey! Do you know where I can get sixty-seven gallons of gasoline?"

"Hmm. That's a tall order. I got maybe ten on hand."

"Where could I get the rest? I need a full tank leaving out, else I'll have to land to refuel." She grinned. "As you can see, that's the tricky part of flying."

"We could scare up empty cans and go to Loving for it."

"Oh, that would be so great! Also, I'm hoping to take folks on joy rides. I told your wife that I could pay you back for your work and your kindness."

"I bet I know what she told you."

Katie laughed. "She said she'd prefer cash or an IOU."

"Yeah, she ain't keen on getting her shoes off the ground. That woman's plumb earth-bound."

"I like how's she's a no bull-hockey kind of person."

"That for sure. You never have to guess what's on *her* mind." Sixty-seven gallons! Harley surely won't take a joy ride as a trade-out, so you have to wonder, what's the plan? And what aviator sets out on a very long flight with so little preparation? One in a big hurry to get off, most likely.

He told her he'd be back soon as he'd had some chow. He heard no footsteps from upstairs, so Wally was still in bed. He brewed coffee for them both, then ate two pieces of toast drizzled with molasses while standing at the sink, taking pleasure in the sun's early beams flooding through the window and warming him. Maybe being right here in this life was his happy place. Put it up against places far away by the clock and the tape. You'd think that the farther west you went, the farther you got from the very ugly history of the nation—unless you considered what happened to the people who were here first, the ones he'd helped the US Army chase into big corrals. But there were pockets of sanctuary, and he believed he'd found one.

He took his time taking apart the damaged elephant ear. The feature was a moving part with moving parts, an assembly of tubular steel, hinges, and wires covered with the fabric of the wings. With unknown machinery with inner parts, you had to track your way with care so's you'd find your way out.

An hour later Jake Bohanan parked his spanking new A Model Ford pickup next to the workshop. Though the richest farmer-rancher around, Bo looked like a hobo, Otis thought. His big heap of black hair went every which away, one coverall tang was busted, so it hung loose like a flapping tongue down his belly. His hands were always filthy, and he was a snuff-dipper to boot, which his wife found especially repugnant. Otis had always found him good-natured, though, and because the Loving bank had turned down Otis's loan request last year, Jake Bohanan had offered one at a fair rate of interest, something Otis had not told Wally.

"Mister Bohanan, how's by you?"

"Fair 'nuff, Otis."

"What happened to that old Essex?"

"Aw, that old bed wouldn't hold more'n a bag of chicken feed and a salt block."

"This one's right handsome."

"Should be. Paid plenty for it." Bo moved his gaze across the aircraft's surfaces, as if measuring it.

"Heard y'all were fixing it up."

"Working at it."

Bo shuffled sideways like a peculiar dance step to alter his perspective.

"That there your pilot?"

"Yep. Strange as it may seem."

Bo strode the length of the airplane until he was standing over the girl. Otis couldn't distinguish the words, but at last the pilot nodded and they shook hands.

He ambled back to Otis. "Be needing your help today, Otis. Gotta run. Arabella's got me on a leash as a messenger boy. Meet me outtha place soon's you can, hear me?"

Walking away, he couldn't have heard an answer, but Otis knew it wasn't a question. He set down his pliers and wiped his hands on a rag.

"What did Bo want?"

The girl stood. "Well, yesterday his wife said she wanted to put on a tea in my honor if I was here today, so she told her husband to make sure I was available later this afternoon." She gave him a look of help-lessness. "I sure don't want to stop working here, but," she shrugged, "she said that the ladies there would likely help me make the rest of my trip if I'd say a few words about being a pilot and all."

"Sing for your supper, that it?"

"Looks that way."

At his workbench he gathered tools to take. Arabella's tea party! He was beset by a hundred irritations at once. Bo hadn't bothered to say what was needed, let alone ask if he had time or interest in helping. Or to mention any remuneration. Bo presumed compliance. That was the thing about the loan. If he'd told Wally about it, she'd dig at him to unearth the details. The single paper he signed claimed he'd borrowed five hundred dollars from Bo at 8 percent interest per annum. When Otis had asked about a payment schedule, Bo had said, *Aw, don't worry. We'll work something out.*

What "they'd" worked out was what just happened: Bo told Otis he needed him. Otis would do the work. Bo would say, I reckon that was worth X or Y dollars, good 'nuff? It usually was. But then came the sticky part: "I'll just check it off that loan if that's all right with you." Wanting to be agreeable, Otis said, "Sure, Mr. Bohanan." But no account statement was forthcoming, not a single scrap resembling a receipt. Everybody supposedly did business based on "a man's word" or "a handshake," but Otis's life-long experience with white folks didn't encourage trust. He had too much pride to raise the issue directly without seeming to insult a fellow who'd been affable and generous. Once, strapped, he'd asked for cash on the spot. Bo had fretted and fumbled and made a bigger to-do of coming up with the currency than was called for.

Today's summons would inconvenience Wally, since Otis would've had to help with the Owl's noon meal. She wouldn't be happy to hear that he'd been pulled off the cook line to help with Arabella's tea party.

"I'm afraid I'll have to desert you," he told Katie. "Bo wants me out the farm to do something he thinks is urgent."

"Oh!"

She looked so distressed that he stopped himself from saying he'd probably been conscripted because of Arabella's party.

"Leonard's most likely working for his uncle or out at that drilling rig. Before I take off, I'll see if I can find him and hijack him for you." He smiled.

"Oh, gosh! That'd be swell."

"If you wouldn't mind, though, Wally's gonna miss me bad at lunch time. It'd be mighty good of you to scoot inside to give her a hand."

"Sure thing."

On the way to the café's back door, Otis steeled himself. Once Wally got riled, he had to meet her ire with the contrary. If she spat hot peppers, he doused them in heavy sugared cream.

She was in the kitchen peeling spuds.

"You in for good or only passing through?"

He sighed. "Well . . ."

"I saw him out there. What'd he want?"

"Aw, you know Bo. Anything he thinks needs done needs done yesterday."

"What's he need done?"

"He was in too big a hurry to say."

"I bet I know."

He waited; he wasn't going to prompt her.

"I bet he wants to dress you up like a monkey and have you walk around in a white jacket carrying a silver tray of them . . . things . . . Them . . . Oh, whatever the *hell* they call them."

He was shocked. "Woman, what are you talking about!?"

"That damn tea party, that's what!"

"He didn't say nothing about a tea party, Wally." For a brief instant, something deep in his history made him imagine she might be right. "He said bring my tools."

"How come you didn't tell him you had other things to do?"

"How you know I didn't?"

"I could tell by the look on your face when you come through the door."

"Well, one reason would be he pays more than I pay myself or what that pilot is gonna pay me."

"I'd have to take your word for that."

She kept peeling spuds with violent sweeps of her paring knife. He knotted his arms over his chest. Her insult burned him; the implication of servility was profoundly unjust and hurtful.

"You know good and well that people around here value that I know how to do things," he said quietly. "I got respect as a man here. You know it."

He could see she knew she'd crossed a line. She flicked a quick sideways glance with her head ducked over the tub of potatoes.

"Yes. I had no call."

He wanted to let her know he was allied with her against Arabella, but it would obviously aggravate the wound to show he knew she was hurt to be left off Arabella's guest list. He moved to her, slipped the paring knife from her hand, gently laid his palms on her shoulders, and pulled her into his chest.

"I told that girl to come help you."

"Devil," she said.

3

THE GAG ABOUT THE WEEKLY *LOVING LEADER* WAS THAT what went on in Noname was so far down on the totem pole that you could drop dead at noon in the street stark naked and news of it would be shoe-horned into the "Goings-On" column that recorded the social motions of Loving's important citizenry. After all, they boasted a municipal power plant, sewage system, three paved streets, and the county courthouse.

The fellow who'd summoned Mabel out of bed didn't normally venture out this way, but, as he told Katie later that morning when he found her behind the Owl working on the airplane, her descent upon this humble hamlet was akin to "the angel Gabriel's presenting himself unto the Virgin Mary." He said that he was also here about that drilling rig, but she was "the paramount story." He wanted a quick interview and photographs if she didn't mind. Also, "a Mrs. Jake Bohanan called to say that you'd be lecturing to a club meeting at her home," and he hoped to be present to gather further material.

"You said your story can't be in the newspaper until next week?" asked Katie.

"Yes, I regret that we just missed this last issue."

He had Katie pose in the cockpit wearing her helmet and waving as if about to depart or had just landed. Meanwhile, a half dozen children accompanied by two mothers and three dogs had arrived to gawk. He then exchanged his camera for pen and notebook and steered Katie by the elbow into Otis's workshop. Leonard blocked the door to keep the kids from rushing in behind them.

Mabel longed to eavesdrop on the interview—as a witness to the landing wouldn't her testimony warrant a quote?—but was too shy to offer it unsolicited. So many things about her newfound friend were still a mystery. Such a contrast between the females Mabel had encountered and this brave and strikingly independent creature wholly void of typical feminine vanities!

She slipped into the back door of the Owl.

Wally got up from the table and poured her a mug of coffee.

"You want toast?"

"Wouldn't mind. Some day . . ."

"Aw," Wally waved her off. "I'll make you cough up sooner or later. I'll wait until you're real strapped so's the bill will really humiliate you."

When Mabel was settled with a plate of toast and a jar of honey, Wally said, "You hear about Arabella's party?"

"Just now. From the reporter."

"Haven't gotten your invitation, then?"

"Nope. You?"

"Course not. You will, though."

True, most likely. And no point in indulging in white lies with Wally (*Oh, I'm sure you will, too . . .*) in an empty effort to make her feel better. What made Wally feel better was having friends be candid.

"Otis's out there now working for Bo. Bo says jump and Otis says how high."

"Let me help, then."

"Love to." Wally lit a cigarette. "Otis told that girl to come work, too."

"She's too famous at the moment to wait tables or wash a dish."

"Fame is fleeting, they say." Wally spat a mouthful of smoke as if it had offended her. "She knows what's good for her she'll decide otherwise. You know what I saw? I saw her hug Leonard this morning."

"She did?" Mabel smiled.

"I got a mind to give that girl a talking to."

Explaining how that had come about would require confessing that she too had hugged Leonard, and she'd already gotten *that* talking to from Wally. Wally would've applauded their union had it been reciprocal.

"Maybe she was just thanking him for all his help."

"Words do plenty good enough for that."

Otis had stayed up late cooking a couple of cauldrons of chicken and dumplings to serve as today's lunch entrée. Wally told Mabel that she had three cabbages from Louise that they'd stew with butter, onions, garlic, celery, and tomatoes, and crowder peas left over could make another side dish long as it lasted. Cornbread and molasses or honey would have to do for sweets. Anybody complains, tell them to go tell Otis, if they can find him.

Mabel went to set the café's six tables, heard a tap on the front-door glass, and saw Bo curling a finger at her. She stepped outside onto the front porch where he was shuffling from foot to foot like a bashful pupil. He offered up a sheepish invitation to the party with a few sidelong glimpses through the front door, and that prompted Mabel to ask, sweetly and innocently, "What about Mrs. Jackson? Would you like for me to pass along hers as well?"

Bo blushed. "Naw. Uh . . . Arabella knows how much this place means to her and how hard she works, and she says she just doesn't see how she'd fit in—I mean fit it in—with her work here and all."

"It's kind of Arabella to be so considerate. And I believe Mrs. Jackson's husband's off working elsewhere today, so you can imagine how that has doubled her chores."

"Yes, ma'am." He sighed, miserable. He looked off toward his idling pickup. To the north, a curl of exhaust rose from the drilling rig's engine, and the morning air was offended by the inharmonious clank of metal at war with a task. Mabel felt a twinge of guilt over torturing the poor man, but he was complicit, so her pity could be measured by a teaspoon.

"Arabella was wondering if you'd bring the pilot with you when you come." He laid the sentence before her like a worried butcher hoping his customer wouldn't notice slick on the ham.

She saw a chance to be offended—now she's playing chauffeur for Arabella?—but she realized she'd be Katie's designated escort! Shy Katie would need a buffer between herself and Arabella's guests.

"Of course, I'd be delighted."

"Mighty fine!" Released, he hopped off the porch, waving goodbye with the back of his hand.

Katie lasted about five minutes out on the floor as a waitress—customers were so enthralled to be served by the aviatrix that they detained her with questions, so Wally quickly shifted her to washing dishes. Mabel took her place out front, suspecting Wally had relished demoting the girl.

Once the dining room cleared out, Mabel helped Wally and Katie clean the kitchen, Mabel standing shoulder-to-shoulder with a dishcloth to dry what her new pal washed and handed over. Sweat glistened on the girl's exposed skin, and her unruly hair sprang wild with curls from the steam. Even in her best humor Wally was a cabinet banger, usually yanked open and slammed shut a drawer, but now as they toiled in a tense silence, the racket she made putting away clean pots and pans hurt Mabel's ears. Clearly, they'd had words while Mabel was waiting tables.

Katie left to resume work with Leonard. Wally sat, lit a cigarette with a kitchen match scratched on the underside of the table, waved vaguely as if to invite Mabel to sit, but the atmosphere was too forbidding. Mabel leaned against the counter instead, poured herself a glass of water from the stone jug.

"Well!" Mabel offered cheerfully. "We got it done between the three of us."

"Yes, and I thank you very much."

"You're quite welcome."

Wally pinched a tobacco speck off her tongue-tip. "I reckon she'll tell you later."

"What?"

"What you're dying to know."

That was Mabel's cue to ask to be told, but, truthfully, she'd just as soon not hear it. She shrugged.

"I gave her what for."

"What about?"

"You know."

Mabel sighed. "What'd you say?"

Wally perked up, gratified by the prompt. "I told her that I saw her hug that boy, and I wanted her to know I consider myself and Otis like an aunt or uncle to him. I make or mend his clothes and I feed him most of the time, and he's got nobody else but that worthless George Purvis to look out for him."

Mabel considered arguing that Leonard had scads of friends in Noname, including her, and that he was fully capable of taking care of himself, but thought better of poking the hornet's nest.

"I told her I saw her hug him, that she'd best not be putting her hands on boys like that, maybe she don't know any better, but she could take it from me that Leonard has a very tender heart and it wasn't one bit fair to stir him up that way and she'd be wise to leave him be, or she'd be answering for it."

Pretty much what you told me, thought Mabel.

"What'd she say?"

"Well, I have to say she didn't get her back up or sass me. I think she'd never for one minute thought what she did would put him in a stew. She looked surprised, anyway. She said she was just being friendly and feeling grateful for all he was doing. She meant no harm, I could see. Just a thoughtless kid. I was about to forgive her, but then she told me I needn't worry because—" Wally's sausage fingers scraped quotation marks in the air—"'I won't be here in Hicksville one second longer than I have to.'"

Mabel writhed with discomfort. She deeply wished Katie hadn't phrased it that way. And she deeply wished her old friend hadn't felt so incensed about what had been an innocent gesture, one she'd urged. She guessed that Wally was put out that Katie's appearance had upset their routine, increased their labor, and led to Wally's social humiliation. The business with Leonard was an easy way to strike back.

Did the occasion call for a big hat and white gloves? Stockings were always de rigueur for schoolmarms for even daily life, and Mabel had enough finery in her wardrobe to be presentable at weddings and funerals. Life out here had fewer requirements when it came to putting style and convention over comfort and practicality, but Arabella once told Mabel she had a moral obligation to "set the tone." She was like a Victorian matron of the British raj dutifully sweating buckets under layers of corsets and cotton in Calcutta.

As she and Katie came into Mabel's cottage, Mabel mentally modeled herself in this or that thing with no pleasure. Did Katie own anything remotely appropriate? She looked a mess, disheveled and damp like a scullery maid, and Mabel's pleasure in playing escort had an underside: she was now *in charge of* making her guest presentable.

Each took a turn at sponge-bathing with the wash basin, Mabel going second. Mabel worried far too long about what to wear, and in the end, she chose a navy school-day dress with a knee-length hem and a wide white collar. It might minimize the contrast between them.

In the "parlor," Katie stood over the sofa where the two clam halves of the valise yawned open. She wore the same stained khaki trousers, tailored like jodhpurs, but had stripped to a clean camisole. She held up a blouse. Pale blue, cotton, vertical pleating down the front, wide collar like spread buzzard wings, four fabric-covered buttons the size of cucumber slices—you'd wear it in the typists' pool at a factory. And very wrinkled. Katie read Mabel's face and returned the expression of a pitifully worried child.

"This one's dry, anyway. All I got besides the one that's all sweaty." She tossed it into the valise and collapsed onto the sofa. "Maybe I ought not do this."

"Oh, dear no! They're going to be so thrilled!"

Mabel eased down onto the sofa and slid her arm around Katie's shoulder. That Katie could be hurt both gratified and frightened her. Where's the tough girl? "I'm just wearing what I go to school in. And why would anybody expect you to go flying across the country all by yourself and still show up like Lady Astor? Remember—you're the star of the show."

"Thanks!" Katie quickly twisted to hug Mabel fleetingly, then sprang up. "You got lipstick, right?"

"You bet! And cologne, too."

"Then let's get dolled up as best we can."

"That's the spirit."

Everybody said that the West was won with the Walker Colt, but it was made livable by the Arabellas. In town after town, headstrong women organized efforts to start or improve a school, fund libraries, recruit doctors and pastors, build hospitals, initiate lecture and concert series and start drama troupes. They hounded their husbands to pave the streets and bring citizens electric lights and running water.

Mabel had to give Arabella well-earned credit: that Noname had a school was due to Arabella's resourcefulness and work, and when

Mabel had declared she was leaving, Arabella had immediately set about raising funds and getting pledges and saw to the construction of the present cottage. Arabella had asked Mabel to join efforts to create a library, and she told her she looked forward to when Noname had a municipal government with the power to tax and issue bonds for basic services. She complained that when she shopped in Loving she suffered remarks about Noname that hurt her civic pride.

A talk by an aviatrix was one thing Loving couldn't boast of, and for that reason Arabella had called the *Loving Leader* to ballyhoo Katie's appearance. Mabel thought that Arabella's salon wasn't meant just to aggrandize herself, as Wally might claim, but part of a wider effort to bring the world in bits and pieces to this tiny, remote spot. Yes, considered Mabel, the guest list need not have been so exclusive, but her bet would be that if given the time, Arabella would've commandeered the church-schoolhouse and sent the word out far and wide. And, truthfully, the attendees would likely give more where they saw themselves as members of an exclusive club and each not wish to be outdone by another.

The ride out of Noname took them past the oil rig, where the whanging and clanking seemed even louder today, and sooty exhaust plumed up around the machinery. Another credit to Arabella—after their recent town-hall meeting, she'd warned the driller not to work after sundown, and he'd complied

Mabel drove a dusty, two-rut road that went east toward the dark high escarpment of the Llano Estacado. They stopped twice to let themselves through gated pastures. As usual for late August, the day was sunny and too warm in full light but cool enough under shade.

Katie was fretting.

"I don't know what to say."

"We don't know anything, so anything you say will be a revelation. People will want to know how you became an aviatrix, of course, all about learning to fly, who or what inspired you, and so forth. Probably they'll have questions that can prompt you more than you think. If they don't, I'll pipe up and help you out."

"Who inspired and taught me, huh."

Tender spot. "Well, you need not say anything personal."

"That's good to know."

As they approached the house, Mabel admired it anew. Unlike pioneers and residents who struck to the woodlands architecture of framed timber and gabled roofs, the Spanish mode used native Pueblo style. Whoever had built the Bohanan's place some time back had sensibly gone adobe and graced the ever-reaching landscape by a low-slung building. With thick walls, tiled floors, and a flat roof, the home embraced its own heat in winters and shut it out in summers. A huge set of wooden doors in the back wall opened into the courtyard that Arabella used as a garden. She'd planted borders of hollyhocks and geranium, and the central surface was paved with flagstone. An elaborate fountain-bird bath that normally sat centered in the space had been shoved aside so that a canopy erected for the event would shade her guests. Under it two girls clad in aprons whom Mabel recognized were snapping out a long white linen tablecloth like a sheet to let it billow, fall, and settle over a buffet table. They looked up as Mabel approached.

"Hello, girls! I see Mrs. Bohanan has found herself some excellent help!" The girls, Johnnie and Bonnie Petersen, never dressed alike because Bonnie refused to.

"These were some of my star pupils," she said to Katie. "Girls, please meet the guest of honor, our aviatrix, Katie Burke!"

The awe-struck twins mumbled and half-curtsied with a knee flex.

As they came to the entrance door, Mabel asked, "Should I have introduced you by your other name?"

"My other name?"

"You said when you're in the shows they call you Skippy Baker."

"Uh, yeah! Jeez, you got a good memory. Yeah, that'd be good."

Arabella surprised them by opening the door before Mabel knocked. She had a tall porcelain vase in one hand. Silk crepe de chine dress in a melon shade, with a U-neck, accordion pleats, embroidered silk floral patterns in vertical stripes, small sailor collar—stylish, Mabel thought.

"At last! My aviatrix!" She called to the twins, held up the vase, and Johnnie hurried to take it from her.

Katie murmured *thanksforhavingme*. Strands of Arabella's bob had lifted and sailed away on their own, possibly disturbed by a hat recently worn. Her makeup might've been applied early in the day, as sweat beaded her forehead and nose, puddling her powder.

"Oh, Arabella! It's so nice of you to do this, and on such short notice!"

Arabella smiled gamely. "Well, I do love a challenge, and for such a wonderful cause!" She beamed at Katie.

"Yes, thanks a lot. Everybody here has been so nice."

Mabel wasn't sure about her reading of it, but Katie's enthusiasm might've been a bit on the wan side. She hoped the girl was up for an afternoon of chit-chat with strangers.

Arabella led them into what she called the library. Two walls had large windows, one looking east to plains that ended abruptly in the distance line of mesa, darkly purple in the haze like a line of thunderstorms, and the other allowing a view of the courtyard and through the wooden doors into the lot beyond, where Mabel saw Otis walking between sheds. The shelves lining two walls were filled with objets d'art, framed photographs, and a few yards of leather-bound volumes, atlases, dictionaries, and a rack of popular novels.

Today the room was a mini lecture hall. Two rows of straight-back chairs were being arranged in semi-circles. The permanent leather armchairs were posted on the ends of the rows like dimples on smiles, and two women obviously dressed as guests were lifting a plant stand holding a potted fern and walking it into a corner. A podium stood off to the side facing a window as if memorizing lines offstage while awaiting a cue. Mabel recognized the women, but by face at church and not by name—if they had children, they weren't her students. Mabel's pal Louise Larsen rushed to Katie's side soon as she entered, asking about Katie's shoulder injury—was it swollen or tender? Even if not, it probably needed cleaning and redressing—and telling her she hoped to get a chance to speak privately with her after the talk.

Within a few minutes, a dozen women had arrived by threes and fours—obviously riding together. Mabel was relieved that none appeared to have dressed for church, and so Katie's pants and wrinkled blouse drew no covert frowns. The guests chatted among themselves in knots that untied and retied themselves as the women circulated. By ones and twos, they approached to introduce themselves to Katie and Mabel. Soon, Arabella appeared with the man from the *Loving Leader* in tow. He took one of the leather armchairs and drew out a notebook.

And so, called to order by Arabella, everyone settled. Mabel took a chair off to the side like an auditor while Arabella drew Katie to stand beside her center stage at the podium.

Arabella had thanking to do, "our aviatrix" first of all, and then her guests whom she knew to be generous patrons of civic endeavors eager to embrace what the future has to hold. She wanted to thank Mr. Wylie Thompson—"our friend from the Loving newspaper"—for gracing them with his presence. She hoped he would take this opportunity to fully appreciate the extent to which *all* his readers—pause, narrow look his way—were progressive boosters regardless of their residence.

Knowing little of Katie personally, Arabella's introduction skillfully transformed her into an emblem of a "modern young woman" whose talk today brings them news from the future and the wider world outside. "As Mr. Thompson himself put it to me, 'She comes like the angel Gabriel announcing the good tidings.'"

"Thanks," Katie said, sidling to the spot at the podium. It came to her chest. "I sure dunno about being an angel." She grinned mischievously. "My ma never thought so, but I sure think flying's a darn good way to get from place to place."

She beamed; they laughed. The sudden upshoot of Katie's poise astonished Mabel. She could breathe now.

"When I started out a week ago, everything here was all unknown to me, and I never dreamed for one second that the folks I've met would be so dad gummed terribly nice, like your friend Mrs. Bohanan. Everybody here has just saved my life."

Was that a tear in the corner of her eye? Was that a minute tremble of her lower lip?

"But I'm sure not used to giving a speech, and I'm pretty darn nervous if you have to know the truth. I told my friend Mabel that I didn't know what to say, and she just told me to talk to you like I was talking to myself about what I do." She paused to favor Mabel with her gaze. Mabel blushed. "But the doggone trouble is that a lot of the times I'm talking a blue streak to myself, so's I just don't think you wanna hear the likes of that."

Chuckles. She has them, Mabel thought. Wonderful. *My friend Mabel.*

"A lot of folks think it queer that a girl like me is in the cockpit of a wonderful machine like the Travel Air so I suppose I can start with how it came about."

She was born into it, she said. Her folks were aviation pioneers early on, and when her pop came back from the war where he'd flown Jennies in France—"that's what we call them from the model number J N 4—" she scribed the characters in the air—they took a notion to buy into an air show outfit. So, by the time she was ten she was helping to suit up, gas up, talk up the shows to folks at county fairs. They traveled all around the country—maybe somebody here had seen their show—Maggie Cody's Flying Circus?—or some other? (One hand went up.) Lived in hangers out of suitcases most of the time, though when they got flush, "a bunch of pilots would pitch in together for a hotel room."

So, it was just part of her life as a kid—she spent hundreds of hours in a cockpit as a passenger—and when she turned fifteen, she begged her folks to let her learn, so they did.

Maybe they'd like to hear what you do when you're in a show, she said. Just like in a regular circus, there's a fellow on a loudspeaker telling the audience all about the "death-defying maneuvers"—she grinned—and you got one pilot who specializes in stunts like loops (she craned back her head and threw up her arms as if do a backwards somersault), and rolls (she bent forward with her arm extended and circled the air with her hand), barrel rolls (spinning her hand to indicate repetitions), figure 8s, and your Immelmans (flat plane of her palm rising, rising, rising, stretching up on tiptoe, then sudden stalling, turning back toward Earth in a nose dive), your upside-down flyers, and then there's the one that really gets them—the falling leaf. "You call it the Death Spiral, too." Her hand slowly shimmered straight up toward the ceiling and Mabel detected her almost mute growling like an aircraft engine. You go up, up, up until your airspeed collapses at zero gravity, and then you start falling backward out of the sky, *tail first*, spinning, and the announcer is yelling all kinds of nonsense (Katie laughed) like *oh my gosh, folks! He's lost control! Watch out down there below! He's bound to crash!* And of course, the pilot knows just how and when to kick the rudder to swing the ship out of the spin then dives headfirst down then into a loop where when he goes right-side up the wheels about hit the runway.

Wide-eyed, she stared at the women as if her next word might be "Boo!" They stared back as if half-expecting to hear that.

So, anyway, she went on. That's one part. There's always a guy who jumps with a parachute, sure—she grinned—he's gonna wait until the very last second to pull the ripcord so's the announcer can pump up the thrills with, you know, *Oh my gosh, folks! Larry's parachute is jammed! He can't pull the cord! This has never happened! Call the medics!* And, sure—you know what happens, he's done this fall a thousand times.

Then they have a guy who's good at standing up in the back of an automobile and jumping onto a ship while it's flying over—"the transfer trick"—and maybe vice versa, both machines speeding down the runway together. Looks really dangerous, she said with a shrug, but not much to it so long as they're both going the same speed. Might as well be parked.

She grinned. "Rubes eat it up, though."

Her listeners chuckled, in on the joke somehow. The moment pricked briefly at Mabel's awareness of an unexpected undercurrent. She'd expected this telling to take a different tone—more serious?

More as if the undertaking were to be discussed like science or indus-try or advancements in medicine, like lectures she'd heard in college. The comic strain Katie'd begun with had shifted. She seemed to be revealing the "tricks" in a cynical way that mocked a gullible public for their manipulated enjoyment and inviting her audience to be complicit. But the women here were an audience, too, and even if you felt favored by being shown what stood behind the curtain, what the joke was, you suspected that when Katie met with her pilot peers, she'd regale them about the "rubes" in "Hicksville" who'd gone wild for all the bull-hockey.

"My mom was a wing-walker. My friend here Mabel told me she'd seen it done in newsreels, and maybe some of you have, too. You want to have a woman do it because they're generally not very tall and don't weigh much. You want someone whose body won't be too much drag at a hundred miles an hour when the wind's full face on, and you want someone whose weight won't throw the ship out of balance. Like my mom. Or me." She waved her hand across her own torso. Katie laughed. "I did it once, but she sure didn't know about it and was hopping mad when she found out. I thought maybe she was scared for me, but then I figured she just didn't want the competition."

Her grin took a bitter twist, and she shrugged one shoulder. It was hard to know if she were joking. "Anyway, she puts herself between the top and bottom wings on one side hanging from the guide wires like she's in a hammock only prone like she's sort of flying like a bird while the pilot takes the craft up in front of the bleachers. He flies around looping and rolling and what-not while the announcer goes into his spiel about this death-defying maneuver and how she's gonna wind up standing on top of the craft and everybody needs to pray for everything to go just right and that kind of malarkey."

Sooner or later, Katie went on, the pilot cuts his airspeed and lev-els out low over the runway, so's the wing-walker can climb out from between the wings then hoist herself up onto the top wing from the fuselage. There's an upright metal post fixed to the top wing, and she crawls around to the front of it, stands leaning against it, and straps a safety belt around her waist. She's got foot things like half-shoes to keep her down, too. Now maybe that sounds like no big deal, okay, so she's tied down, so what? Well, the pilot starts revving up to a hundred and starts doing those same rolls and loops and dives and tail spins while she's standing up there—it's a really strong wind, it'd knock you silly if you were on the ground in a storm that big—and then the ship turns upside down and he's flying level right above the ground right in front of the bleachers, and you're thinking uh-oh!, her head's gonna knock the ground and get ripped off!

"Oh, my heavens!" blurted out Millie Archer. "That must be dangerous! It has to be! Weren't you terribly worried because it was your mother!?"

The unexpected outburst stirred the room.

"Only every minute of my life." No grin this time. "Especially when my dad started drinking again. He was her pilot. We were at this county fair outside Atlanta, and they were doing that stunt and he couldn't keep the craft level when they were upside down over the field in front of the bleachers and she had to double over and hug her knees to keep from scraping. They had a big fight about it. She said she'd never stunt with him again. They broke up, and he went off with another outfit."

The room fell so silent Mabel heard a clatter of dishware from the distant kitchen. They watched Katie for a cue for responding in a way that could spare her embarrassment. There'd been no chuckle or shrug to cue them to treat this lightly.

"Whole thing depends on trust," Katie went on. "Everything we do. You gotta trust the machinery, the weather, the gas jockey who fills your tank, the friend who's supposed to clean your carburetor, the promoter who's supposed to pay you, the fellow who packs your parachute. And you gotta really trust your stunt team. Nobody's got the gu . . . *intestinal fortitude* for doing this if you're worrying every second that somebody's gonna let you down, not do their job, because your life depends on it. I don't blame my ma at all. I felt a lot better when she started stunting with . . . this other pilot."

Millie Archer's heart-felt question had gotten a heartfelt answer, so full and seemingly from deep inside Katie's experience that they were eager to hear more. Here's another way she's fearless, thought Mabel. To stand there in front of strangers and say such things! It was a very enviable quality.

"Something I'm wondering now," said Blanche Burnett, "is how I've always had this picture in my mind of these glamorous aviators with their scarves and their leather jackets and their derring-do. They always seemed so . . . *dashing*! Like the stars of moving pictures, you know, like Douglas Fairbanks or Mr. Valentino. That isn't true?"

Katie snickered. "Well, the ones I've known—and I've known a bunch—about half of them are drunk half the time when they're not in the air and some are often looped on anything else they can find, and they're always broke because you can't make much now in an outfit 'cause there's so many around, and they waste their pay and their time on poker games and dice, so they have to sleep on the ground or on somebody's floor, and they eat what they can get when they can get it, which is never often enough, and they don't take baths so they stink to high heaven, and they don't know much about anything in the world except for flying because that's ALL they care about, believe me, even the ones with wives and kids, and they're willing to put up with everything else if it means they get one more minute in the air."

She took a breath. Her hands trembled minutely. She stared at the podium and not at her listeners.

"I tell you what's really sad." She looked up. "Most of the fellows were flying in the war in France. They talk about it and talk about it until you're sick of hearing it. It's like they can't get over it. And they loved it! It was when all the stunts they did were *really* death-defying. You add all the danger and risk of flinging yourself about at three thousand feet in the sky in a junk-wagon that might fall apart any second and you add to that somebody's shooting a machine-gun at you trying to kill you. It made their blood boil, it was like opium or something. *That* kind of flying really mattered. Somebody *else's* life depended on it. Nothing's been so exciting since, and so when they're doing loops and rolls and what-not over a bleacher of rubes, they feel like clowns or circus ponies, like they're nothing now but a cheap show. Hurts their pride and there's nothing they can do about it."

She did favor them now with a steady gaze and an inviting half-smile. After a moment, Wilma Gray spoke up. Her daughters Marcia and Elizabeth were Mabel's students, usually ahead of their peers thanks to Wilma's tutoring.

"Please forgive me for saying so, but this doesn't seem like a proper world for ladies, I mean women and girls, or children. I do think it's wonderful for young *women* to become aviatrixes like that Amelia Earhart, I really do, I'm not like some people who don't believe it's right, but . . ." She drew a breath for courage. "I'm wondering and worried about how a child growing up that way would be able to go to school or have a regular life where the clothes get washed and ironed and the food gets on the table and there's church and friends to play with when you're moving around all the time and there's just no . . . no *home!*"

The comment struck a critical note despite the plea for indulgence at the outset, and it showed on Katie's face.

"Yeah, I dunno. I've heard stuff like that before. I guess people want everybody to be respectable. We're not. I'm just not. I didn't ask to be born into a family of flyers. And, yeah, to answer your question—it's not just hard to have a 'regular life.' It's impossible. I learned stuff when and where I could learn it and people were willing to teach me. My ma read books to me. And, sure, I saw kids walking to school together and I wanted to be there, sometimes. But see—I couldn't do anything about it. And all I could do is take advantage of what I could and did learn, and that's why I'm standing here right now as the pilot of that Travel Air and those kids who went to school are sitting in the bleachers paying to watch somebody like me. And the ones who were boys back then now go dig ditches or fit shoes to people's smelly feet or sit behind desks writing their name over and over, and the girls are washing and ironing and sweating over a stove while some little ape is screaming at her from the nursery in their *home* and another's hanging on her . . . sucking at . . ." She broke off with a shudder. "Well, you know. You get the idea."

Another new note, thought Mabel, and a sour one. Now she feared this all might loop out of control with the women inching away from sympathetic interest. Did Katie now seem vulgar, bitter, and hostile? An urge to defend her new friend welled up, and she rose to take the floor before too much damage had been done.

"As a schoolteacher, I just want to add," she let her gaze sweep the audience, "that just from the short time I've been with you, Miss Baker, I've become aware of how you seem quite versed in certain fields related to aeronautics, as I am sure that your flying requires many mathematical calculations and knowledge of both geography, cartography, meteorology, and astronomy, as well as engine mechanics." She paused to baste everyone with a big smile to signify that a jest was merrily making its way into the mix. "And just yesterday I also saw you *sewing* on the fabric of your aircraft to mend a tear! And so I would say that you seem to know many of the same things I and all mothers here teach our children, only you seem to have come to them by a different path. This is perhaps something people wouldn't realize without knowledge of your experience."

"I guess that's true," said Katie, uncertainly.

Arabella gamely sprang up to stand beside Katie at the podium.

"Miss Baker, I know we would be delighted to hear about this particular expedition, if you don't mind. Many of us have been talking about how eager we are to *participate* in whatever enterprises inspire us and our children."

"Oh, yeah, sure!" Katie piped up. "Sorry! I didn't mean to get on my soapbox."

In her world, she said, people are always trying to beat each other. Who's flown the highest, who's flown the longest in time or the longest distance, or who's flown the fastest. Partly they're always at this just because it's in their nature, they're just the kind of people who if you say you've done something once, well, then, they've done it twice, whether you're talking about crashing your craft in a backyard goldfish pond or eating at Joe's diner. Even if you're just trying to go out the same door together, they have to try to cross the threshold first. They're just that way. And the ones who can almost make a living at it are the ones who get their names in the newspapers and record books because people will pay to see them defend their titles or break their own records. Or crack up. They get sponsors and even aircraft, just like winning racehorse jockeys go to the richest owners and the fastest horses.

"I'm a new pilot. And I need to get in the books to get ahead." She explained that next year at Santa Monica, California, there will be an air derby at the National Air Races just for women pilots like there has been for men.

And though you might think she was unique, she could name at least two dozen aviatrixes older and more experienced who will compete—Pancho Barnes, Ruth Noyes, Louise Thaden, Phoebe Omlie, Ruth Nicols, and lots others, including the one somebody mentioned, Amelia Earhart.

To qualify for the air derby, you have to have at least a hundred hours of flying solo and at least twenty-five hours flying across the country.

"I'm also going for a record. If I make it all the way to California, I believe I'll be the youngest aviatrix to make a successful solo transcontinental flight."

"Bravo! How inspiring!" Arabella patted her palms before her bosom and others picked up the cue. "And do you have a sponsor?"

"Well, not exactly. I had some savings, and there was somebody willing to help with basic expenses, but truth is, I don't have much left for emergencies like this one. I guess I was gambling I could make it all the way on what I have."

"Well, you are a very brave young woman!"

Katie ducked her head, blushing, as Arabella cued the applause. To Mabel the presentation had gone well enough, as the rough spots had been smoothed over by a very skillful hostess, and the implicit plea for donations had slid easily into the proper moment without seeming gratuitous or crass.

Arabella turned toward her guests and slyly edged Katie away from the podium, and Mabel sensed a wind-up—tea would be served. Before Arabella could go on, though, Wylie Thompson spoke from his armchair.

"If you wouldn't mind, Miss Baker, I have questions for my article. Would you please tell us about the aircraft itself?"

There might've been inward groans. Everyone could feel that the natural ending—and the coming tea and refreshments—had been delayed by a question they had no interest in.

Sure, said Katie. Her craft was built by the Travel Air people in Wichita, Kansas. There followed a flurry of details about the aircraft's handling characteristics and performance, and much about its specifications—engine size and type and manufacturer, top speed, cruising speed, fuel and oil capacity, range, "service ceiling," weight, length, width, wingspan, range, weight, and so forth. Katie seemed eager to flaunt this knowledge as a damper to the implication she was uneducated. Mabel sensed eyelids drooping, and she yearned to coax her friend to cut it short. Her bet would be that after having sat for the talk, some needed relief by way of Arabella's touted indoor plumbing.

"Thank you kindly, Miss Baker," said Thompson. "Now you please correct me if I'm wrong, but isn't your aircraft a new model for the company?"

"Yes."

"Earlier this year, I believe."

"Yes. It's a great aircraft. Probably a lot of flyers will use it next year at the races."

"Will you be using this one?"

"Oh. I dunno. Maybe, I guess. I have to qualify first."

"Isn't that a very costly machine?" Thompson seemed to be consulting notes. "I'm told upwards of six to ten thousand dollars would be the price tag."

Katie's eyes narrowed. "I suppose so. I dunno for sure. If you say so."

Arabella's features were slipping from "gracious hostess" to "annoyed moderator." She shifted her weight from foot to foot and gave Thompson a challenging look.

"Just a couple more questions if you don't mind," he said, reading her pose. "I mean no disrespect here, but it does strike me that you seem very young and by your own admission inexperienced to have been put in the cockpit for a solo journey clear across the nation in so costly a machine." He let the question hang a moment while they all watched Katie. Mabel grew irritated. The question seemed insulting. But it also brought something to the fore that had been buried in Mabel's mind under her impetuous admiration.

Before Katie could reply, Thompson added, "But I'm sure it must mean that some benefactor has complete faith despite your youth and inexperience. Would that be the 'sponsor' you mentioned?"

"Uh. Yeah. I've been really lucky."

"Thank you, Miss Baker! And if you'll kindly indulge me for one last query. I'm told that when you arrived, the word BEECH-NUT was on the flanks of your aircraft. But I also see that the words have since been painted over. Was the Beech-Nut company your sponsor? Has their sponsorship run its course?"

"Uh," said Katie. "Yeah, you got it."

During the tea in the garden, Mabel thought it best to let her charge off the leash, and so she circulated under the canopy with a teacup and saucer in hand, a crustless mini sandwich of cream cheese and chive tucked under the belly of the cup. Katie's glamour as an exotic seemed to have rubbed off on Mabel as her escort, and she heard questions that implied an intimacy—*What is your aviatrix really like?* And *Do you think she is upset with her mother?* Blanche wanted to know more about the break-up between her parents. And did she think the pilot had a beau?

Mabel watched Arabella glide from guest to guest reminiscent of a bee pollinating flowers, and the image made her hopeful for a beneficial outcome for Katie. She kept a furtive protective eye as Katie stood, hands in her trouser pockets, teacup-less, while being approached by twos and threes who exchanged polite pleasantries to judge by Katie's little nods and half-smiles of pained toleration. Louise had hovered on the fringe of the interlopers, apparently awaiting a chance to corner her alone, and when she did, whatever their conversation was about it brought a troubled look on Katie's face that piqued Mabel's curiosity.

Mabel wondered if anyone would raise the reporter's prickly questions with Katie. However impertinent, his questions brought Mabel puzzling information about Katie's relationship to the aircraft. Katie had told them yesterday that she was delivering it to its owner in California. She'd not mentioned this in her talk. And wouldn't it have been natural to say that when she was asked about using it in the upcoming race?

4

AFTER THEY CLEANED THE KITCHEN FROM LUNCH AND MABEL and the flyer had left for Arabella's party, Wally had gone upstairs for a nap, and when she came back down it was going on five. She wondered what was keeping Otis so long at Arabella's. She stood at the front windows, waiting, and her vigil was rewarded in an unexpected and troublesome way: Mabel's automobile chugged by with what looked to be several passengers, and to her that meant that Arabella's shindig was long over.

She believed that working for Jake Bohanan had a hand in bringing on Otis's dark spells, and it was too easy to picture him right now lying in his truck bed out in the vast nothingness around their hamlet. Once when she'd asked where he went when those moods got heaped up and drove him to hootch himself into oblivion, he said he went "out to the boondocks where nobody'll see me, nobody'll hear me, and nobody'll try to help me." He'd meant he wanted to spare them both of any embarrassment, but to her it just meant more risk, more danger. He could stumble away from his truck, trip and fall into an arroyo, knock his head, break his back, and lie there paralyzed for buzzards to pick his eyes out and rip his flesh apart and rattlers and scorpions to get their revenge. And she couldn't do one damned thing about it!

Made her absolutely furious. He'd throw a horrendous hissy fit if she up and disappeared and didn't come back until the next day and said, Oh, well, I just walked halfway to Carlsbad and sat down in the sand dunes and knocked myself in the head with a hammer so's I'd be dead to the world for a good while so anything and everything that had a horn or a stinger or fangs or claws—or a rotten fellow with a rut on his mind—could do whatever with me!

He'd say, Aw, you wouldn't do that.

Well, of *course* she wouldn't!

He'd never said so but she'd felt it too many times—that she had no right to make a federal case out of his comings and goings because ... she ... was ... not ... his ... wife. They'd met and fallen in love in Texas years ago where getting hitched was unthinkable and legally impossible, and she'd thought they came out here to New Mexico because nothing stood in their way.

She might reply if anybody asked—Well, just haven't got around to it, I guess. What she could but wouldn't add is that they'd both had a spin on that merry-go-round.

But nobody had asked. And better not, by God.

But truth was, Otis had a stubborn streak that led him to do things that he kept apart from her. She'd never pried into his past, just let him give her what he wanted when he wanted, and he respected her right to reign over her own history. They were old enough for the story of all they'd done before they'd met to be a long one with many a dreary chapter. But the one they'd been writing here together was the very best, she believed.

Standing at the window watching the light fade from the street as the sun sank behind the café, she squeezed her fists around an invisible object, sent a hiss through clenched teeth.

God*damn* that Arabella Bohanan!

Trembling, she went into the hallway where the telephone was posted on the wall, yanked the receiver off its hook, danced with impatience like a kid needing to pee while the operator in Loving took forever to connect her.

The telephone rang and rang on the other end.

"Good afternoon," purred Arabella at last. "This is the Bohanan residence. Arabella Bohanan speaking."

Wally about exploded. So syrupy! Like she's the world's nicest person!

"This is Wally. I guess your . . . *thing* is over."

"Why, yes, it is, Wallace. It was a great success, even if I say so myself. Thank you for asking."

"I wanna know is Otis still there."

A rustle and a pause on the other end. Wally's heart pounded. She did not want to hear that he'd left hours ago.

"I just checked. It seems that he and Jake are still dismantling the canopy I had them put up in the patio."

Hearing that Otis was still working did more than reassure her of his welfare—it gave her leave to feel indignant. "Well, he's been out there *all the damn day*, then, Arabella! It's not like he doesn't have his own work to do, and because he was gone today, I had to handle that lunch crowd all by myself. You need to know that when you put him to work, you put me to work, too. Y'all are always taking advantage of him, and I've got half a mind to put a stop to it!"

"Well," said Arabella after a moment. "I'm very sorry you feel that way, Wallace. I would've thought you'd be grateful that Jake so often gives Otis the opportunity to pare down your debt."

"My . . . *debt*?!" Wally blurted, feeling tricked and bested without knowing how or why.

"Why, yes!" Arabella sounded genuinely surprised.

Wally's thoughts reeled, ricocheted inside her skull. She was afraid to ask for details—that would put Arabella gleefully on top—and she was caught between denying something unknown and feeling foolish or just hanging up and leave Arabella smirking at her hasty retreat.

"I don't know what you're referring to," Wally said coolly as she could manage, as if this "debt" were owed by a distant, unknown party. "But I pay my bills and live within my means and always have. And I do *not* owe you or your husband a single blessed cent. Not one, you hear? Not one!"

"Oh, dear me!" gushed Arabella. "I fear I've let the cat out of the bag! I suppose you might want to speak to Otis about this."

While Wally was still wrestling with this news, Arabella beat her to the hang-up.

5

LEONARD LONGED FOR A REPEAT PLEASE ON THAT HUG. FOR sure he hadn't known it was coming. Somebody tosses an apple at you without a warning whistle, and you see it looming and at the last second throw up your hands to catch it or block it from smacking your honker. Just standing there with a paintbrush in his hand and she comes walking up *and just keeps walking right into him!* Giant nest of that fiery red hair billowing up around his chin, and her arms slipped around his ribs and her palms spread on his back while he stood half-frozen holding the paintbrush out so it wouldn't drip on her, and she pressed close. He felt what he now imagined were her warm breasts on his belly and his thigh brushed between her legs—

Oh, so briefly. Like a blink.

So now, hours past, he'd turned into a huge pink throbbing member, like a Leonard-sized dinger with his head and its hormone-drenched brain bobbling atop it. It was a deliciously painful condition. He'd worked alone for hours while Katie and Otis were gone, mooning feverishly, wallowing and swooning, going over and over that millisecond before she'd mumbled something and pulled away. He was happy to work alone; the absence of interruption gave his imagination full authority to rollick like a drunk along his nerve ends, gallop unchecked like a mad horseman through his sensitive tissues, kicking over his melee-rattled heartbeats.

Oh, if only he'd had the tiniest smidgeon of warning! He'd *ready* that spot on his belly to absorb the warmth of her breasts, *ready* his thigh to feel her soft legs brushing his, *ready* his chest to cuddle her cheek—making his body wholly receptive and *expectant*.

They'd expect him to make progress, and he wanted to please her with his dedication. But each motion to repair the craft brought her a step closer to flying off. He'd not had nearly enough of her, and it pained him that Louise Larsen and Mabel had enjoyed her overnight company—hogged her, really—and one was sure to get another helping.

Of course, he couldn't offer that. And he did feel miffed that Arabella Bohanan's party had shut him out. He might've offered to help Otis, but it would've left the airplane unattended and wasted what Katie felt was precious time.

At a point in the afternoon, he fixed on the fact that the craft had two cockpits. She'd said she planned to give folks joy rides, and he'd been thrilled by the notion, but that mysterious force pulling him into her orbit and his yearning to have that hug again roiled his imagination—result was he dreamed himself into that front cockpit, and not for a "ride" like a trip on a merry-go-round, but longer, farther, into the future.

That notion wrote itself into a story. He was not so creative a storyspinner that he could fashion himself as the flyer's beau—a stretch that required a higher estimate of himself as her equal and equally desired. But maybe a helper or sidekick, a mechanic seeing to the health of the engine and the airplane? Like a groom for a jockey, he'd do whatever she might need done.

Mabel once said, "You should consider going where your talents and skills can find greater opportunity to develop."

He'd taken that to heart. At the time he was sweet on her, and if she'd handed him a train ticket to that "where," he'd have stepped aboard without a second thought.

But that had been before his heartbreak. Overwhelmed by a heady mix of fondness, tenderness, and desire, he'd pushed himself at Mabel and tried to buss her cheek. She'd stiff-armed him, reeled back, apparently repelled, but spoke as gently as possible, he supposed, because she was a kind person. Told him he was way too young, and she needed to remain his teacher and friend. "And I won't say nothing more than that, Lennie, because I prize my students and my friends beyond all measure."

So, while it was richly rewarding to relive his hug from Katie, he didn't dare put his filthy paws on her back or push against those breasts or urge his thigh deeper into that silky hollow. Held his breath and waited, again and again, for the fleeting sensations to alight.

After Katie and Mabel had left around three, Wally had brought him a bread-and-butter sandwich, a glass of milk, and a chicken drumstick. They sat on upturned buckets, and she smoked while he ate.

"Saw what that girl did."

"What?" He felt a blush seeping to the surface.

"I'm talking about her grabbing ahold of you."

"Aw, Wally, heck fire! She was just being polite."

"Polite my foot! Lennie, you gotta give me credit for living over sixty years and knowing a whole lot more about females than you do."

"Well, you don't have to be so suspicious. Good golly, she just, I mean—" He burned. Wally might as well have one of those new X-ray machines.

"Well, you can think she was just being polite, and I'll credit her for it. But I just want you to know that the human female's always at a disadvantage in a way, and a lot of them are gonna use whatever powers they have to equal things out, get what they want."

Embarrassed, he felt sulky. "She don't want nothing from me except what help I give her like I'd give any darn stranger stranded here in this, this—"

"You'd best not say Hicksville."

"Hicksville!? I wadden gonna say that! Why would I say that?"

"Okay. I can see you're sulling up on me."

"Well, heck, Wally! How many times are you gonna give me this same lecture?"

After a moment, she leaned over and stroked his cheek with her palm. Smiled.

"Don't pay me no mind. I'm a bitter old busybody."

"Aw, you're not. And I do listen to you." He grinned. "That's why you don't have to tell me the same thing so many times."

Around sundown, Otis drove into the yard, parked, and came to inspect Leonard's progress, graded the work as "A number 1."

"Is Katie coming back?"

Otis shrugged. "I saw her leave Bo's place with Mabel."

Leonard waited, fruitlessly, tidying up their tools, and at one point, he gingerly stepped up on the trailing surface of the lower wing and, looking about, crept forward, ducking under the upper wing until he was right by the front cockpit. The polished aluminum dashboard with its trapezoidal shape nested several black-faced dials and gauges with sharp red or white numerals or needles, and the masculine aura they radiated filled him with a yearning to understand their functions, to master their use. The control stick, the rudder bar—this cockpit also had a full set of controls. He was tempted to ease down into it but resisted and settled for picturing himself seated. Then he noticed that the seat had two indentations for backs and two for butts—this cockpit took two passengers, and that was disconcerting.

Then he heard Wally's angry voice from inside the kitchen, and that rattled him, so he scurried across the wing and dropped down to the ground. Wally and Otis were having a heck of a fight. He couldn't distinguish their words in part because he didn't want to know, and their discord saddened and confused him, so he walked home in the twilight, disappointed at not seeing Katie again.

For a time, he lay on his cot fretting and restless. He tried to read more of *The X Bar X Boys on the Ranch*, a book Mabel had given him for his last birthday but couldn't keep his mind on it. He knew Mabel believed it would appeal to him: *The Manley Boys, Roy and Teddy, are the sons of an old ranchman with a thousand head of cattle. The lads know how to ride, how to shoot, and how to take care of themselves under any circumstance.* And he supposed he should've taken to these fellows since their lives were a bit like his only a lot more exciting. A lot more. But these "lads" had absolutely no interest in radios or automobiles or motorcycles or aircraft or dynamos, or how bridges or skyscrapers are built, or oil wells were drilled, so he found their concerns old-fashioned. Horses and cows. When they weren't very boring, they were very annoying.

He slipped the radio's headset on and tickled the crystal and tuning rod to bring in WBAP. The weekly "barn dance" show was in progress, with fiddler Capt. M. J. Bonner whooping it up on "Wabash Cannonball," followed by a number by the Hilo Five Hawaiian Orchestra. He listened for a good while. Normally he found this weekly dose of music uplifting, and he often pictured dancers doing a do-si-do and a Texas Star while he put his own feet through lively paces as he lay bootless in sock feet on his bunk.

But not tonight. Everything around him had crumbled to flakes like blossoms dried too long between pages. Envy poked at him, distracted him from enjoying the music. It just was not fair that Mabel or Louise or Arabella Bohanan should have laid claim to so much of Katie's time.

What were they doing right now, anyway?

And so, along this path, the hug snuck back to him, her cheek against his chest, her breasts on his belly, her thighs so briefly pressed to his own. Desire seeped up and saturated his memory, dousing it with heat and made him groggy and yet alert, woozy yet jumpy, the florid sensations dampening his thought and recharging his blood; he felt it beat in his temples and his breath went shallow. Where earlier he'd not allowed his imagination to fabricate a back pat to match her own, a counter pressure against her soft mounded torso, or an inching forward of his leg between her thighs—now the poor fellow was helpless to hold anything back, and he went at it whole-hog, like a starving stevedore on a T-bone steak, bending her this way and that, caressing her here and there, returning the favor to himself until almost as quick as her fleeting hug, he shot himself in the eye.

6

HOWARD STAYED AWAY FROM THE HOUSE, CLEANING IRRIGA-
tion ditches. The chore was necessary, though it need not have been
done today nor in one day-long effort. Working alone soothed him; it
put physical and psychic distance between himself and conflict with
others, chiefly Louise. He wouldn't have said he was fleeing from it; in
his defense, he could rightly argue that in this space he'd made, he let
his mind rest like calm pond water so that thoughts could bubble up
from the muck and pop on the surface. This time for reflection might
offer him knowledge of his truer, deeper feelings about things. In the
Orient they called it "meditation" when you stood back and let your
mind run its own business alone, so he supposed that was what he did.

He'd caught Louise stripping Izzy's bedroom—the "just a thorough
cleaning" excuse was a big prop behind which she was hiding her real
intent. Maybe it had been to protect him; maybe it had been to dis-
arm his objection. He could read her better than she gave him credit
for. Partly because of his lifelong habit of keeping his observations to
himself, he rarely confronted her with what he felt to be true if it meant
getting into a wrangle, so he'd simply acquiesced to the lie. Well, not
exactly a lie, he supposed—the room no doubt did need cleaning. But
it needed cleaning the way these irrigation ditches needed dredging
out with a spade.

The aviatrix's visit had rattled them both. The instant that pilot had appeared and he learned she'd be staying the night, he'd felt
himself *contract*, evaporate if possible—the memories assaulted him
ferociously and without warning. And arriving by way of that infernal
aircraft. He'd been mean, he knew it. It came back: Izzy's blithe indifference to his love, to his attention, to his care—wholly inexplicable
when she and her mother had been all he'd thought of in France, all
he'd longed to return to. He had no way to account for her atrocious
behavior toward them both, and no amount of solitary reflection
would offer any better explanation than that she felt both her parents
had deserted her: he to go to war, her mother to her death. And the

pair of parents he and Louise offered her were a poor substitute for those in that pre-war Eden of her childhood, and the new "home" in what she persisted in calling a "desert" would never live up to the one in the green woodlands of Eastern Tennessee.

And he'd been powerless to fix it. The fix she'd made herself by running off with a fellow she hardly knew—that was desperately pathetic and so obviously of no real lasting value that Howard's heart had ached for her ever since. She'd most likely been deserted again, and her pride would never allow her to say so and come back. It pained him to think that she was miserable and unhappy, even now.

The sight of that room upended stopped his heart. Louise very well knew what effect it would have. She'd tried before to drag them out of the morass of his sorrow, telling him, "You know I don't know why you're not angry with her. I think you should be furious to be treated this way. She had a right to be snotty to me—it's what you'd expect—but it makes me really mad on your behalf that you never think to blame her or let yourself off the hook for her terrible decision."

To which he'd said, "She's just a child, ignorant and innocent."

And she'd said, "Apparently not so innocent."

Those had always been their postures. Sometimes he wondered this—if Louise would ever say anything in Izzy's defense, it might free him to be angry on his own account. But for them both to be against her, that would be ganging up on his motherless daughter and only child.

To insist on keeping that room intact wasn't rational. Though he'd come out into the field shaken with the notion of that last shred of connection being lost, over the hours he'd recognized that if Louise had not done that, it might never have been done, and people would start to talk, if they already hadn't been, about how he insisted on keeping the room like a shrine to a dead person though Izzy wasn't dead—or so he presumed—she was just . . . just so *inconsiderate and thoughtless* that she never bothered to let them know how she was.

He rode Mildred slowly back to the house a little after five. Mabel's T was parked there, and she and the pilot were standing beside it talking to Louise. As he sat a-saddle watching, Pal hustled up from his dig by the barn and flung himself at the girl; she hugged him and bent to kiss that smelly old canine's head.

That kid was absolutely nothing like Izzy. Pal's approval of this scrappy, ill-groomed aviatrix was a mark in her favor, for sure. It crossed his mind that he'd always adored Izzy, appreciated her female vanities, her shallow pursuits, her empty headedness. They were oddly reassuring. You wanted to protect her, you wanted to applaud her dance and piano recitals, you wanted to be proud of her liking for frills and fuss. Izzy would make your heart beat faster to see her in her wedding gown and to walk her down the aisle. You could be half in love with her yourself.

But weren't you always a spectator? This pilot with the wild red hair that never seemed to have been brushed and with the gumption to fly that aircraft—if you were stove up with a bum leg, she'd be happy to climb the windmill for you to grease the rotor bearings. This daughter would go into the fields with you and take a turn with the ditching spade, go fishing and hunting, be happy to sleep under the stars and eat beans from a can heated on a campfire.

She might take up where you left off some day. And with pleasure and appreciation for the legacy.

How old am I, Howard?

He'd been very rude to the pilot and regretted it.

When he went into the barn to slip his saddle off Mildred, Louise came up behind him.

"Mabel gave me a ride home from Arabella's."

"How was the party?"

"It was interesting to hear Katie talk. And I think Arabella did her a big favor by passing the hat. I gave her five bucks from my rainy-day tin."

She watched him remove the bridle and hang it on the wall, pick up the curry brush and gently sweep it down Mildred's gray flanks.

"Since she brought me home, the least I could do is offer them dinner." Her voice was guarded, cautious.

"Oh, sure! Good. Always a pleasure to have Mabel." He looked her in the eye. "And that girl is pretty harmless, after all."

His enthusiasm made her brows lift. "I'm glad you think so."

7

KATIE WAS COUNTING HER MONEY. SEATED ON THE SOFA with her valise open beside her, she parted the lips of the envelope and thumbed through the currency. Mabel tried to pretend she wasn't watching; she busied herself with getting out the glasses they'd used last night for the wine. That bottle, half-hidden under a tea cozy, would still fill two small glasses, so she should propose to finish it.

She was eager to know how much Katie'd been given, but her mother always said you don't ask people about their religion, their politics, or their money. She was still mulling her own contribution. Her annual salary of $950 was lower than what her counterparts in Eastern cities were paid, but the cottage was gratis, and her overhead low. Over the past two years, she'd tucked away over $250 in a biscuit tin under her bed. With so few places to spend, she spent little. Train fare to Ohio and back was around $30, and when she was back home, she spent nothing. She'd always been frugal.

Unable to restrain herself, she said, "I hope your benefactors thought to give you bills and not checks! But please let me know if that's not so. I can take you to the Loving bank to cash them."

Katie looked up. "Looks like Mrs. Bohanan already thought of that and told people to give me cash!" she reported happily. "Hey, how much does a gallon of gas cost in Loving?"

"Twenty-three cents a gallon."

"Uh. I need sixty-seven gallons. That's—" Katie squinted at the ceiling. Mabel reflexively started calculating, but Katie beat her to the total. "A little over fifteen dollars! Yippee!" She held up the sheath of bills and waved it like a fan. "They gave me ninety-three dollars! This has been the best forced landing anybody ever had!"

"How wonderful!" Mabel gushed. About the equivalent of one month's salary. Envy and irritation pricked at her though she hastened to master it.

"My ship has a range of about six hundred miles on a full tank. I wish I knew how far it was from here to Los Angeles by the crow-fly."

"A lot farther, I'd imagine."

Katie nodded. "How much do you think Mr. Jefferson and Leonard will expect to be paid?"

"Oh, gosh, Katie. I have no idea." Her guess would be that the obviously smitten Leonard would sooner die a thousand deaths than to charge her a penny.

"Well, I want to pay them!"

"Of course."

Katie buried the envelope under the clothes in the valise and closed the cover. Mabel said she couldn't keep the wine around without risking her reputation and her livelihood, so they better drink it up. Katie happily concurred, and Mabel poured them both the rest of the bottle.

"I hadn't thought of this before, but I guess I need to get rid of the evidence." She nodded at the empty bottle.

Katie took tiny sips from her glass, seemingly to savor and make it last.

"Outhouse."

"You think so?"

"Why not?"

"I guess nobody'd go digging around for it."

They laughed. "Every few years, though," added Mabel, "they have to either clean it out or dig a new hole."

"Ugh!" snorted Katie. "I vote for a new hole."

Mabel tried to keep down with Katie's rate of consumption, but the wine spoke to her blood in an unfamiliar and tantalizing way, and it was all she could do to keep from gulping it in one greedy swallow.

"Yes. And if they do root around in there, it'll be years from now."

"And you'll be long gone?"

"Well, my God! I hope so."

"You don't like it here?"

"Oh, I didn't mean to imply that." She was confused herself; she realized that she'd feared Katie might think her provincial if she didn't seem eager for new horizons. "I just mean, well, I never thought of it as a permanent position. Most people around here expect that their schoolteachers will work so long as they're single, then when they marry, they quit and leave. They make it a point to tell me that with great regularity."

"Is that your plan?"

"I'm afraid I don't have a plan."

"I know you said Leonard wasn't a beau, but is there somebody else here that, you know—"

"Gosh, no!"

"Somebody back where you came from, one of the Valentine co-tillion boys?"

Mabel shook her head. She shot Katie a wry grin. "I have maybe one more year of age before I get the label 'old maid,' I guess."

"Well," said Katie, "to me you seem like the kind of girl lots of fellows would really go for."

Mabel blushed, murmured a thanks that seemed a pro forma denial. She yearned to hear more about this "kind," but modesty prevented urging it.

"I do like it here," she offered, "and I don't mean to sound as if I'm champing at the bit to leave. People here are kind and generous and they have tremendous respect for a woman in my position."

"I'll sure say they're generous."

"Did Arabella tell you who gave what?"

"No."

"That makes it pretty hard to write thank-you notes."

"I wouldn't even begin to know how, anyway. Don't you have to have special paper and envelopes and things?"

Katie didn't seem particularly ashamed of either her ignorance or her lack of proper materials, as if writing such a note were a species of professional endeavor acquired only after training. It came to Mabel that Katie had no idea if she'd contributed.

"Excuse me a moment, please.'"

In the bedroom, she went to her knees, pulled the biscuit tin from under the bed. She popped the lid. The bills were mostly ones and fives, most bills soft as cloth from use. She'd been saving for—for what? Simply a lifelong habit of holding back, expecting if not disaster at least a downturn in fortune. She was simply not a female who pined away for baubles or haute couture, and, if she didn't already own one, the one material item she might've sacrificed to get would be that automobile her father had given her.

She'd once had vague thoughts of going on to California, though she couldn't have said why then and had no answer now. It was just where young people went who left their homeplaces and had any ounce of restlessness. She had no desire to be in the movies in any way. She'd pictured a richer cultural life, that's for sure, concerts, plays, lectures. Friends with other single girls with similar interests. Going to the ocean, sitting on a beach, and feeling the sun and the salt breeze.

Mabel counted out some bills and slid the tin under the bed. What she'd give wouldn't be missed—to her surprise, it seemed to her then that if she gave Katie the entire bundle, that too wouldn't be missed since it had no dedicated purpose.

"I wanted to give you something, too." She held the bills between her thumb and fingers. "I know it will seem maybe an odd amount, but you said you had to spend fifteen on fuel, and you said you had ninety-three, so I thought I'd give you enough that when you'd bought your gasoline, you'd still have an even one hundred."

Katie's eyes bloomed with surprise. "Wow! Mabel! That's twenty-two dollars!"

"Is it?" Mabel shrugged.

"That's like . . . 23 percent of what I got at Mrs. Bohanan's! Holy cow! That's way more than your fair share!"

Katie leapt from the sofa and flung herself at Mabel, clutching her and squeezing, her cheek just under Mabel's chin, then released and said, "Oh, you are so super!"

Rattled, Mabel said, "Well, it's not so much, really. I seem to make more than I need. And besides you need it. There's no telling what you might encounter, like another emergency. I just thought that for me it's money well spent. And—" She felt as if she were babbling. Her need to justify her gift was inexplicable and embarrassing.

"Well, thanks again."

"You're welcome."

"Let's drink to you."

"No, let's drink to both of us. You were superb today out at Arabella's. I wish school were in session—I'd love to have you talk to my students. They'd be so thrilled and inspired!"

Katie took another tiny sip for the toast, but Mabel tossed down the rest of her glass. She held it up to the light and squinted at it.

"Wish there were more." A whole lot more, she wanted to add. Feeling that surprised her completely.

"Always," said Katie. "For everything."

On their way home from dinner at Louise's, Katie had told her that Louise had asked her earlier at the salon to spend another night with her and Howard, as a favor. "She said she hoped that her husband could get used to having someone else in their daughter's room."

Mabel was surprised at Louise's candor, since it brought to the surface things everyone said about their using the room as a shrine, and signaled a new turn, she thought.

"What did you say?"

"Well, I said I'd already promised you."

"Katie, if you wanted to stay there, I sure would understand!"

"No. It just felt weird, you know. Like too much was depending on me that I didn't know anything about."

"Well, I'm really happy to have you as a guest. I guess I hadn't really realized how much I missed talking just to another kindred soul."

The long day full of charged events had drained them both, apparently, as when Mabel suggested they retire for the night, Katie readily agreed. The routine from the previous night—a trip to the privy, a wash-up (that included Katie's need for a fresh sanitary pad), a change of wardrobe, seemed familiar now, and Mabel welcomed the absence of anxiety over how to manage these preparations: Katie now had "her" pajamas and her side of the bed, her glass of water on the stand by her pillow. On their privy visit, they'd both peered into the dark and odiferous hole while Mabel pitched the wine bottle into the maw, heard it splash in the muck, and both had cackled with horror.

They lay side by side in the dark. Although only moments ago Mabel had felt fatigued, the instant the lantern was snuffed, the darkness aroused her, and she felt twitchy and anxious. Not sleepy, that was for certain.

"Thanks again for being so helpful," said Katie.

So she was alert as well! "It has been my pleasure and my honor to know you and have you here." Mabel giggled. "Sounds like a luncheon introduction!"

"Well, I'm not giving another talk."

Mabel turned on her side to face her guest. "I do mean it, though. I do get lonely here sometimes, and to have somebody to talk to—like this, you know, I miss it terribly."

After a moment, Mabel said, "May I ask you something?"

"Sure."

"What did you mean when you said I seemed like the kind of girl that fellows would go for?" Katie could not possibly imagine what it cost to ask that, she thought.

"Well, jeepers! You're so warm and smart and funny and helpful, and like I said you have really beautiful eyes. You know things. And boy howdy, I bet this is going to sound odd, but you smell good, too!"

They both erupted into clamorous laughter that shook the bed.

"I don't know if any of that is true," said Mabel, getting her breath. "But it sure is wonderful to hear. Because after a while you start to wonder if there's something wrong. Poor Leonard had a crush on me, I'll admit, but he'd have had one on any young schoolmarm."

"You sure you didn't have beaus back home when you were in school?"

"Not any that count. I hope you don't mind if we talk about this."

"Fire away!"

"I've never even been kissed. And I'm sure not bragging!"

"I'm really surprised."

Encouraged, Mabel plunged on. "You remember I told you about my friend, Elizabeth? Well, she'd had this cousin—he was a little older—and she said he'd taught her how a man kisses a woman. And the summer her family went to France, she had a fellow there kiss her. So, she knew how. And she taught me. We played silly games where we'd make up dialog about Francoise and Mariette being lovers in Paris and such nonsense. She said there were a lot of ways to kiss. About all I know came from her. We practiced it." A thought came that she left unuttered: *We got to be awfully darned good at it, too.* Instead, she added, "It turned out that there's a lot more to it than I'd thought."

In the silence, Mabel feared that Katie would think that she was hinting at something. She was trembling minutely from the memory of their games. But when Elizabeth deserted her to be married, Mabel swore she would never again kiss a member of her own sex. It was far too . . . *disturbing* in far too many ways that she didn't understand.

Katie said, "Sometimes there's nothing to it. Or behind it."

"That fellow, the pilot, you don't believe he felt anything for you?"

"He felt something for me, but it wasn't what I wanted, and it wasn't what I feel for him."

"You still love him."

"I hate his guts! If he was here right now and I had a shotgun I'd blast his balls off!"

"So, you do still love him."

"Oh, don't be so . . . wise!"

"You said I was smart."

"That was before I learned you'd use it on me." After a moment, Mabel heard a muted mewling, a sniffle. She leaned toward Katie, felt around for a hand, and took it in her own. She was on the verge of tears herself, she was just that happy.

"I don't know what I feel, I feel everything at once all the time. I feel like I'm going to explode, I feel like if I get that airplane back up into the air, I'll just put it into a nosedive and let it smash me into the ground. And when I'm not feeling all those things that have to do with him, I'm scared, really scared."

"What of?"

"I don't know what I'm doing. I was so hurt and mad when I took off all of a sudden that I wasn't thinking straight and I wasn't ten minutes in the air before a thousand things came to me that I should've done to get ready to fly that airplane, and it was too late, and I was too proud to turn around, and that's how and why I wound up crashing here, and it makes me so ashamed of myself and scared."

"Well, if you had to land, I'm glad it was here. We can put you safely on your way again."

"Oh, I'm so very grateful! But the first thing I realized when I took off was that I'd never be able to land at an airfield. So between here and California . . ."

"But why not?"

Katie sighed. And sighed again. "Promise not to tell anyone!"

Mabel wriggled closer and took Katie's other hand. "I promise."

The pilot she mentioned last night—Curly—he joined their outfit just before her mom and dad were starting to have trouble. And, like she said, he'd been really super about teaching her to fly, for nothing. And that was really important, because flying lessons at an airfield were way out of her reach, and her parents weren't eager to pay for that, either. So he'd taught her. She flew maybe at least a hundred hours with him. And he was so great about sticking up for her when the pilots would razz her about being a girl and give him the business about teaching her.

"He's really good-looking, too. The way those women today said they thought about how pilots were dashing and handsome and all that junk? Well, that's just how I saw him, then."

She had a terrible crush, followed him around like a stupid cocker spaniel. She wrote love notes but didn't give them to him. She did buy him a big Valentine, though, and worked herself up to write a really gushy note in it. She spent hours lying awake making up stories and pictures about a future together, a couple of pilots, barnstorming all over, sleeping and eating and just living everything together. What was the word? Vagabonds, vagabonds of the air. He was always friendly, and he even threw an arm around her shoulder and jostled her for a joke, or came up behind her and massaged her neck, gave her a hand up onto the wing, and so a couple of times they'd been so full of good spirits and fun that she'd just reached up and grabbed him around the neck and kissed him under his chin. And one night she did that he'd had a couple and she'd had her first shot of whiskey, and so when she leaned up, he leaned down, and that's when they kissed. Then, later ...

"He took advantage of you."

The bed jiggled slightly with her violent shake of her head. "No! If he hadn't made it happen, I think I would've asked him."

It happened three more times over the next two weeks. She felt even closer because this was when her dad left the outfit and Curly started being her mom's pilot for her stunts. So he was like a big brother as well as her fellow. He was still really sweet, but she could tell he was getting nervous because she was so young. He didn't want anybody to know about them because people would get jealous, and you don't need that kind of stuff when people's lives depend on each other.

"You can see why I'd think I meant something to him, can't you? I wasn't just making it all up? I told him over and over that I loved him. He'd always say, well, you're really special to me, too, and the times we have together are really special, too. Or he'd say, you're so great!, or he'd sort of scruff up my hair like I was a ten-year-old and laugh. He never said it back, but I just thought—" Mabel heard a sharp intake of breath, a muted whimper. "Just thought it was because fellows, especially the pilots, are nervous or embarrassed about saying tender things when they really feel them."

Mabel let her quietly weep without urging her on.

"Oh, I hope I can trust you!" Katie blurted out after a bit.

"I *hope* you will."

What happened was this—this company, the Beech-Nut people, well, they'd bought the new Travel Air, and they were looking for a pilot to fly it around to shows and fairs and the like and do stunts to promote the company. Besides having the name on the fuselage, they had a big banner to tow, and they were going to give the pilot a lot of samples of chewing gum to pass out. Curly was really jazzed about it—it was good money.

She could see it would mean he'd go off on his own and "that really tore me up." She couldn't stand the idea of not seeing him every day, not being his special girl, not having those *special times* together.

"So, I told him that I had a good idea. He could take me as a wing-walker, or I could also parachute, I'd done that, too. It would just add to the attraction, and I told him I bet the Beech-Nut people would go for it. I knew how to be in a show. I was born into it. It fit perfect with all my dreams about how we could be together in the future. I told him he didn't even have to pay me.

"He was really excited about the idea. He kept saying, 'Boy oh boy, Katie, you've got a good head on your shoulders. That's a really smart idea!' He was really impressed and of course I was so pleased about that. I'd done something great for him and for both of us. He said he'd talk to the Beech-Nut representative about it, but he couldn't see any reason that they wouldn't be happy to get an even bigger show at no extra cost."

A week went by. The outfit did shows in Akron and Cleveland and Memphis. She kept asking Curly if he'd heard anything from the Beech-Nut man, and he kept saying no. Because they were moving almost every day, she hadn't had a chance to put herself before him in a way that might spark one of their special times. The Beech-Nut people delivered the ship to the outfit so's he could get used to it before taking it on a tour. They had a three-day county fair in Chattanooga, so there was time and the chance for rest between shows, and so she went where he was staying in a hotel with a couple of other flyers and just waited around until they took the hint—they knew what was up—and left them alone.

She tried to smooch him up, "but he just seemed so cold, like it was torture to him to have me touch him, so I had to ask what was wrong. He said he had some bad news for me. He was really down in the mouth. I thought it might be that the Beech-Nut company had turned down my idea, and so I asked if that was it. He said no, not exactly, but they were worried about my age and lack of experience. He said they just didn't want to take those kinds of risks. They thought it was a very good idea, though.

"He said that like it was a consolation prize. And then I saw what was coming, and sure enough, he said, 'I had to ask your mom to go with me. We stunt together almost every day. I know you're disappointed, but . . .' and he went on and on about how talented I was and how smart and that in just a short time I'd be ready for anything in the shows. I could tell he was just trying to soften the blow. I was trying not to break down. Even as horribly sad and disappointed it made me, I could see why they'd told him I was too young, and I could see why they'd think my mom was the right choice. She had a billing on the posters as a wing-walker and a reputation.

"So, for a couple of days, I moped around and tried to get over my disappointment. They still had a show to do with our outfit by way of their contract. The night before they were supposed to leave for the Beech-Nut tour—this would be just last Wednesday—my mom told me that she'd been worried about how silly I was about Curly, and she'd been afraid I'd be hurt by expecting too much, and it was a good thing for me not to see him for a while."

"I guess she was trying to protect you."

Katie snorted. "You might think so. What I found out next was that she and Curly were doing one hell of a lot more than stunting together! They'd been having their own *special times*"—she sneered—"behind my back. And that explained everything. I was just completely knocked to the ground. I must've sobbed for eight hours straight. That just tore my heart out of my chest."

"Oh, I'm so, so sorry," murmured Mabel. She squeezed Katie's hands.

"And then I got hopping goddamn mad! I've never been so furious in all my life! So the next morning I just jammed some things into that suitcase and went out to the field. I knew they'd gassed up the ship the night before, and so I just climbed in it and told the mechanic I was there to start it up and check the engine, so we hand-propped it, and when it was warmed up, I just flew it off the field. They weren't going to sashay about in this ship together and have those 'special times' if I could help it!"

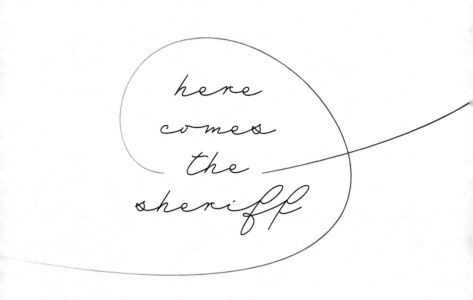

here
comes
the
sheriff

1

THE DRILLER BANGED ON THE DOOR ABOUT DAWN THIRTY. Said his helper had run off, the well was about near to gusher, and he desperately needed somebody to wrangle both the drill stem and the casing and weld the joints, because the hand that Miz Larsen bandaged when that finger got crushed still wasn't strong enough to do more than hold his pecker when he pissed.

Otis told him sorry, he'd promised that aviatrix he'd go to Loving for gasoline, but he suggested Johnston wake up Leonard—the boy could do what needed done, including welding. "He's slow at it and still learning, but he's careful and thorough."

A couple hours later following a dustup with Wally about helping the pilot, a skimpy breakfast, and twenty miles of bad road, he pulled up at Harley's one-pump place behind a vehicle that—wouldn't you know it—belonged to Sheriff E. J. Browne.

Otis knew Sheriff E. J. Browne by sight, but he didn't know if Browne remembered him. If you were colored folks and kept your head down, that's pretty much the way it always was.

But Otis hadn't always kept his head down. At the moment, he was standing in his truck bed unscrewing the stopper to an empty fifty-five-gallon drum, and as soon as Browne pulled his T sedan with the star insignia away from the sole gas pump at Harley Johnson's Oil & Gas in Loving, he'd ease up and fill the barrel, another five-gallon cannister, and the tank on his truck.

The sheriff had one hand on the gas pistol poked into the gullet of his vehicle, and the other gesticulated as he jawed with Harley. Otis watched, though with his head cocked in case they looked up. He was caught between looking where he damn well pleased and a reluctance to draw the sheriff's notice. That seemed cowardly, and the struggle made him stew. Annoying how the mere sight of one particular peckerwood could taint your day with dread and buried rage. With age, though, he'd learned to let some things sail on by.

He'd seen Browne on his infrequent patrols of Noname and

environs. Now, up closer, he noticed that the sheriff had packed pudge around his belly and his hair had turned a sickly gray. Now he wore specs with gold wire rims. He looked more benign, less capable of harm. When Otis and Wally lived at New Jordan, the sheriff, then a constable in Roswell, made regular trips out to their community every time a white rancher's cow, horse, dog, sheep, wife, child, wagon, feed sack, pitchfork, fountain pen, or teacup went missing. Stood to reason one of the "Knee-grows" at New Jordan had filched him, her, it, or them. He'd haul somebody back to Roswell to the Chavez County jail to put the fear of God in them. Never apologized when that stolen thing turned up misplaced or overlooked.

They had big Juneteenth celebrations at New Jordan. The community had been founded before the war by a preacher and his congregants who'd hoped to settle where black folks could live as farmers, merchants, blacksmiths, haberdashers, teachers, and bankers free of white folks' interference. Otis and Wally had arrived there from Texas just after the war, and by then it was a thriving community of several hundred citizens. Otis had come to New Jordan for the reasons others had, though pairing up with a white woman gave them both an added impetus. In Texas, anti-miscegenation laws prevented marriage, and many cities had made interracial cohabitation, sexual conduct, and even social contact a crime. And although the state of New Mexico was free of a punishing legal apparatus, in nearby Roswell, as in many American cities, the Ku Klux Klan had swept up civic leaders and white trash alike in its frenzy.

For Juneteenth celebrations, they invited neighbors near and far regardless of color, and dozens of white families attended. Singing, dancing, eating, and some secret sipping went on, everybody on their best behavior, and rarely were there shows of incivility. E. J. Browne came with other Roswell constabulary, and while he generally behaved, he also gave the impression that the amusing hijinks of darkies were like those of circus chimps.

But once when Otis and Wally were doing the hopped-up version of the foxtrot called The Toddle, he caught Browne's eyes fixed on them as they bobbed and swung. Browne and pals were ringside in wooden folding chairs chawing cigar butts and nipping at flasks. Otis felt just saucy enough to cruise himself and Wally right past his nose. He knew Wally'd relish poking him. It felt reckless to flaunt themselves, but flaunt they did, stayed on the floor through three tunes, one a waltz that asked for dips and a good deal of rubbing on one another.

He'd gone to the punchbowl, then, and got bumped from behind, an unexpected shoulder in his back, someone tripping into him?—and when he spun, holding cups of punch that had sloshed all over his hands, Browne was close to his face.

"Excuse me!" he chortled. "Didn't mean to jostle you none."

When Otis didn't respond, he bent an inch closer. "Just a friendly warning. Y'all don't wanna come into my town and parade yourselves around. Some folks don't like it."

"You the law, ain't you?"

"I am some of it."

"Ain't you sworn to serve and protect?"

"Duty-bound. But I ain't never every place at once."

"I appreciate the caution. I'll bring my old pal Samuel Colt to help me out in case there's a ruckus. We served together."

Browne tsk-tsked. "Not wise."

Otis thought that was the last of it, but two evenings later Browne and two others caught him in Bobby Farin's barn shoeing a horse and said they needed to "investigate" him on suspicion of selling hootch. They stripped him to his black skin and poked at his orifices as if he had a vat of moonshine tucked up his bunghole, tittered about his flaccid member. He wasn't hurt. He reckoned they could've dragged him out to the boonies and hung him, cut him up, or set him afire. But it deeply humiliated him.

New Jordan was a fine place—so long as the artesian wells held out, the worms didn't find the crops, and the soil stayed sweet and didn't turn alkaline. Then most everybody left, and Otis and Wally moved to Noname. The very moniker seemed to guarantee anonymity, their skills were needed, and the village was so remote as to render its inhabitants scarcely visible to any authority. Browne, in the meantime, moved from Roswell to become the county sheriff based in Loving.

Being in Browne's sphere of attention now got Otis worked up inside. The humiliation from—what, eight–nine years back?—burned anew, as if they'd stripped him and mocked him just yesterday. His hands shook, hair on his nape tingled and itched. He kept the wrench gripped tight in his fist. The sheriff apparently was telling a joke to Harley, Browne's head cocked and bobbing, Harley leaning into the narrative stream with an expectant grin, easy to guess there'd be a darkie in the story too dumb to catch on to a prank or a con, or maybe a high-yella whore with a piquant twitch.

His rage at seeing Browne surprised him. He'd had a lifetime of such humiliations, so why should this old injury flare up? Growing up in Texas, his boy Delbert had suffered much the same himself. And too many times his boy had been with him when a peckerwood had insulted him, and he'd just shuffled and mumbled like a beat-down fieldhand. When Delbert went overseas with his cornet in a Negro division as part of Jim Europe's jazz band, he stayed on in France after the war. *Sure, they got crackers here, Pop, but they few and far between. Folks nuts about our music.*

In Noname he rarely faced an open insult. He was known and respected, though under the normal civility ran a current of prejudice like the bed of cold water in a river beneath the warmer surface. Few approved of their sharing quarters like a man and wife. He was sure they ragged about it behind their backs. No doubt some choked back their disgust to picture a black man putting hands on a white woman and she welcome it, let alone set up housekeeping. But Noname wasn't Southern, so no law prevented it, and they did have genuine friends. He guessed some wouldn't set foot in the Owl for it, no matter how starved. Wally was keenly on guard for signs of disrespect; he talked her down from a high dudgeon when they got slighted—he'd had a lifetime of it and knew what that rage did to your spirit, your essential energy for getting through a day with an iota of pleasure. You summoned up your equanimity to keep your head from exploding. Wally was more or less new to it. But she was mistaken if she thought he wasn't upset to be degraded and disrespected.

Glaring at Browne, his body went woozy, his breath shallow. He waited out the passing wave, looked off toward a nearby mesquite thicket bordering the rutted sandy street. When Browne and Harley went inside the station's office, Otis climbed down from the truck bed. He took the bills the aviatrix had given him from one overalls pocket and counted out twenty bucks. In another pocket he had assorted bills and change from two others who'd asked him to purchase items in the mercantile.

Though Harley recognized him as a customer, Otis knew he'd have to pay in advance. He could wait until Browne had finished his business, or he could interrupt them and get about his errands.

God . . . BLESS it!

He sighed, rolled his shoulders, strode to the screen door, opened it, stepped over the threshold. Harley was behind the counter, and Browne was on the customer side, leaning a hip against it. They stopped talking when he entered and looked at him.

"Mornin', Harley." He nodded. "Sheriff."

They nodded back. In a pleasant merchant's voice, Harley asked, "What can I do you out of today?"

"Just needing some gas."

Harley took a step left to his cash register. "How much you needing?"

"About seventy gallons."

They both drew back in surprise. Harley whistled.

"That's a bunch." He bent to scribble on a pad. "That'd be sixteen dollars and eighty cents." He peered at Otis over the top of his glasses. "You sure you got that kind of cash?"

Otis peeled two fives and seven ones off the roll in his fist and laid the bills on the counter. Harley picked them up and recounted them, set them back down.

"You know, that's gonna deplete my stock. Can't be refilled myself for another two weeks. I can't short my regular customers."

Though he knew better than to object, Otis said, "I am a regular customer, Harley."

"True, true." Harley shook his head sadly and stared at the bills. Otis then understood. He uncoiled his fist, unrolled the other two one-dollar bills, set them atop the stack, opened his palms to show them empty.

"That help ease everbody's pain?"

Harley nodded. He rang up a sale, took the stack and recounted as he placed the bills in the drawer.

"What you need so much gasoline for?" This was Browne. The tone seemed civil enough, but there'd been no *If you don't mind my askin'*, and the presumption that Otis had to answer galled him.

Otis sorted through various responses before finally, without looking at Browne, said, "This and that. Getting it for other folks back in Noname."

"Buyin' it here and peddlin' it there, are you?"

"Only what it costs me," he said, though that was fudging.

"Well, you are a noble soul." Browne took his elbow off the counter, stood upright with a hand on his holster.

"Noname? You that *Knee-grow* runs the café?"

"Do a lot of things. Bit of this, bit of that, whatever folks need."

"You ever stay up at New Jordan?"

"New Jordan?" Otis turned to look at him. "Ain't that place a ghost town?"

Browne nodded. "But you at Noname?"

Otis hesitated, then nodded.

"Fellow at the newspaper told me an airplane landed right plop on your main street—that right?"

"True enough."

"I also got a report this morning from Texas to be on the lookout for an airplane has the word Beech-Nut on the side of it. Like the chewing gum. You read?"

"Yes," said Otis. "I can read and write."

"That airplane down there have that word on it?"

"Not since last I saw it."

"What's the pilot like?"

"Aw, like a lot of them, I reckon."

"Don't be thick with me. They looking for that aircraft because it was stole off an airfield back East." Browne turned to Harley. "Girl took it, believe it or not."

"A girl!!?"

Browne nodded. "What they say." He turned back to Otis. "What you say?"

"Well, I ain't had a close enough look to say one way or the other. Don't know nothin' about no stolen airplane."

Browne sneered while shaking his head—typical darkie.

"Reckon I'll go have a look-see for myself, then."

It would take a good spell to extract that much gas from the underground tank. You had to hand-pump it up and into "the scarecrow" until the glass head showed full-up. Otis had to fill the five-gallon can by setting it on the ground so gravity could pull gas down the delivery hose, then climb into the bed to pour from that can into the drum. He had to repeat this more than ten times.

It allowed plenty of time to gnaw on that worry bone. *You that Knee-grow?* What he didn't add—*that's shacked up with that white trash?* If he hadn't said it, that meant he didn't know that Wally and he lived together in Noname. He'd never been in the Owl, though apparently believed Otis ran it. He had little curiosity about anyone there.

What you need so much gasoline for?

None of your god-blessed business.

You ever stay up at New Jordan?

Yeah, and you and a couple other peckerwoods stripped me down one night just for fun and someday I'm liable to put a bullet right through your brain pan for it.

You read?

Do I read??! What do you think, you ignorant cracker?

Don't be thick with me.

Don't be thinking you can ask me any old thing any old time. I'm done giving the likes of you straight answers.

Browne came out of the office and stepped to his automobile, put a foot on the driver's side running board, turned to peer up at Otis. He shaded his eyes with his hand.

"Where you reckon I'd find that pilot?"

"Ain't sure. Could be gone already."

"Suppose not."

Otis appeared to consider Browne's options. "Well, you know the Bohanan place out north of town?"

"They the ones with that Spanish house?"

Otis nodded. "The missus out there—she generally knows everything that's going on."

Browne jerked his head as if that stood for a thanks, boarded his vehicle, and pulled away. Otis watched the auto disappear toward the center of town. Browne seemed to carry some of the animus away with him; Otis's heart slowed, and his mind cleared enough to replay their exchange calmly.

The girl had stolen the aircraft! That sure explained why she and Lenny painted the flanks of it. No doubt a story lay behind how a kid like that happened to run *away* from a circus and took a pricey airplane with her. You had to laugh.

The list of items to be bought for Mildred Price and Hank Goforth was short, but as he was topping off the barrel, he was weighing the information he alone seemed to possess. He knew just where the pilot was. He knew Browne would look for her. Big fat white folks' business. Browne apparently was not headed immediately for Noname, though, and it was possible to skip the added purchases and drive to Noname with the fuel.

A smart prosecutor could easily link his denial at Harley's with a later meet-up with the girl to gas up her airplane. Helping her flee the law. Hard to argue that he'd been ignorant that the law was looking for her, for sure.

Did he need more trouble—or any trouble—with the likes of Browne? No. Of course not. Did he owe that little white girl any favor, especially one that would put his and Wally's carefully secured safety at risk? No. He'd already done work on that airplane that he most likely would see no return for, to judge by how the girl had only feinted in wishing to pay him.

So why stick out his neck for her? She'd stolen the airplane. She was a thief. She'd not told him he was helping a thief by repairing that thing and getting her fuel. What did he have to gain by—what's the crime officially? *Aiding and abetting.* He'd already jeopardized himself by denying everything in that conversation with Browne—just from a half-baked impulse to be unhelpful. Did it without thinking of the consequences.

It's a wonder he'd lived free this long being that stupid.

2

THOUGH LEONARD WAS RELUCTANT TO BE AWAY FROM "THE excitement" (being with Katie), repairs on the aircraft were complete, so he agreed to work with Johnston but told him he needed to be back at the Owl when Otis returned from Loving—he put it that way rather than admit it would break his heart to miss Katie's departure.

Also, he was excited to roustabout for the driller. He was no longer on the sidelines in the hot debate about the value of the enterprise. At the town meeting ten days ago, those who, like Leonard, favored the arrival of modernity, spoke of lifting Noname out of a Luddite swamp by embracing the prospect of finding oil. That might bring the railroad, a bank, a "real" mercantile such as Loving had, maybe a barbershop, and for certain a gasoline filling station. A hotel, even! Maybe a café open for dinner. (Wally guffawed.)

Noreen Forrest had seen boom towns in Oklahoma, creeks running with oil and then catching fire. Whores and gamblers, she said. Indians buying grand pianos and using them for their hens to roost in and brand-new automobiles that they just leave in a ditch when they run off the road when they're licckered up and just go buy themselves a new one.

Somebody snickered. Then the other argument came to light. Dry farming around these parts was tough, and a man has to put food on his family's table, and if a rig in a far pasture makes up a little for what the weevils took from the cotton and the drought sapped from the grain sorghum, what fool would turn his back and make his family suffer?

Leonard had no interest in the economics. He loved the machinery; the internal combustion engine was enshrined in his mind as a world wonder, and the neat equation that required its use to find and extract its own fuel from the earth had a pleasing symmetry. Whatever helped to bring that nebulous thing called "the future" had his enthusiastic endorsement.

Now he'd come to the heart—albeit mechanical—of it all.

Operating a spudder rig involved stretches of tedium while the bit on the end of the weighted drill stem is lifted and let fall. After every four or five feet of penetration into the soil, the cogged bull wheel pulled the drill stem and bit out of the hole so that a hollow bailer could be lowered to bring up the ground-up earth and rock mixed with water and dumped into a pit.

After every ten feet or so, a new outer shell, or casing, must be lifted from a stack using an attaching tool, welded to the casing protruding from the hole, and pounded down.

Being new to the experience and immensely flattered to be thought worthy of the tasks, Leonard was thrilled by everything he did. Nothing made him feel more engaged as an eager journeyman than gas-welding the casing joints. They'd stopped by Otis's workshop to pick up the acetylene and oxygen tanks, hoses, torch, lighter, rods, heavy leather gloves, and goggles. Leonard didn't know if Johnston were aware that he'd had never done a gas-weld without Otis's looking on. He blossomed with pride to think that Otis sent him out with confidence that he'd do it properly, and so though it pricked his conscience, he stayed mum that this was his first professional job.

The time came for it. While Johnston fiddled with the rig engine, Leonard wire-brushed the metal surface around where the pipes were to be joined. Then he drew a hinged, clam-shell clamp around the ends of the joints, closed and wrenched it tight so the pipes wouldn't move while he welded. His hands trembled minutely. If the welding rig—the red and gray hoses, the torch held in one hand, the rod with its clamp-handle in the other—had been a musical instrument, this would be his first recital before an audience.

He slipped the goggles down, sucked in a breath, tweaked the gas feed, clicked his sparking tool to light the torch, adjusted the flame to a hot white point, aimed it at the metal where the seam showed. He let the torch heat the metal to a ruddy sheen, touched the rod gently to the joint like dabbing a cut with mercurochrome, began inch-worming along the seam, pointing the torch a tad ahead of the rod so it would preheat the steel.

So far, so good. He eased back and pulled the goggles up to inspect his first scar of weld. A little wormy, maybe, but definitely covered the gap. Johnston must not be worried about him, he thought. He was back of the rig out of sight. Leonard considered calling him to check his work (he was proud enough to want a compliment), but then decided to finish before showing it off.

Johnston had been right about the well's being close to "coming in." A few hundred feet below the surface lay a lake of crude captured in a formation of stone, capped by a huge, trapped balloon of natural gas. Their last foot of drilling had minutely fractured the ceiling, and the gas had been seeping and rising up the hole while Leonard was welding.

When he moved the torch back over the casing to continue to weld, it was his last conscious act of the day.

ONCE AGAIN, WALLY'S DAY GOT UPENDED BY OTHER PEOPLE'S needs. First that driller fellow had banged on the door before she was hardly awake and tried to lasso Otis into working for him, then she learned too late that he'd already promised *that girl* that he'd drive to Loving to get her gasoline.

Wally wasn't against her getting what she needed to get gone. But he hadn't said diddly-squat beforehand about being AWOL from kitchen duty this whole day. Again. Left her in the lurch. Again.

Early that morning, after Otis had left, she'd looked out her back window. That aircraft filled the frame, spoiled the view, and she'd seen that girl moving around it. She'd considered asking for her help, but she sure didn't want to stand in the way of getting that machine and that girl out of her yard fast as possible. The whole rigmarole had been a giant pain in the patootie.

She had to enlist Mabel's help. Again.

She complained to Mabel about Otis's habit of not letting her in on his thinking until it was too late for her to have any say on what he'd come up with on his own.

"He's just not a man to talk about himself," offered Mabel, making it sound like a compliment. Sitting at the table, she'd peeled one big Idaho and was holding it up to admire as if it were a work of art. She waggled it at Wally—this ok? Wally nodded.

"Well, that's one of them understatements. I think he just doesn't want to hear a lot of guff from me about what he wants to do." Wally was chopping carrots and onions, and she blotted her leaking right eye by ducking her head into the shoulder of her blouse. She normally wouldn't air out family problems, but the occasion seemed ripe for it.

"I wanna ask your opinion."

"Shoot," said Mabel, pleased.

"Otis borrowed money from Bo Bohanan a while back. To this day I don't know how much or what for, and I only know because that damned Arabella had such a big party with herself telling me about it. You wouldn't believe how much fun it was for her to tell me something like that I didn't know."

"Is that what bothers you the most?"

"Lord, no. I don't live with her."

"Did you tell Otis she'd told you?"

"You bet! And I wadden any kind of quiet about it, neither."

"What'd he say?"

"Oh, he made up some bull-hockey about he didn't want to tell me because it was going to be a big surprise."

"Well, that sounds nice!"

Wally scoffed. "I told him sure as Hell's on fire it was a big surprise."

"You think he was fibbing?"

"Well, of course he was!"

"Did you tell him you thought so?"

"Sure. You know me. Unlike him I say what's on my mind."

Mabel looked as if she might comment but thought better of it.

"He got his back up, then. He said a man's got a right to his own business without other people poking their nose in it. 'A man's got a right.' 'A man's got a right.' Kept saying that until I thought he might take up a banjo and set it to music."

Mabel chuckled.

"It's like when he takes a notion to go off, you know . . ." Wally hadn't meant to add that complaint, and she instantly regretted it. Otis was easy to shame about this, and she felt she'd betrayed him. Mabel must've heard the undertone of that reluctance and chose not to push for more. She'd now done three potatoes; she laid them in a pan of water at her elbow as she'd been instructed and half-rose to pull more toward her from a pile on the table.

"I suppose a lot of wives complain that their husbands don't talk to them enough. Not that I'd know."

"Might be." Wally paused, then pushed ahead. "We ain't married."

"Oh. Sorry! I forgot!"

"Understandable," said Wally. "But I ain't forgot, believe me. That's what comes next after 'a man's got a right.' A bachelor's got even *more* of a right to be left alone."

Wally had a sudden hitch in her breath like a muted sob. Mabel leaned up from the table as if to hug her, but Wally went palms-up like a traffic cop.

"No! Now don't be encouraging me to be a sob sister!" She blew her nose on a tea towel hanging from a rack, wadded it up and tossed it into a corner.

"I thought that was why we came here from Texas. Law wouldn't allow us to marry there." After a moment, Wally added, "I reckon what I want to know is what you think I ought to do about it."

"About getting married?"

"Uh. no, I was thinking about that loan. But what the hey—you can just toss that in there, too." She gave Mabel a pained smile.

"I dunno. I'm not an expert, for sure! But do you think maybe if he's been a lifelong bachelor, he's just set in his ways?"

"He was married long time ago. Got a son lives over in France now."

"Huh! Maybe he wasn't happy then? Could it be that's why he's shy now? What happened to his wife?"

Wally shrugged. "You'd have to ask him. And good luck finding out."

A pop like a huge hand clap, the windowpanes shivered, then they heard a whooshing noise. They both scurried onto the back stoop and saw the huge fiery column boiling over the near horizon, black-topped and swirling like a charcoal dust devil.

"It's that oil well!"

"Oh, my sweet Jesus!" cried Wally. "Lenny's out there."

Mabel got her T running quick as she could, and she and Wally and Katie rumbled out of the Owl's back lot, Mabel shakily pushing the automobile down a rough two-rut wagon trail that led into the pastures, jouncing them as the wheels fell into ruts, swaying wildly against each other when Mabel had to jerk the vehicle to and fro.

"Oh, hurry!" urged Wally, peering ahead. "Lenny's out there!"

They felt the heat as they approached. But the gas that exploded had brought up the black gusher behind it, and the volume of it had extinguished the flames but poured like an upward-rushing river into the sky and showered in a torrent down onto the rig and the surrounding earth. The wooden structure was smoldering. Mabel stopped the Lizzy, and they jumped out. The driller Johnson was seated cross-legged on the ground, dazed, shaking his head as if to clear his ears of water, but with no visible injury, Mabel saw, but Wally had already run under the arc of the shooting dark crude to where Leonard lay on his back yards away from the drill site. His gloves had apparently shielded his hands, but his goggles and hat had been stripped by the blast, and a huge gash in his forehead gushed blood mixed with oil all over his face, his throat, his chest. He was moaning.

Wally sank to her knees beside him and kept screaming, "Lenny! Lenny!" Though it was hard to determine where he'd been injured, Mabel also went to her knees pressed the cut on his head to stanch his bleeding.

"We need Louise!" she shouted.

Katie said, "I'd go but I don't know how to get there!"

Mabel ran to her automobile, started it, and turned it back toward the town, but she'd soon encountered Louise and Howard racing along in their buggy; Louise hopped down and into the Ford, and they went back to the well. Howard followed and went to the driller to assess his condition, while Louise ran to where Mabel knelt beside Leonard.

The roar of the gushing torrents made it hard to hear or be heard, and Louise signaled for Wally and Mabel to lean back so she could examine the boy. It was hard to determine anything for sure—her first impression was that his injuries were beyond her skills to diagnose and treat. Leonard's shirt was half-burned off his torso, and the mixture of blood and oil slathered over his body kept her from seeing the injuries. The arm that was still covered by a shirt sleeve seemed crooked at an angle that suggested it was broken. He might have internal injuries. Burns and terrible deep gashes for sure.

"He needs a hospital!" she shouted to Wally and Katie and Mabel.

4

THE DRILLER WAS SEATED CROSS-LEGGED, HEAD BOBBLING. The women had left him there and gone on to Leonard. The driller's face was splotched with crude oil, his hair spiky with it. Howard bent into his face. His eyes were glassy, unfocused. His lips parted and he said something unintelligible.

"Are you okay?"

The driller didn't answer. Howard guessed the blast had deafened him. He had a pink-jowled face with a red nose and glistening eyes a murky indeterminate color. Concussion, thought Howard. He leaned to the side and vomited, wiped his mouth on the back of his hand.

Fifty yards away, the women huddled over Leonard. Mesquite shrubs were aflame, and a huge mat of blackened pasture grass smoked in fiery ruin, pushing mirage-like waves overhead. His head swam. He judged that the women were far more capable than he at this moment in attending to the boy. The heat from the smoldering derrick pushed at him in waves; the shrill scream of the escaping oil from the pipe and the constant whoosh of the spouting column of it arching high over the derrick like the Earth's ripped artery—it was hallucinatory, hellish. Dizzy, he went to his knees beside the driller.

"Can you hear me?" He pointed at his own ear.

The driller looked bewildered.

"You probably got a concussion. You're probably in shock!" He laid his hand on the fellow's shoulder, and the sensation of the man's solid form under his palm coursed up through his arm and spread through his torso, evoking pity, a familiar nausea and panic, and a terrible responsibility such as he'd wished to never have again.

He stood and urged the driller up by scooping under his armpits and lifting. The driller struggled up, stood wavering and wobbly, so Howard slung the man's left arm over his own shoulder to walk him toward the buggy. They were about the same size, Howard thought, weight too and maybe age. He'd been in the war?

Helping the driller this way, the intimate contact of another injured fellow, of his hip to Howard's hip, his arm over his nape, Howard's palm cupped around the fellow's ribs, felt horrendously familiar, frightening—as if this fellow's condition were contagious, that as they stumbled they might fall together, trapping him, and lie helpless and vulnerable to another explosion, bombs, mortars, cannon shells, as if fate would make no distinction between the two human forms since they were joined.

At the buggy, he nudged the driller up into the seat—he seemed to understand what was wanted—and Howard, with his hands shaking, eased along Mildred's flank, stroking her firmly in an effort to dampen that trembling, working his way up her withers, her neck, her gray jaw, kissed her long bony muzzle.

"S'okay, s'okay," he murmured. Her big brown orbs watched him warily. He grit his teeth, closed his eyes, and whispered this mantra until his hands stopped shaking.

When they reached the Larsen farm, Howard said, "Can you hear me now?" The noise from the rig was distant. Pal rounded out from behind the barn and barked with happy excitement; hearing that, Howard almost burst into tears.

"What?" asked the driller dreamily. It was as if he were drunk.

"You're in shock. You have a concussion. Were you in the war? I was in the war."

The driller shook his head, squinted as if concentrating.

"You need bedrest. You better hope they don't say shellshock."

Howard raised his arms to coax the fellow to rise, and the driller roused himself and climbed down from the buggy. Howard steered him up the back stoop and into the kitchen.

"Sit here. Wait. You've got oil all over your clothes."

The driller stood placidly while Howard unlatched the hooks on his coveralls and dropped them down to his ankles. He pushed on the fellow's shoulders to get him seated in a kitchen chair, unlaced and tugged off the fellow's boots, yanked the coveralls free of his heels. His undershorts were filthy, yellow-spotted, the waistband grimy. He wore a stained sleeveless undershirt.

"Were you in the war?"

The driller blinked.

Howard filled a glass with water, rummaged in the cabinet of Louise's medical supplies, shook out two aspirins, brought them to the driller. Like an automaton, the driller took the water, drank half, looked at the aspirin in his palm, put them on his tongue, and swallowed the rest of the water.

"Good! Now stay right here and I'll get you something else to wear."

He came back with a pair of his pajamas, and, after a struggle, got the driller changed into them. They were cotton, white, with a pattern of hunting dogs. The driller held a forearm before his face, pressed an index finger on one of the brown canines.

"Luther," he said.

"Good. You're coming around a bit. Were you in the war?"

The driller's head made a diagonal motion that might've been a yes or a no.

"Bedrest. Let's get you settled."

He led the fellow into Izzy's room. It ruffled his sensibilities to walk through that door thinking what he was about to do. But he himself came here when he thought Louise wouldn't notice to lie on the bed and stare at the underside of the canopy.

"Here. Lie down here. No, wait! Sit a minute. We need to clean you up a bit."

Howard steered the driller to the edge of the mattress, then he left and a moment later brought back an enameled basin half full of water, a cloth, a bar of soap, a towel. The fellow hadn't moved though he'd spaded his hands into their opposite armpits as if they'd been very cold. He took the washup on his face, ears, and neck like a child enduring a nanny's rough scrub, whining a bit, grimacing, but the result pleased Howard—his scoured cheeks were peachy fresh beneath the stubble, suitable for a wounded fellow in a field hospital.

"Okay, lie back now." He palmed the fellow's chest and pushed back gently until the man was lying fully supine, his head on a pillow. Howard scooted his feet and legs onto the bed and centered them.

"Okay. Good! There you go! Bedrest is best rest, what they told me."

The fellow was staring at the underside of the canopy.

"Better than a cot on the ground, huh?" The stretchers had four stubby legs hardly a hands-breadth long, and he remembered being barely conscious in the hospital tent and flinging out his arms and how his knuckles sank in mud, and he thought he was half-dead lying in the bottom of the trench.

"Go ahead. Close your eyes."

The driller complied, but his body stayed tense.

Howard eased back into the wing chair, reached behind him expecting to feel the big stuffed bear usually enthroned there. Vaguely, he wondered where it had gone. He sighed, let his hands fall limp onto his thighs. Disaster averted. Safe. Louise would know what else needed to be done to fix this fellow.

He better hope they don't say shellshock.

"You better hope they don't say shellshock," he said to the driller. "First, you know, I had a concussion and they said bedrest. Bedrest is best. Somebody sleeps for two days and seems okay, then they could send us back into service. Were you in the war? If you don't seem okay . . ."

If you start blinking constantly and fidget and have nightmares and headaches and can't sleep or that's all you do, sleep and sleep, asleep on your feet, or you're dizzy and can't eat or that's all you want to do or you go deaf for no reason. Or all of a sudden you stop being able to talk.

"There was this one doc at a ward I went to with other fellows having the same troubles. He had to test first whether you were just putting it on to keep from being sent back in. Were you a yellow coward. Test is what I call it, anyway. He said it was supposed to help. Like getting back up onto that horse when it bucked you off. One fellow kept ducking, you know, whenever he heard a door slam or somebody put something down hard on a table, and so the doc strapped him to a wheelchair and rolled him out beside a road where the tanks and trucks kept roaring by. Oh, he screamed something awful."

If you couldn't talk, they had a big wooden box with wires they hooked to your throat, turned on the juice.

"Pretty soon you got to talking, all right. And if you had a stiff leg wouldn't bend, they'd bend it for you or know the reason why."

By the time he got to the hospital at Fort Sheridan, they'd gotten smarter about it. A drug—opiate-based—and hypnosis. *Tell me all about it.* They trained the nurses to encourage you to spill your guts. Put you to work in the gardens.

He remembered the day he stopped blinking incessantly, happened soon after the night he slept all the way through.

"You're lucky if you get a good woman to look after you," he told the driller.

Then, as if coming awake from a dream, he remembered Louise, the flyer, Wally, and Mabel bent over Leonard's inert form, the horrendous noise, the crescendo of cascading oil, the smoking turf. He prayed they were all okay. Maybe he shouldn't have left; had he run away? Would they feel he'd abandoned them? A *deserter*?

He lay his head back, closed his eyes. He was suddenly exhausted but likewise so tense his flesh felt electrified, fingertips buzzing. Moments later, the wasp-rasp sound of that aircraft's motor startled him upright, and he stared at the ceiling as the airplane rose over the house and flew on north toward the Carlsbad hospital.

5

THE CRAFT TRACKED TRUE ON TAKEOFF, SOMETHING SHE'D worried over because the strut had been so damaged. By that time every citizen in Noname had rushed to witness the burning of the rig and the departure of the airplane, some still arriving as Katie had gunned the engine and roared along picking up speed and scattering them as they surprised themselves in her path, the prop wash flapping skirts and sending up billows of sandy dust. She'd cursed as a laggard wagon driver barely got his rig to the side as she blasted past.

The strut, the milling spectators—only two of many worries, what with the basting glue on the repairs still sticky and no telling how that rigged-up aileron would behave, but by far the biggest headache was fuel. When they'd moved her ship to the yard behind the café days (it seemed years) ago, that fellow Jefferson had put maybe three or four gallons in the tank. In the workshop she found a hose she used to siphon maybe five or six gallons from Mabel's Model T, and meanwhile Mrs. Larsen was wedged in beside Leonard in her forward cockpit crying for them to hurry.

They'd said it was maybe fifty—sixty miles, maybe less by air, she thought, since they were calculating distance on a dirt road that passed through many gates to fences marking off ranchers' ranges; the airplane could span six hundred miles on a tank of sixty-seven gallons—that was less than ten miles per gallon, so she probably had fuel enough to reach the road they'd supposedly blocked off behind the hospital.

But maybe not enough to get back.

The sky was the washed-out blue of a white-sun summer day, cloudless in the immediate vicinity, big dark-headed Stratos to the southwest, sailing this way she guessed. But the heated air helped the engine be its most efficient, and she was cruising at around two thousand feet, tracing the road beneath her to Carlsbad. Mrs. Larsen's head poked above the cowling in the forward cockpit, and the blow-back from the prop wildly whipped her hair. Katie couldn't see Leonard. Since the moment they'd run up to him out at that oil well, he had stayed unconscious, and it had taken all four women to move him into the Model T then up into the cockpit, Wally and Mabel fretting loudly that they might be doing more harm and Louise insisting that they had no choice and that it was just a blessed thing he was dumb to whatever pain his injuries would be causing.

For once do something useful with that contraption.

When Wally said that, Katie'd had no space to consider it. Right now, she struggled to keep on a course over a plain featureless except for the beige thread of sandy road. With no map, setting a compass heading was pointless. Her heart was pounding and sweat drenched her blouse and oozed off her back down into her trousers. The gushering well had sprayed crude oil onto their hair, their clothes, and coated their exposed skin with a greasy stench. She'd had no opportunity to change into flying togs, though her helmet had been in the cockpit.

For once do something useful . . .

She prayed the sweet fellow they were ferrying to the hospital would live. She had a part in his survival or death, and never had her skills and knowledge seemed so vital. This was no stunt; there was no gawking audience to fool and thrill, no phony theatrics, no prize or race to win except to get him there before it was too late.

For once do something useful . . .

For once? A bitter echo, resentment. It hadn't dawned on her how much she'd taken from these people, how she'd become a burden. She'd been helpless, yes, but also, she'd imagined she deserved their help. She was a novelty, a celebrity of sorts equated with the likes of Earhart through no fault of her own, and if no one had asked for her autograph, they had treated her with great deference, asked her to speak before them as someone whose experience was outside their own and wondrous, admirable.

She'd gotten the swellhead. How kind they'd been! Mabel, especially. In just this short time she'd grown so comfortable using Mabel's name, allowing Mabel to use hers, and she suspected that her dire circumstances had made her yearn even more for the comfort of a sympathetic ear. She'd been so lucky in where she'd had to land! She could only hope that getting Leonard safely to the hospital would erase the stain of having been so selfish.

She wished she could communicate with Mrs. Larsen to see if Leonard were still alive. He'd wormed his way into her tender regard—not like the; hopeless angry passion for Curly—but what a sister might feel. And Mabel—the comfort they had together, a girlfriend—not something she'd known before. How Mr. Jefferson had worked so hard so that she could fly the Travel Air and find it air worthy. Mrs. Larsen and her concern for the gash on her shoulder, her offer that recognized Katie's need for room and board, and Katie'd been so dismissive of it.

She'd arrived here with a set of obstacles and problems and saw these people as merely ciphers in the equation that might put her back in the air. Now they were real to her. And they were a community unto themselves, giving mutual aid and comfort. They belonged to one another. They leaned on one another.

They had a life together, and she'd disrupted and shred it like a June bug dancing on a spiderweb.

Since they'd worked their way into her awareness, she'd never felt so alone, and that seemed odd. She'd been happy to be an outsider, she believed. Her attention had been solely on getting what she needed to be on her way. Whatever feeling of belonging that she'd grown into with that air circus, whatever expectations she'd nursed about a future as a flyer and member of that fraternity, well, that had blown up in her face, and she'd exiled herself.

If she never saw Curly or her mom or those bums again, that'd be fine with her.

But it did mean she belonged nowhere to no one.

Getting back into the air now made her wonder where she'd been heading in the first place and why. The story she told Mrs. Bohanan's group about needing to qualify for the Nationals at Santa Monica was true enough.

But it left out so much. *Sweet Pea, I'm so sorry and disappointed, they just don't think you're seasoned enough yet, and you know, your ma, well . . .* Fought back her tears and tried to see it from their point of view, oh reasonable girl, and sure, Mom had the billing, the savvy, and the skills to put the sponsors' minds at ease. They were in the hanger, in the lounge, just the two of them, and he hugged her close and kissed the top of her head the way you'd do a kid with a boo-boo. She'd sulked and pouted a good two hours, then went to his hotel looking for more consolation, maybe a last special time together before they left, and when he answered her knock, she caught a glimpse of her mother scurrying to hide, half-naked and clutching clothes to her chest, and the complete betrayal reeled itself out for her.

She spent half the night walking the dark lanes around the Chattanooga airport, sobbing and screaming, and as dawn came and the hour drew near for them to set out on their tour, her fury burned so deep it overwhelmed her.

So long as she could draw a living breath, they weren't taking that Travel Air! Without a plane they were just two bums without a job, two sorry sacks of crap, pretty much penniless, and that was only half of what they deserved.

But landing at Noname had broken the rhythm of that crazy dark impulse. Getting back in the air now meant the plane was sound enough to lift off from Noname for good, but that supposed need to qualify for the Nationals was childish and absurd. Pointless. She'd *stolen* the airplane! She'd damaged it! Sure as God made little green apples, nobody will reward her for this. She'll be disqualified. Arrested.

She'll go to jail.

Mrs. Larsen had scooched up in the cockpit to wave at her, then she pointed toward the approaching horizon. Katie'd already spotted it—a cluster of irregular interruptions in the plain, boxy, clearly manmade. She'd been told to follow the Pecos River that ran alongside the town where she'd see a bridge taking the road she was following into town. Just south of it lay the hospital, they said, next to a church, and their impromptu landing strip would be stretched out behind it to the west.

The river was a caramel snake threaded through a hilly barren landscape the color of rawhide, and the water had nourished a line of cottonwood trees, mesquite, and salt cedar shrubs as well as irrigated outlying fields of wheat and sorghum along its banks, so that its green-edged meandering course was a navigator's blessing. Katie came down low over its route to watch for her landmarks; Louise too had arched up over the cockpit gunnels to peer ahead and below. Then the bridge was visible carrying an automobile and a wagon with two horses, and then the hospital attached to the church with a bell tower, and then the road alongside empty and expectant with a cluster of vehicles at one far intersection.

She looked for a flag or smoke or a vehicle's dust trail to judge the wind, found none, but when she banked to come around again, she could feel the tug of the breeze tilting her right wing up into a steeper bank and so guessed a southwesterly breeze. The road seemed to run north-south more or less, so she could approach and come down on the northern end.

Perfect landing! Worth a gold star, for sure. Oh, but too darned bad that son of a motherless goat Curly couldn't have witnessed it.

A squad of orderlies swarmed over her craft soon as the prop stopped turning and heaved Leonard up from the cockpit and carried him away, then she and Mrs. Larsen were led into a changing room. A nun named Sister Margaret pointed out a large shower stall and invited them to scrub the crude oil off their bodies—she made no mention of the blood on Louise's arms, her blouse, and skirt—gave them washcloths, towels, and bars of soap and told them she'd come back with clean dry clothes, "though you might find the styles a tad dowdy and the sizes maybe not a tailored fit," she joked. Katie was reluctant to turn loose of the soiled khaki pants and blouse, even though they were not the least bit wearable in their oil-drenched condition. She had little in her valise back in Noname, so every garment counted, and she didn't know when or where she might next see them. "Don't worry, hon," crooned the nun. "We'll do our best."

Sister Margaret brought Katie a pair of boy's corduroy trousers and a frilly yellow blouse meant for, say, a picky twelve-year-old girl who probably owned a pony, Katie thought. At least she didn't stink from the oil, as the soap she used to wash her hair carried its own perfumy personality. It was just Mrs. Larsen's good luck as a lifelong beauty to be brought a beautiful silk dress sporting big red hibiscus blossoms set against an ivory background. The dress fit her form perfectly and the colors set off her dark hair and eyes, made her look even a bit more exotic. Stick a rose in her teeth and she'd be ready to tango.

Then Sister Margaret said she'd take them to the waiting room. Their friend was still being examined.

"I was a nurse during the war," Louise told the nun. "Fort Sheridan, Illinois. Hospital number twenty-eight."

6

LATER THAT AFTERNOON, AT THE PLACE WHERE THE ROAD TO Loving crooked to avoid a patch that stayed muddy from a spring-fed seep, Mabel ran her automobile off into the muck at the bottom of the bar ditch. When she was able to back out of it, she ran down into it again. She rocked the vehicle to see if she could free it and managed to root the front wheels deeper, almost to the hubs.

A rabbit zoomed across the road, and she'd swerved to miss it, maybe.

Her watch said 2:45. She'd brought a book—Willa Cather's *My Antonia*—that her sister had mailed to her. She'd planned to read it immediately, but Katie had arrived. Her plan was to sit in the auto and read, but now the Ford was canted with the driver's side down, and she had fallen against the door.

She gathered her purse and the book. When she opened the door, she almost tumbled headlong into the muddy ditch. She had to set one foot into the muddy water to climb up onto the road. She stood in the road feeling sorry for her poor, oil-splotched auto, deliberately mired and immobilized.

She had no idea how long she might have to wait. On both sides of the road, a farmer's barbed-wire fences prevented trespass. She should've brought a blanket so she could comfortably sit. Her left shoe and foot were mud-coated up past the ankle, and the wetness was irritating. Her hair itched and stunk, even though she'd tried to clean the oil from it; she and Wally had swabbed their exposed skin after they'd seen to getting Katie, Louise, and Leonard off, then she'd scurried home to change, but she still felt sticky and filthy. She'd needed a very long, hot bath, but Otis said she'd best not waste a minute getting gone.

An antelope zooming across the road had startled her, so she'd wheeled down into the ditch to miss it, maybe.

She walked up the road. Her wet shoe squeaked, the stocking inside was soaked, a horrid sensation. Around her were grasslands spiked with century plants, Spanish dagger, and mesquite, flat enough to appear endless. It was too sunny and hot for comfort, and she was glad for her hat. A herd of cows in the distance, not moving, heads down. Not a habitat in sight. She hadn't thought to bring water. Maybe this wasn't such a great idea.

Inexplicably, as if a taunt, a tin pail with a rusted bottom lay on its side just off the road, and she retrieved it. She turned it upside down, tested the firmness of the bottom with her hand. The rust was holey like torn lace, but the rim would likely hold her.

She eased into a squat onto it. It held, though the seat was too low to be really comfortable, and the metal rim soon cut into the flesh of her bum even with the padding of her skirt.

Last summer I happened to be crossing the plains of Iowa in a season of intense heat, and it was my good fortune to have for a traveling companion James Quayle Burden—Jim Burden, as we still call him in the West. He and I are old friends—we grew up together in the same Nebraska town—and we had much to say to each other. While the train flashed through never-ending miles of ripe wheat, by country towns and bright-flowered pastures and oak groves wilting in the sun, we sat in the observation

The flies annoyed her. She was holding the book with both hands and had to release one to bat them away from her face. It was hard to fix on the words. When she'd left the Owl, they'd still not heard anything from Louise and Katie in Carlsbad. Surely by now the doctors had told them something. If they even made it there, that is. Katie had worried about the fuel. When Otis had shown up from Loving bearing his news about the sheriff, he'd given Mabel back a few gallons so that she could safely execute her plan.

the observation car, where the woodwork was hot to the touch and red dust lay deep over everything. The dust and heat, the burning wind, reminded us of many things. We were talking about what it is like to spend one's childhood in little towns like these, buried in wheat and corn, under stimulating

A coyote. That's better. Bunny's too little, antelope's too big. But aren't they pretty much nocturnal?

stimulating extremes of climate: burning summers when the world lies green and billowy beneath a brilliant sky, when one is fairly sti- fled in vegetation, in the color and smell of strong weeds and heavy harvests; blustery winters with little snow, when the whole country is stripped bare and

She shut the book. The bucket's metal rim knifed into her flesh. She heaved herself up from the squat, dusted off the back of her skirt. Too bad she didn't smoke. It'd be something to do. Her bladder twitched a bit. Another annoyance.

Far ahead on the eastern horizon, a vehicle appeared in the road. She saw the ruddy sand plume rising over it. Standing just off the right of way, she watched it approach. Not an automobile, a truck. Her lips twisted into a little moue of disappointment.

She had no need to flag it down. It stopped just beside her. A fellow leaned over from the driver's side, keeping his engine running. In the bed were cages of chickens, a bale of hay. It was a good sign he didn't stop his motor and didn't get out of the cab.

"You all right, Missy? What happened?" he called through the opened passenger window.

Old fellow, lips altogether covered by a big droopy moustache stained with snuff or chewing tobacco syrup. Ghastly.

"Oh, I'm so silly! A . . . rabbit ran across the road in front of me, and I just flew into a tizzy and jerked the wheel and ran right off into the ditch there."

He turned to face the road ahead as if deliberating how much time he had available.

"Well, I can try to pull you out. I got a chain."

"Oh, no! Don't worry! My husband and his brother are coming in their truck. They should be right along soon."

"I could stay a bit if you need."

She heard the reluctance and was grateful for it. "Oh, no. I'm fine. Won't be long." She waved the book. "I have entertainment."

"All righty then." He clutched and the gears clashed in protest as he tugged on the lever. "Just a word to the wise—probably best to let a bunny come to a bad end under your wheels than to run aground and be stranded out here."

"Yes, thank you. I'll remember that." Patronizing clodhopper.

She was about to ask if he had a spot of water to spare, then decided her pride was too delicate to risk another humiliating lesson, and instead turned and walked out of his sight back to the bucket.

A while later, a man and a woman came along in a buggy. She successfully fended off their Good Samaritan efforts but likewise struck out in her request for water. Ironically, and to her great irritation, the need to empty that twitchy bladder eventually became unbearable, so she goat-footed back down into the ditch just far enough that her body wouldn't be visible from the road and did what needed doing.

Two young cowboys on horseback had too great an estimation of their own gallantry to take no for an answer and tied their lariats to her back bumper in spite of her protests and spurred their mounts to pull her auto out of the mud while she worried that the poor horses would collapse from heart attacks. Luckily, she'd stuck the auto deep enough that they couldn't budge it. She told them several times that help from her two brothers was on the way, but they seemed to imagine they were in a competition to save her.

She said, "Please don't worry! They've got a big truck! But I would appreciate it if you'd leave me that canteen tied to your saddle there. I'd be happy to pay you for it."

The cowboy grinned sheepishly. "Aw, ma'am, I'm awful sorry but what I got in here ain't fit to pass the lips of no lady."

"I'm not particular!"

"Well, I'm sayin' it's not water, ma'am."

Another miserable half hour. 3:30. Surely by now Louise had called the Owl to report from the Carlsbad hospital.

Then at last she saw it. At first it was indistinguishable from another vehicle seen at this distance, but then gradually the little hump on the roof was apparent, and her heart beat wildly. Her hands sweat. She jumped from the bucket, leapt into the road, waved wildly as the automobile bore down on her, slid to a stop.

She scurried to the driver's window.

"Sherriff Browne! Am I glad to see you!"

"Well, howdy to you!" he crowed. "What's your trouble?"

She pointed into the ditch. The automobile's roof was visible from his vantage.

"My! How'd that happen?"

"I'm afraid I was startled by a . . . coyote running right across my path here, and so I just went into a tizzy and wound up down there in the mud and I can't get out!"

He turned off his engine. His door creaked when he opened it and stepped out. The flank bore a painted silver star surrounded by insignia she was too rattled to read. She felt breathless and trembly, hoped he'd think her panicky manner came from her mishap.

He stepped to the shoulder, put his fists on his hips, and frowned as if working on a mystery.

"What's a lady like yourself doing out on the road all by your lonesome?"

"Oh, well, sir, I'm Mabel Cross. I'm the schoolteacher down at Noname. I was on my way to Loving to see a very sick friend. An emergency."

"Well, Miss Cross, I'm wondering if you got a license? Is this your vehicle?"

"Yes, sir, to both."

He pointed at the car. "Did you have lessons?"

She bit her lip. "Yes, as I said—a coyote ran right across the road in front of me, and I yanked the wheel to keep from hitting it." How annoying this person was!

He gave her an oily smile. "Well, let's see if we can get you out of this jam."

He opened the trunk of his vehicle, reached in, and drew out a chain—it clinked and clanked against the rim of the trunk as he pulled several lengths of it free of the litter and gathered it in his arms. A hook was fixed to both ends.

"Let's give this a try!" His manner was all good cheer now that it was settled a young woman needed his help.

"Oh, thank you! I don't know what I'd have done if you hadn't come along!" she gushed, hating herself for it.

"Just doing what I'm paid for."

His comment might've suggested an unwillingness if his smile of "modesty" hadn't been so pronounced. Okay, then, he could play saving the damsel, and she'd play helpless maiden. Her tongue was like a rawhide glove in her mouth. At the first sensible moment, she'd ask if he had water.

He side-stepped his way down into the ditch, wrapped one end of the chain around the rear bumper, backpedaled up the ditch, paying out the chain as he went. Then he hooked the chain to his rear bumper.

"Here's what we'll need you to do. Go ahead and start your engine, put it into reverse gear, and when you feel me pulling on you, try to use your engine to help back out."

"Oh, dear! I'm so sorry, but that's still another problem."

"What is?"

"Well, after I'd come to a dead stop down there in the mud, my motor died, and I just could not get it started for the life of me!"

177

He frowned. "Hmm. Guess we'll just have to investigate that, too. But I'll still need you to get behind the wheel so's when your Lizzy gets up off her knees and starts coming at me derr-ee-air-first, you can steer her right. You'll need to put the gear into neutral first. Think you can manage that?"

Whatever reservations she'd had about lying to an officer of the law vanished completely.

"Why, yes. I think so."

"Good!"

He turned to move toward his driver's door, and she said, "Oh, dear me, before we venture into this salvage operation, I have to confess that I am so very parched that I'm afraid I can't think straight! Is it possible you might have drinking water in your vehicle?"

He chuckled, shook his head. That shake didn't say he had no water—it said, *never ceases to amaze me.* He turned and smirked.

"Now, Miss, you are telling me you set out on a journey alone in your automobile without thinking of how you might need water in this country?"

"Yes, I know it was foolish. But as I said, it was an emergency."

"Well, you're not the only one. That's why I carry it."

"You are a godsend."

He opened the passenger-side door, lifted a gallon glass jug from the floorboard, pulled out a stopper, and held it up by the ring in the neck. It was water, sure enough, and her every cell cried out for it even though bits of chaff were floating on the top, and the color—not crystal clear, to be sure—was suspect. He pointed it at her as if for her to take it, and, puzzled, she took it in both arms. It was as heavy as a sack of potatoes. Clearly, he expected her to drink from the jug. No telling who or how many . . .

"Oh, sorry, miss! Of course, you'll need a cup." He bent into the vehicle and came back up with a V-shaped paper Dixie cup, which he opened for her. They traded jug for cup, and he poured it full for her. One swallow. She held it out again. He poured. Her hand was shaking, spilling water from the cup over her wrist.

"Oh, dear! I'm afraid I'm making a mess."

"Not to worry, Miss. Go ahead, drink up."

She took two more cups full. He set the jug back into the floorboard of the vehicle. She smiled big at him.

"Okay, that's better! I'm ready for action now!"

He saluted her, walked around his vehicle while she went down into the ditch, grabbed a hold of the fender to steady herself, climbed up and into the driver's seat.

First, she set the handbrake. Then she put the gear into reverse, knowing full well that this would create even more resistance. She couldn't get away with riding her shoe on the foot brake, as that would light up her tail lantern.

"Ready!" she called out.

She heard his engine, then felt the tug, his automobile straining, then she heard the whine of his tires spinning against the hard-packed sand on the road. She smiled. Oh dear, ha, ha, ha.

He went at it again, reasserting the power of his engine against the sucking muck that gripped her wheels. Same result. He tried a third time. Then she heard his door creak open and slam shut, and after a moment he appeared beside her window holding a shovel.

"I'm gonna dig out around the back of your front wheels—I think that's gonna make it easier."

"Wonderful idea!"

The shovel blade went *chunkslurp* in the sopping earth. She heard huffing, grunting. After few moments, he stuck his head through the passenger-side window.

"There. That's gonna help." He looked at the gear shift. "Is that gear in neutral like I said?" He frowned.

"Oh, no sir! You told me reverse gear."

He shook his head. "Well, I meant if the motor was running and you were trying to back up. If it ain't, then I'm trying to drag that dad-blasted transmission along with the rest of this crate. You see? Can you put it in the neutral?"

"Yes, sir." She clutched and shifted the gear. "So sorry!"

"And that HANDBRAKE?"

"Oh, I'm so sorry about that, too! I guess when I was sliding into the ditch, I did everything I could to stop myself and just grabbed it and am just now seeing what I did! Oh, I am so addle-pated! Having this *catastrophic* accident has just made me so upset! I can't think straight." She turned her head to sniffle.

He sighed. "It's all right, Miss. Just take it off, all right? We'll try again now that the wheels are free."

He went back to his vehicle. She shifted into reverse again and let the handbrake remain set. After a moment, his engine revved, then she was jolted by the tightening chain, and then, despite her efforts, she felt the car sliding upward, unstoppable. She gripped the wheel helplessly, wondering *all right—what now?*

When he towed her up onto the level road, he backed up to put slack in the chain, stopped his motor, got out. She watched him in her rearview mirror as he bent over and disappeared, unhooking the chain. Smiling, he then came to the driver's window.

"There! We did her!"

"Oh, yes! Thank you so much, Sheriff! I'm deeply in your debt."

"Now let's see if we can get her cranked up."

He stood beside the car while she pretended to turn the ignition key, then she mashed the foot starter, let it grind on and on uselessly for a while, then stopped. She turned and put an *oh dear* squiggle in her brows, shrugging.

"Let me give her a whirl. We don't wanna run down that batry."

Reluctantly, she got out of the driver's seat and stood by with the door open while he slid behind the wheel, turned on the spark, pressed the starter. *Aruh aruh aruh* it went. He stopped. Sniffed. "Smell that gas? We've done flooded her. You know what to do when that happens?"

She shook her head slowly, sadly.

"Well, strange as it may seem—when you crank on it, you put the foot feed all the way to the floor!"

"Really?!"

"Yeah. Ain't there a word for that—you know, when you do something seems like the opposite of what you should do? You're the schoolmarm."

"Paradoxical?"

"Yeah! That's it. Paradokable! Learn something new ever day."

He was certainly in a jolly good humor now that his efforts to free her automobile had succeeded. He jammed the accelerator to the floor and stomped on the starter. After several seconds, her motor coughed, cleared its throat, then caught its big breath and roared as he revved the engine. He turned and gave her a big grin.

"Say howdy to Mr. Ford!"

He turned it off, slid out of the seat, and held the door open for her to resettle. She stepped into the V, but paused, put her palm on the window frame, bowed her head, closed her eyes, shot out the other palm to brace herself against door, whimpered.

"Miss! Are you alright?"

She gave it a couple of beats, then opened her eyes, stood upright, inhaled deeply. "Oh, yes! I'm sorry. I was just a tad light-headed there for a minute. I don't think I'm quite up to this sort of catastrophe! My nerves are just ajangle!"

"Well, maybe you'll feel better when you get to where you're going."

"I certainly hope so." She leaned against the automobile and fanned her face with her hand. "Sheriff, I am ashamed to say that I'm in need of a further favor if it would at all be in your person to grant it. I realize that you're a very busy man with many tasks, and I have no doubt you were on your way to perform an important official function when you were so kind as to stop and give me aid." She was really laying on the teacher-talk. "But I have to confess that I'm quite afraid of continuing my journey unescorted—I can no longer trust my own abilities or the dependability of my automobile. Would it be possible at all for you to follow me to Loving? I hesitate to ask, please believe me, but if I were to stall or be stranded once again, and night fell . . ." She shivered minutely for punctuation.

He was frowning. Weighing it, she hoped.

"You're from down there in Noname, right?"

"Yes."

"Well, I was on my way there to check out a report we got that an aircraft had landed right on your main street couple days ago. Then this morning Texas Rangers wired to be on the lookout for an airplane—it was stole from an airfield back East."

"Oh my! And you think this might be it?"

He shrugged. "One they're looking for has the word BEECH-NUT on the side of it."

"Like the chewing gum?"

"Yeah."

"Huh. Last time I saw it, there was no such word written on it."

"They said a girl stole it."

"A girl?! A child took an airplane? What a remarkable thing!"

"No, I reckon older than that. Is the pilot of the one y'all got female?"

"Well, indeed she was. But she was a full-fledged aviatrix with much experience, just as nice as nice can be! She came and talked to our ladies' literary society about her life as an aviatrix—it was beyond interesting, I tell you, Sheriff, it was *absolutely inspiring*! I just cannot think for one moment that she would've taken her aircraft without authorization! Besides, she came to us from Los Angeles, lost her map and ran out of fuel, and is on her way to New Jersey, I believe."

"On her way, you say?"

"Oh, yes. She took off just this morning. Made quite a stir, of course. Not quite the Bijou show as her altogether unexpected arrival, of course."

She waited. He frowned, staring at the pointed toes of his western boots. Finally, he raised his chin to meet her gaze, and she could tell by the look on his face that he'd congratulated himself already.

"Well, in that case, it'd be not just my duty but also my honor to make sure a constituent stays safe and sound!"

On the way to Loving, she drove very slowly, pausing before each little bump and rut, zigzagging as if unable to manage a straight course.

At one point, she turned off the ignition, the motor died, she coasted to a stop, ground on the starter, etc., and he had to stop, get out, hear her complaint, take her place behind the wheel, flood the motor himself, restart it finally, slide out from under the wheel, go back to his vehicle. She estimated that took ten to fifteen minutes on its own.

By five o'clock, they'd reached Loving. She pulled to the curb, stopped her motor, dug into her purse, found a dollar bill. She got out. He'd stopped as well behind her, and she went to his driver's door, thanked him profusely, assured him that she felt safe now.

"Can I donate to your favorite charity?"

"Aw, now. No need!"

"Please!"

He took her bill—a bit sheepishly, she noted.

The telephone office was still open, so she called the Owl to let Wally and Otis know—she could hardly contain her glee—that their scheme had worked. Just as Otis had feared, Sheriff Browne had been on his way to investigate when she'd intercepted him.

"Still ain't sure about getting mixed up in this," Wally said. "I reckon Otis don't mind spending his old age chopping cotton on a prison farm."

"Have you heard from Louise?"

"Yes, she called a bit ago. Lenny's alive, anyway. She didn't know what all was wrong with him yet, but the doctor told her he'd pull through. 'Young and strong' he said. That goes a long, long way."

"Thank God!"

When she hung up, she was ravenous from her crime spree. She went to a café and sat at a counter eating an enormous T-bone steak, a baked potato, and a bowl of beans. Then she had apple pie with a scoop of vanilla ice cream heaped on it. And though she never drank it past noon, she had two cups of coffee with cream and sugar just to fortify her for the trip home—keep her awake.

By the time she got back on the road, dusk colored the air, and soon full dark came on, and she turned on her headlights. Night prowler.

Night hawk. Secret spy, jewel thief. Her brain was crackling with caffeinated energy. She and Katie, sinister sisters, compañeras of crime. Oh, how heady it was!

She picked up speed, relishing the delicious rush of the cool dark wind through the open windows, the reckless headlong plunge of her automobile into the night, the lights wavering and shivering with the auto's jitttering over the washboard sand as she mashed the feed to the floor and urged the auto up beyond where she'd ever pushed it—how thrilling!

7

LOUISE HAD TO EXPLAIN TO THE HEAD NURSE—NUN THAT SHE was the closest thing that the poor injured boy had to a next-of-kin right now.

"I was a nurse in the war, am one now, his nurse, he's actually been under my care, and there are a lot of folks anxious to know how he is, so I need to see him so I can let them know."

Probably the extraordinary manner of their arrival made her case better than the fibbing. In any case, a doc so old he looked as if he'd stopped using leeches just last week came hobbling with a cane to their waiting room to report that Leonard would likely survive. Young and strong. Young and strong, he said again, as if those words were medical procedures to be repeatedly applied. And of course, getting him here so quick was likely 80 percent of why he survived; otherwise, he'd have bled to death.

"Oh!" blurted Katie, then she mewled quietly into her palms. Louise patted the girl on her shoulder.

"What is the extent of his injuries?" asked Louise. "I know there were cuts and gashes, and if I'd had some Dakin solution like we used during the war, I'd have irrigated them before we came to prevent infection, and same goes for how if I'd had cocaine hydrochloride maybe we could've saved him so much agony. But right now, I'm just a medicine-cabinet nurse. I'm guessing concussion for sure, and his left forearm . . ."

"Yes, and cracked ribs," put in the doctor. "Some metal fragments in one shoulder. Lots of gashes. Burns and cuts on his forehead and cheeks. Lost a lot of blood. A lot." He paused, clearly irritated. "And yes, of course, concussion, as you'd expect."

He was sedated, bandaged, resting peacefully but groggy if not fully asleep. Best to keep him that way.

Louise insisted to the doctor that they needed to actually set eyes on their dear friend.

They went down a hall on the heels of a nurse wearing not a habit but a civilian nurse's uniform that caught Louise's eye—bright white cotton, a mid-calf hem, short sleeves, pleated skirt, and an open collar.

"I like your uniform," she called out to the nurse's back, then surged ahead to stride with her. "So practical. When I was in service at Fort Sheridan, what we wore probably had two more yards of material, and some part of my uniform always seemed to be getting in my way." She stroked her own forearm. "You know, those long sleeves and the cuffs. When big-wigs were around they made us wear those darn capes."

The nurse half-turned to grant her a polite smile.

"But I guess there are a lot of changes."

"This is the only one I've ever worn."

Right. If she was twenty yet, that'd be a surprise. Louise was about to ask where the girl had gone to nursing school, but she turned abruptly into a large room with many beds, about half occupied by patients. The girl led them to a patient at the end of the row on their left, and if Louise hadn't been led there, she'd not have known the patient was Leonard. His head was swathed in gauze, and his torso—the portion visible above the top of the sheet—was likewise wrapped in bandages. Mummified, thought Louise. His left forearm was in a cast and bound to his shoulder with a brace. An intravenous bag hung from a hook and a tube ran into his good arm.

"Poor boy!" she burst out. Katie started bawling. Then they fell into each other's arms and did it all up proper before running out of breath and were both trembling. Louise eased backward into a straight-back visitor's chair, and Katie eased a hip up onto the footboard.

Some of the ward's other patients had visitors who were murmuring to the patients, studiously avoiding the muted latent drama at other bedsides. Louise wiped her eyes with a tissue from a box on the bedside table and passed another to Katie.

"Is he asleep or in a coma?" Katie whispered.

"Oh, I'm sure just asleep! They'd have given him a sedative and probably anesthesia when they did all the work. I'd guess they had to . . . do some incisions to get at that metal in his shoulder."

Katie winced. Louise tried her best to smile away Katie's fears. "He's gonna be fine. You heard the doctor. You were a lifesaver, Katie!"

"I'm so glad I could do something."

They sat for a while in silence. Louise felt antsy, frustrated. It was strange to be in a hospital and not be performing any ministration or even simply housekeeping duties. Some patients here in this ward had no visitors. A few were reading, others napping, still others staring at the ceiling. She wondered if the staff here would think it inappropriate of her to volunteer while Leonard was recuperating. At the least, she could do what hospital volunteers had always done—cheer up the sick and injured, dole out books and magazines, read and even write their letters to loved ones. She suspected that nursing might've undergone many changes since the war. New ways of dressing wounds, new potions, new notions. If she could stick around, she might freshen up her skills.

Her spirit brightened to remember the hurly-burly, the nerve-tingling rush of that busy wartime bustle at Fort Sheridan, the camaraderie between working nurses, the tears when fellows didn't make it, the huge upswell of joy when one pulled through after a night on the edge. Sneaking that Everclear into the nurse's quarters and adding orange juice, bawling in each other's arms when things went bad, celebrating when a gal got engaged—especially to a doctor.

Those memories made her present life a sad arrangement of boring chores and tasks she could do in her sleep. Or as if she were asleep.

That's what it felt like. Those things serviced only her and Howard. They had no meaning beyond the boundaries of their farm. She could not even lay claim to raising a child. While she wasn't useless altogether—she knew people in Noname counted on her rudimentary and (she now believed) antiquated skills for simple measures applied to simple problems, what she did was hardly a step above the granny folk cures people applied on their own. She did still love Howard, and she had to appreciate his hard work, but she had long since acknowledged to herself that when they first hit it off, half of her attraction was that he was a patient and she a nurse. Though he no longer needed nursing, he did need understanding, and that was much harder to give, it required a patience she didn't always feel.

And then there was Izzy. You could say that Izzy was like a disease that Howard had contracted that lay embedded in his cells, dormant until blooming sporadically and ravaging his spirit. She had no idea how to treat that. Just when she'd think he was in remission you could say, he'd fall into a purple funk. It wouldn't incapacitate him, just alter his mood, turn him inward. All talk of having their own child then was beyond consideration.

Katie was looking about. She pointed to a clock high on the wall above the door leading to the hall. 4:55.

"I'm thinking we should leave. I can't fly out of here after dark. And I've got to ask somebody about getting enough gas to get back, too."

"You go on back to Noname. I think I'll stay just to keep tabs on what they're doing, how he's doing. Tell Howard I'll call Wally to keep him abreast of my plans, okay?"

Katie's brows arched up.

"He can come later with the buggy, or I'm sure Mabel will want to come in her auto. The nuns here will find me an empty bed when and if I feel I need it. You know, one nurse to another. We do have a kind of sorority."

"A what?"

"A . . . club. Unofficial, you know, just a kinship you feel with another one."

8

KATIE FLEW BACK FROM CARLSBAD ALONE, AND WHEN SHE reached Noname, the sun had set, the glimmer in the West glinting pale in the gusher of oil that wavered like a trembling finger over the smoking remains of the derrick. News of a gusher had already brought sightseers as well as prospectors, land men, and speculators, so she had to buzz the street to chase off the traffic long enough to land.

She taxied her craft behind the Owl and threw a tarp over the cockpit to discourage intruders. Inside the café, she found Otis, Wally, Mabel, and Howard. Howard had brought the driller, who, on coming out of his fog of bewilderment, decided it was urgent to get to his gusher, and he'd telephoned an associate from the Owl who'd bring equipment needed to stopper it; otherwise, it would run wild for days.

Wally had tacked blankets up over the front windows—they'd never had a need to shutter them—and had made a CLOSED!! sign with a slat from an orange crate and a piece of charcoal.

"Maybe I should add one that says 'DO NOT KNOCK!,'" Wally was saying, after she'd shouted, "Go away!" through the door to the third person who'd knuckled it. People wanted to eat; people wanted to use the phone; people wanted to know whose well it was. Lights from vehicles glowed sporadically like mysterious lanterns, appearing and disappearing as ghostly orbs on the fabric.

When Katie walked in, they all babbled at once, though Mabel rushed forward to hug her. Trembling, Katie sat at a table drinking the coffee that Wally brought, and she told them about Leonard's condition, even though Louise had already called to report it.

"And Louise stayed?" Howard seemed baffled by the news.

When Katie arrived, Wally had been putting leftovers out on the kitchen table—buttermilk and stale chunks of cornbread, pinto beans, cabbage and bacon, molasses, butter, a bit of peas and ham hock, half an apple pie. Except for Mabel, who'd eaten that enormous steak supper in Loving, they all took plates to the dining room, where they sat in stunned bewilderment. So much had happened in the last twenty-four hours!

Otis said, "Something you don't know, girl. When I was in Loving getting your gasoline, I bumped into the sheriff and heard him say folks back East were looking for you and that airplane." The look he fixed on her had the dark weight of a weary judge. She set down her fork, sighed.

"Figures," she said. "Sooner or later."

"He aimed to come looking."

"That figures, too."

"He ast me what I knew."

"Can I ask what you told him?"

Otis nodded. "I told him I didn't know much, which is God's honest truth, because you ain't told us diddly."

"And you're making a fool out of everybody here!" exclaimed Wally.

"Tell them!" Mabel burst out. She turned to the others. "She's got a reason, all kinds of reasons."

Katie shrugged, seemingly helpless.

"I tried to throw him off," Otis said. "Mabel drove all the way to Loving to catch him before he got here, and she just got back. She lied for you, too. Turned him right around."

Mabel blushed. "I didn't mind."

"You might when he comes tomorrow because of that oil well spurting all over the place," said Wally, "and believe me, he'll come running because of it, and if finds out the two of you were—what's it called?—betting and aiding? In cahoots, anyway. And lying?"

"Katie . . ." said Mabel.

"Okay, yeah, I'm sorry I didn't tell you all. I did . . . take the Travel Air. I mean I took it without anybody giving me permission."

"Called *stealing*," put in Wally.

"Whose airplane is it?" asked Howard.

"I dunno for sure. Maybe the Beech-Nut Company owns it, and maybe they just leased it from Travel Air. Soon as I got airborne that first day, I knew it was the wrong thing."

"So why not turn around?" asked Wally. "Pretty clear you can land the damn thing good as you can take off in it."

"Well, Judas priest! I didn't want to give them the satisfaction of seeing me grovel."

"Who you talking about?"

"Nobody."

"So—just too darned proud, that it?"

Katie shrugged. "I guess. I told myself at the time that I needed to get to Los Angeles, just to prove I could fly that far by myself. I think my dad's there, in Santa Monica, anyway, working as a pilot and mechanic."

"Tell them the whole story," urged Mabel. "Tell them why you did it, you know, about that fellow."

Katie sighed, ducked her head. "That's the part I'm most ashamed of."

The version that she told, Mabel saw, was missing the details of her mentor's seducing her and *taking* her. Mabel wanted that revealed because it would outrage them on her behalf but understood why Katie held it back. She'd been tricked and betrayed. Curly had led her to believe that they had a future as not only business partners but also as a couple. Katie'd imagined marriage, even.

Then her rival turned out to be her own mother! And her mother and Curly were going to use that airplane to further betray her!

Mabel thought surely everyone could understand how Katie's rage and sorrow had pushed her to do something so rash.

"Good honk!" Wally slapped the table. "When will you girls ever learn?!"

"She's not the first to get fooled by a bounder," said Howard. "And run away."

"You're just lucky you don't have a bun in the oven," Wally added.

Katie made a nest of her crossed arms, laid her head on it. Her shoulders shook. Mabel felt tears running down her cheeks. For a bit no one moved, then Wally leaned across the table and stroked her shoulder.

"It's okay, hon. I shouldn't be barking at *you* about it. You had a tender young heart and that . . . *bastard* just tromped all over it."

Katie gulped a few ragged breaths, lifted her head, sniffed, slid her nose across the sleeve of her blouse. Mabel passed her a napkin, and she wiped her face with it.

"I'm sorry. You know, about lying. I know it wasn't fair."

"I'm not worried," put in Mabel. "I didn't say anything to that sheriff that I couldn't stand behind in a court of law."

"Likewise," said Otis. "Though he and I have a history, and if he comes to remember it sharp enough, he might decide to go over my p's and q's with a magnifier."

"Let's hope not!" Wally dug a cigarette from the pack in her apron and lit it.

Katie heaved a sigh that was half moan.

"So what's your plan?" asked Howard.

Katie shrugged. "When I set down on the street out there however long ago it was, I was just thinking about fueling up and getting some grub and sleep and getting back in the air. I guess in the back of my mind I knew they'd be looking for me, but I thought I could get all the way to California, you know, like that's *olly olly oxen free* or a foreign country."

It pained Mabel to see Katie in such distress. She got up to carry her dirty plate into the kitchen. She set it on the counter there, heard Howard say, "No plan, in other words."

Katie murmured something. When Mabel returned, Otis was saying, "I've got your gasoline. If you get out at first light, you'll be gone by the time anybody who matters might get here."

Katie bit her lip and stared into space, brow furrowed.

"You don't have to go!" declared Mabel. "I mean, we could maybe find out where things stand . . ."

"Where am I going?" Katie asked Otis. "Sooner or later, I'll have to land at an airfield for fuel, and they'll know the second I touch down that I'm the one who stole that Travel Air."

No one had an answer. Wally got up to retrieve the pie tin from the kitchen; meanwhile, Katie twisted her lips, bowed her head, frowned into the plate under her nose.

"I think I'd like to try to call my dad." She raised her brows at Otis. "Would that be okay?"

Otis nodded. Wally, standing in the doorway with the pie tin between her hands, rolled her eyes behind the girl's back.

Katie went into the hallway. While they sat finishing off the pie, they could hear her voice but not distinguish the words, only the volume rising and falling, at one point muted sobbing. As the time went on, Wally kept looking pointedly at Otis and miming punching a key on their cash register, but he just shrugged.

Eventually, she reappeared, cheeks tear-stained and flushed, but smiling weakly as she slid her bicep across her face to wipe away her tears.

"He said just get out there best as I can, and he and some pals would do what they can to help me."

Mabel said, "Oh, I know that must be such a relief for you!" The rational part of her didn't have much trust that the "help" would keep her from being arrested—unless they planned to help her stay a fugitive. Pity surged up for her new friend; her situation seemed hopeless to Mabel despite how hope was glowing in Katie's tear-damp face.

"We oughta gas up your plane tonight," said Otis.

Katie nodded. "There's one thing, though." She turned to Mabel and Wally. "I want to fly you both over to see Leonard tomorrow morning. I promised you a ride. I owe you all so much."

Wally's jaw fell open; her eyes bulged. "Whoa, girl!"

"But . . ." Mabel shook her head.

"I know," Katie said. "I've got it figured out now. If that sheriff is around when we're coming back, I'll just land up the road a few miles or so, and Mister Jefferson can come get you in his truck." To Wally she said, "It'll be safe, I promise. We'll be there before you know it!"

departure

1

MABEL AND KATIE LEFT HER COTTAGE BEFORE DAWN, KATIE
carrying her valise, and Mabel carrying her only winter coat and a head
scarf because Katie had told her and Wally that it would be windy
aloft and maybe cold early on. After their voyage through the clouds,
they'd be at the hospital in late summer heat.

Most of the sleepless night Mabel lay tormented by clanks, groans,
shouts, cars, and trucks rumbling along the street outside the cottage,
making for a surreal, disorienting sense that she'd been transported
from Noname to a location where no one could sit still, where citizens
were afflicted by worries and a horrific restlessness. The world outside
her cottage turned jerkily like a gear with a chipped cog as a rapacious
future set upon them.

Katie fairly radiated an anxious uncertainty but didn't seem to
want to talk about it, no doubt feeling things close in. Mabel wanted
desperately to set her at ease, and there'd been a spell when they'd
spontaneously rolled into a spoon with Mabel's larger form curled
about Katie's and her arms around the warm slim girl. That sweet,
delicious intimacy had less of the self-conscious tension of their previous nights, and it brought back tender memories of Elizabeth. But
it was bittersweet to have discovered this friendship only to have it
yanked away.

The upheaval had torn Mabel loose from her mental moorings,
she felt. She'd manipulated a gullible lawman: lying awake, she wasn't
nearly so pleased with what she'd done as she was shocked about that
possibility in her, though maybe the episode with the salesman and
the wine had brought out her darker side. She'd been glad to "save" her
friend, though she knew that safety was temporary. In cold light, she
had to wonder if the risk of losing her job and facing possible charges
was worth taking for a friendship that might, literally, fly away.

As they left the cottage, even at this hour, strange men were moving
in the street, sitting on automobile running boards and fenders, talking

loudly, and smoking as if it were half past noon. They passed close to three men huddled over a small fire, apparently heating a tin can.

"Hey, gals, where are y'all coming from this time of night?"

Another cat-whistled. The third said, loudly kissing the air, "Come over here, sweetheart, I'll walk you home."

"Aw, up your hole with a totem pole!" Katie called back.

They laughed.

"Double that, you clodhoppers!" Mabel chimed in, astonishing herself.

They hurried to the rear of the Owl, where they let themselves into the kitchen.

Wally had coffee and toast for them. Like Mabel, she wore a house-dress but planned to wrap herself in a blanket. Within minutes, Katie had settled them in the aircraft's forward cockpit and had taken her own place; Otis cranked the propeller, and the raucous engine coughed to life, and Katie brought the craft around the building and into the street. People scurried aside, but Katie had to taxi a good quarter mile out of town before the road cleared enough to lift off.

They climbed, then the aircraft banked and turned north. Wally had completely covered her head and torso with the blanket, but Mabel was eager to experience the view. The sun was just glowing over the eastern horizon above mesas that marked the rim of the Llano Estacado, and as they passed over the city, she marveled at the toy-like buildings, the cars, the ant-like humans, the way the waking light struck the second story of the Owl and its roof, which, she realized, she'd never seen. They flew over the oil well—the inky fluid still spurting, the rig surrounded by trucks, tiny men carrying lanterns, and the huge dark stain spreading over the landscape like spilled paint, filling the arroyos, making rivulets and odiferous swamps, she thought—a hellish wetlands where no plant or animal could ever live.

Being flung through the sky jarred her sense of time, space, and her identity. To think that only one week ago, she had no notion of these volcanic upheavals to their lives. The vivid presence of *unconceived* reality made her anxious—where nothing is stable, anything might happen. She couldn't control events in her life any more than control this aircraft hurling her headlong through the air at a pace she could never have imagined. It made utter folly of any notion of rational deliberation. You might as well throw up your hands.

Have faith, saith the preachers.

Easier said than done.

She soaked in the fresh perspective of the world below, marveling as the sun rose and flooded the Plains with warm yellow light, but it seemed they'd hardly been aloft when she could distinguish the green thread of the Pecos River banks ahead, the irrigation canals spreading out like veins in a leaf, a cluster of multistory buildings, and a girder bridge spanning the river. When Katie turned to land on the dirt road lined beside the hospital, Mabel spied figures standing where the road stopped at the hospital grounds. Once they'd taxied to that entrance, Louise waved merrily as the airplane rolled to a stop.

They left the blanket and coat in the cockpit, then climbed down to the ground. Louise met them clad in a nurse's uniform and seemed jazzed up, frenetic, introducing her companion, a Sister Something, and thumbnailed them each ("Wally owns and operates our only café, and Mabel's our schoolteacher, and of course you remember Katie our aviatrix"). Chattering nonstop, she led them into the building, striding along corridors and climbing stairs to the upper stories, pointing out the maternity ward, the reception room, the doctor's and nurse's lounges, a cafeteria, as if, thought Mabel, she'd worked here for ages. It was oddly jarring—shouldn't Louise be wondering about Howard? But that someone should suddenly behave uncharacteristically no longer surprised her—everything had been upended, and no one was who they were supposed to be, and nothing was the way it had been or should be.

According to Louise, Sister Something had agreed to mentor her for a brief "refresher workshop" while Leonard was recovering, and he's doing just fine, by the way, and all the nurses here are topnotch and so nice about letting her look on. They'd even lent her a uniform. And even though no nurse here had her wartime experience with burns and shellshock and the like, there were *tons* of new developments she was *absolutely thrilled* to be adding to her . . . medicine cabinet, you could call it.

When they turned into the ward, Leonard gave them a wan wave with his free hand. He tried his best, Mabel could tell, to smile as if he weren't in pain. They gathered around his bed, and Wally obviously yearned to hug him but only waggled the air with her opened arms out of fear of doing harm. She kissed his forehead. Katie patted his shoulder. Mabel struggled to keep pity out of her smile but knew she failed as she reached for that waving hand and squeezed it briefly. She was afraid she might burst into tears. It was so good to see that he was alive. Different. (Of course! The pattern was establishing itself in a most thorough way.)

Sister Something left them, and Louise prattled on about Leonard's injuries, his progress, his treatment, like a docent describing a sculpture to museumgoers. Leonard watched her with an odd detachment. The "happy fellow" who was Mabel's Leonard was not in this injured young man's body at the moment.

"Our Lenny is getting the best of care!" Louise made an unnecessary adjustment to the sheet around his bandaged torso. "Aren't you?" She didn't wait an answer. "He's already a favorite!" She beamed at him as if he were a prize pupil. "There's this one little nurse—she's most adorable—and she's been flirting to beat the band with him, and I think our dear Lenny has come down with a case of heartthrob!"

"Aww, God!" groaned Leonard. "Don't say that!" His cheeks were glistening with salve for his burns, and a bandage wrapped around his head at the level of his brow, but, even so, Mabel saw his eyes squinch and his lips twist with annoyance.

Louise flushed quickly, embarrassed to have teased too far. "Oh, pooh, Lenny! You know it's true!"

He shrugged and looked away.

A silence settled. Other voices rose to fill it, a laugh, someone complaining. Floor fans kept up a murmured whir. Louise had been talking so ferociously ever since they'd stepped down from the airplane's wing that her sudden muteness left a vacuum.

"Well, I'll let you all visit and go help in the waiting room. People get awfully anxious and sometimes they need someone to talk to who understands."

Louise strode away. Wally and Mabel exchanged a glance. Wally said, "Lenny, you gave us such a scare!" She tried to smile and tsk-tsk to suggest what happened was the result of his being naughty.

"Sorry," he said.

"Oh, hon, I didn't mean you meant to do it! You know that."

Mabel said, "You look like you don't feel very well. Are you in a lot of pain?"

"It comes and goes."

"Is there anything we can bring you?" asked Wally.

Leonard tried to scootch himself up a little more upright. "Listen, y'all, that's a lot of hooey about that nurse." He turned to gaze at Katie.

Wally said, "Oh, I think Louise was just joshing you."

"The one she's talking about is getting married next month. She's just friendly. I don't know why Miz Larsen would want to say something like that."

"I'm sure she didn't mean any harm by it," put in Mabel. She could've added that Louise was just too darn full of herself right now to think of someone else.

"Well, just please don't go repeating it, especially around here. It would make her feel bad. She's a nice person and she's kind to me. That's all. Okay?"

"No, of course," said Mabel.

After a moment, Wally asked, "Have they said when you might leave?"

"Not really. But Miz Larsen is keen on having me recuperate at her house until I get okay to do things on my own. She wants to make her spare room into a kind of hospital for anybody who needs nursing."

Wally and Mabel locked shocked gazes for a moment.

"Really?" asked Wally.

"What she said."

"I'm sure that will be very good for your recovery," offered Mabel. "Everybody worries about your being so much on your own, anyway. Well, not that your uncle George wouldn't do what he can, of course. But Louise, she's trained. Is *training*."

"Pretty clear to me she's dying to put that peaked hat on again," said Wally.

Leonard wanted to know what all had happened since the gusher blew. They told him how they'd been besieged by strangers. Wally was particularly graphic about being pestered all night by yahoos banging on their door, and Mabel told him about Howard's helping the driller, which, she realized now, Louise didn't know about.

Sister Something returned carrying a trifold screen of white muslin and told them that soon it would be time to tend to Leonard and that the cafeteria was serving breakfast. Wally and Mabel rose to leave.

Katie said, "I'll be along in a bit."

2

LAST NIGHT, AFTER WALLY HAD GONE UPSTAIRS AND MABEL and the pilot had left, Otis went out to fuel the airplane. Howard offered to help, and Otis was grateful, and the two men made short work of the job, Howard siphoning gas from the drum and into a five-gallon can, then passing it up to Otis, who stood on a stepladder to funnel it into the engine's fuel port.

Around them in the night came shouts and hoots, motors, the faint hiss of the gusher spewing in the distance. Light from vehicles on the street, reflected and refracted, struck their faces and the aircraft as they worked. Otis had the impression of being on the periphery of a festival, say, or a circus, and he and Howard were roustabouts working behind the tents for whom the event was employment and not enjoyment.

When they finished, Otis said, "Got a reward for you."

He led Howard into the workshop, lighted a kerosene lantern, pulled two cane-bottom chairs up to a wooden crate, rummaged in a workbench drawer, came up with a bottle.

"Ah," said Howard.

"Sorry I got no water for it."

"Who cares."

Otis poured two tin cups half full.

Howard sipped from his. "Oh, say, that's the real thing."

"Seagram's," said Otis. "Special occasion. I got rotgut too if you'd like."

They laughed. Howard told him how he'd taken the driller home, cleaned him up, tried to treat him, but before long the fellow had come around and started worrying about his well. Howard had notions of what to do when a fellow takes a blast like that—from being over there, you know—but Louise knew a lot more. She might've made the fellow stay in bed.

"It's good we all got somebody around like her," offered Otis.

"A good wife can be a blessing, all right."

Otis took a big slug, swallowed. No time like the present, he reckoned. "They *can* be, true enough. Lord knows there's what's under that rock, too."

Howard put his tin cup up to Otis's to be clinked.

"Wally's put out with me right now."

"Why's that?"

Otis sighed. "My boy—the one over in France, still—I got a letter from him a little while back. Getting homesick, he said. Wants a quiet life. He said he was thinking about having a little farm." Otis laughed. "Well, that's a sweet dream, but that boy never spent a minute of his life with his eye on a mule's bunghole. Got no earthly idea what it takes. He grew up in St. Louis, about as citified a fellow as you can imagine. Plays jazz music on the cornet. I wouldn't try to talk him out of it, though."

"Farming's got its . . . surprises, that's for damn sure."

After a minute, Otis said, "So I had an idea. I bought a piece of land out near the Linam ranch for him, and I can help him get a start. It's got a couple playa lakes, old buffalo wallows you know, and I'm carving off a good bit of it for me and Wally, too."

"Getting your boy back here!? Sure, that's a swell idea. I envy you."

"What I thought. So, I went to the bank in Loving to get a loan though I *knew* all along they wouldn't *go* along, but I figured nothing ventured. Then I went and asked old Bo Bohanan for it, and he said he knew I was good for it, said he'd even take it out in trade—sweat off my brow kind of thing."

"Good of Bo to do that."

Otis grimaced. "Well, that part gets complicated, but I won't go into it. My problem was I didn't say nothing to Wally about it, and she found out about that loan from Arabella before I got around to it."

"Uh-oh!"

"Uh-huh."

"She and your boy . . ."

"Well, she's never met him. He was off to France before Wally and I got together, you see. I got no reason to think this wouldn't be a good thing to her, but I still haven't worked up to telling her what the money's for."

"Where's the boy's mother?"

"Aw, she up and left when he was just a tyke. As far as being my wife goes, I can't fault her for it—I reckon I was way too much of something and way too little of anything else. But I was pretty bitter on my boy's behalf."

"If you don't mind my asking, why keep Wally in the dark?"

"I'm just jittery about it. Kept thinking I would wait for the right time to spring it, but sure enough the right time just whizzed by and the wrong time came running up, instead."

"I know what that's like."

"Thing is, the trickiest part would've been telling her I got the money off Bo. You know how she is about Arabella."

They sipped companionably in the lull. The lantern burned steadily though the wick was smoking. Needed trimming, Otis noted.

"I reckon you can guess how much it'd mean to me to have him back here."

"Oh, yeah."

"You suppose your girl's ever gonna want to come home?"

Howard sighed, set the tin cup on the table, put his elbows on his knees, his chin between his palms.

"There's always hope."

"In the meantime, though, you ever thought about starting all over? I mean, Louise is young and healthy. Wally tells me she's got what she calls baby fever."

"We talk about it. Some. I just can't seem to get ready for something like that."

"Well, if you ask me—and I know you haven't—I'd just say any child of the two of you would be a lucky duck. And if Izzy took a notion to come back, having a little sister or brother could be a bonus for her."

"It's possible."

"Well, I won't say another word about that. Pardon me for butting into your business in the first place."

"Oh, no, no, Otis. I appreciate it."

Good, thought Otis. Louise, I've done my duty. Hope it helps.

In the morning, after he'd helped Katie crank up her airplane's engine, he made a big vat of coffee in a stockpot—not the tastiest joe anybody'd ever quaffed, for sure—set it on a table by the front door, added cups (no saucers) and glasses, a tin of sugar, a spoon, an empty tin can for "donations," and went back inside. Folks could at least help themselves to that.

Howard showed up just after first light with a slab of bacon, five pounds of potatoes, three dozen eggs, and two pounds of butter. No, it wasn't all from his larder—when he'd gone to query the Petersen girls about coming to work, their ma had volunteered about half of what he'd brought.

By eight o'clock the Owl's lantern light drew the famished like moths; no sooner did they discover the coffee on the porch than they were coming through the door for grub. Soon every table was taken, and some fellows sat on the floor and held a plate in their lap.

Howard, Otis, and the Petersen twins held their own for an hour or two, and eventually the crowd thinned out. They'd run out of bread first, then the eggs, then the hash browns, and were down to the last half pound of bacon when the sheriff showed up. Otis spotted him standing on the porch jawing with someone.

Otis scooted into the kitchen and busied himself scraping and washing plates. Sure enough, though, the sheriff walked to the rear to find him. He looked up from the sink.

"Mornin', Sheriff."

"Morning. Otis, ain't it?"

"That's right. Can I get you a cup of mud?"

"Naw, thanks. Had some."

Otis turned back to the vat of soapy water.

"I'm still looking for that airplane, like I said yesterday at Harley's. Like I told you yesterday."

"Well, Sheriff, I don't believe it's still here. Like I said yesterday, there was a chance it'd already gone."

"They're telling me out yonder that it's been parked in your lot, and it took off early this morning."

Otis jerked his head back as if KO'd by an uppercut. "Sheriff, that's the first I've heard about it! As you know, I was over in Loving and when I got back, I'll swear on a stack of Bibles ten miles high there wasn't no airplane out there, and I spent most of the afternoon at that burning rig trying to keep folks from getting hurt and came back last night plumb wore out and didn't hear scratch. You been out there?"

"It's the main reason I came. On my way."

"Well, stay careful."

"We ain't through talking."

He left out the back door as if wanting to take still another look around for a missing airplane. When he was sure the sheriff had gone, Otis told the Petersens and Howard that if the sheriff came looking for him later, tell him Otis was out fixing a leak on the workshop roof. The plan was for him to nail a big red towel to the peak if Katie needed to fly on by and land five miles back up the road at a dry-creek crossing, where she could leave her passengers and then be aloft again before the sheriff could catch her.

3

LEONARD'S DENIAL WAS A HALF-TRUTH. LOUISE SAID HE HAD "a case of heartthrob," but things were more complicated than they might imagine. Cooped inside his fractured form, Leonard itched with agitation to be forced to lie still hours on end, day and night, although Adorable Nurse had promised to help him walk about soon as he felt like it. Right now, with a few broken ribs taped up, it did smart when he moved his torso, but out of their scrutiny he'd already been sitting up and practicing steps around his bed, probing, wincing, and grimacing, to check how each little move might reverberate in his pain center.

The torture started when he lay still. When Adorable Nurse leaned over him to change the dressing on his forehead, her pert Adorable Bosom loomed like a ripely waxing moon in his vision, and her Adorable Womanly Scent made him swoon. Her Adorable Fingers gently stroking the salve onto his raw and tender cheeks—it hurt and yet didn't hurt. When Adorable Nurse swabbed his neck and legs and stomach with a soft cloth, soap, and warm water using her Adorable Hands, her Adorable Chestnut Hair glistening where it poked out from under her cap, her Adorable Little Bow Lips curling to smile, her Adorable Chatter about her Pekinese named Kong, all the while swabbing, swabbing, his thighs . . . 11 times 11 are 121, 11 times 12 are 132, and so forth because it was too easy to start at 1 x 1, and the strain on his brain to calculate the results beat back the swelling desire. *My, how you're sweating!* Adorable Nurse observed. *Would you like to me turn a fan a little more your way?*

He'd watch her walk away. Couldn't help it. Wasn't his fault he was trapped in bed and couldn't go hoist a calf or ride his bike ten miles or do his nightly pushups to leech off that energy. Was it? When he was plumped with desire, it did at least keep his mind off other troubles, but, really, when you came down to it, when Adorable Nurse came nigh, his first thought was: *I sure don't get much pleasure from this pleasure.*

What baffled him: just three years ago as Mabel's pupil, he was always agog to watch her lips speak, her neck turn, her thighs move her skirt from side to side, her brown eyes glisten, and there was her throaty laugh, her gentle teasing mockery when she caught him skylarking. Oh, Lord! There'd never been such a female in the entire universe! It would about make him burst into tears to imagine her sitting on a sofa and letting him put his head in her lap and looking up into her eyes as she fingered the tendrils of hair falling over his forehead, the nerve ends in the back of his scalp like a thousand tiny fingers absorbing the heat of her thighs, that secret place massaged by the weight of his cranium, her arching over and her bosom pressing his cheek, his face . . .

She'd been his first, and it shook him to his core when he dared to imagine that he might kiss her—this was long after he was her pupil—and she'd gently put him off. Broke his cotton-picking heart. To him, Mabel and desire were married, and he mistakenly presumed that no other could ever arouse him. He was stuck with her whether she returned his ardor or not.

Then Katie showed up. And that stupid fickle desire just said adios to Mabel like it was merrily off on a vacation and stepped right over to this red-headed pixie whose freckled face lit up his heart. Same mess. Again. It seemed awfully . . . *unfair* really, that he'd been caught so off-guard by the sudden shift. No warning whatsoever! This weird thing inside had its own mind, its own plans, and would go willy-nilly turning his head this way and that with no regard for his personal loyalty to the previous object of his desire, using his whanger like a divining rod.

So, when he blurted out to Louise, "Don't say that!!" about his yen for Adorable Nurse, he hadn't meant it wasn't true. He'd meant he didn't want it to be true, didn't need for it to be true, and calling attention to it made everything worse and more confusing. If other people noticed, then he was trapped with it.

So, the first thing he said to Katie when Mabel and Wally had left for the cafeteria was, "I swear to God about that nurse, Katie."

"I believe you." She scooted her chair up close to his bed. She leaned back and dug into her trouser pocket. "I want you to have this."

She handed over a pewter-colored disc to his free hand. He lifted it up to his face.

"What is it?"

"Something I've been toting for a while. Kind of a good luck charm."

"Don't you need it?"

She shrugged. "You've been my luck in so many ways."

"Aw, gee. Thanks!" He turned it over. "Who's Curly?"

"A pilot. He taught me to fly. Anyway, I just thought this could be something to remember me by."

"Are you leaving?" His heart thumped, and he heard his fear in his voice.

"Yeah."

"When?"

"Well . . . today. After I get Mabel and Miz Jackson back to Noname, I'm flying west. I hope to make El Paso by sundown. Yesterday when I was here checking the craft, a couple of fellows came out to see it. They've got a Jenny they take out now and then. They flew in France. I asked them about getting to El Paso, and they said I could fly the railroad and the highway from here to Artesia, then follow the highway west to Alamogordo over the mountains, then I could pick up the railroad and the highway south to El Paso. They said if the weather holds, I could probably make it in five hours. They gave me a highway map and gas to get back to Noname yesterday."

Her plan was so detailed it stripped the maybe out of leaving. It seemed a feeble hope, but he said, "I sure wish you'd consider staying. Noname's got no airplanes. You'd be a big frog in a tiny pond, you know. Bring people to the train depot in Seagraves or here—be a flying ambulance and a taxi."

She took his hand—fisted over the medallion—and held it with both of hers. Her face wrinkled up. He thought she'd start crying.

"I wish I could. I really do. I want you to know that I never had much of a chance to be around kids my own age or around people who weren't like carnival folks, always putting on shows somewhere then pulling up stakes. I never had much of a chance to get to know other kinds of people. Like you. You are *so* super! You might be the nicest person I ever met." She grinned. "Even if you did tear a big hole in my elevator."

He tugged his hand free of hers and pulled the sheet up over his face.

"Lenny?"

After a moment, he let it fall back down to his chest. He sighed. His eyes felt raw, his vision a little blurry.

"Now I wish more than ever that you'd stay!"

She looked toward the entrance to the ward. "It's not exactly a choice. Here's what everybody else knows now that I need to tell you. That airplane's not mine, I mean, you probably figured that. I took it without the owner's permission. And so now they're looking for it. And me, I guess."

"You *stole* it?"

She winced. "Well, I guess you could say that *technically*."

"Why?"

She whooshed out a big breath. "I was mad at my mom. And I felt like she had stolen a big chance for me. And she was going to use the Travel Air in a special tour I was supposed to go on. There's more to the story, but that's basically it. I just wanted to get back at her."

"Can't you just tell her you're sorry and give it back?"

"I wrecked it. Well, damaged it, you know. And she doesn't own it, either. So, she's not the one who'd need the apology. It's just a big mess. I called my dad in Santa Monica last night, and he told me he'd help me. He's never been all that reliable, but he's my best shot."

At the far end of the ward, a nun was approaching with a tray of paraphernalia, followed by Nurse Adorable, who stopped to chat with a patient, and those two were trailed by Wally and Mabel, returning from the cafeteria.

"Promise you'll write to me, okay?" he put in hurriedly.

4

LEONARD WAS IN LOUISE'S KITCHEN WHEN WALLY BROUGHT Katie's first letter to him. He'd been enjoying three days of recuperation. Leonard had insisted he didn't need anything special now that he could walk, but Louise argued that there was no need to take chances, fractured bones needed rest and time to mend, germs abounded, etc.

Louise hoped to use Leonard to test how far she could go in colonizing Izzy's room. She was hoping Howard would adjust to it. And she could argue that he'd put that filthy, oil-drenched driller right into Izzy's bed without a second thought or consulting her.

She wouldn't say that she'd plundered the supply cabinets at St. Francis for her "homemade hospital." No outright thievery. She'd put on her best bonnet of persuasion with Sister Emilia, chief warden of the medicinal pantry, and told her of the great need the inhabitants of Noname had for modern medicines, braces, crutches, splints, rolls of gauze and tape, alcohol and iodine, and the makings of Dakil solution and biochloride of mercury for surface sterilizing, and how she herself was always in despair for wanting to help people and simply not having the resources, *especially the little children, Sister*, it just plain *wrecks me* to see them suffer!

She was about to mention Jesus as an implicit endorser of her scheme but bit her tongue. The nuns were, after all, members of the order of the Sisters of the Most Precious Blood, so they shouldn't need a reminder of their vows. Sister Emilia was sympathetic, and together they walked the shelves to identify overstocks or items seldom used or things so common the hospital regularly restocked them, Louise holding a big cardboard box between her arms while the nun plucked items and laid them in it. Later, Louise snuck back on her own and doubled her booty, telling herself that she had "permission" and that Sister Emilia had been interrupted before they'd finished.

These efforts helped to heal the wound that had opened in her during her stay at St. Francis Xavier. The sharp memory of being useful and being among colleagues day in day out kept biting at her. The hospital had four floors, had recently undergone renovations and additions, was burgeoning with surgical personnel, attendants, orderlies, and auxiliary staff, as it struggled to cope with the city's growing population from the potash mines and the opening of the caverns. That, too, was part of her misery—Carlsbad was a *town*, of around two thousand souls, with a multistory red brick county courthouse with its spire and a "downtown" boasting several other brick buildings. A library! A post office! All the amenities that Arabella had hopes for bringing to Noname. It seemed silly to be so awed by these most fundamental features of a bona fide city. After all, she'd grown up in Kansas City and gone to nursing school and worked in Chicago! But she'd grown so used to being isolated, with everything that once mattered withering away bit by bit, that she'd apparently become only half-aware of the loss. That airplane flight was like a time machine whipping her into the future and the past simultaneously, ripping her right out of her present circumstances.

Her humble "hospital" in Noname was a little pathetic when you got right down to it, she thought, but it was all she could do. She'd already scouted out possibilities for when Leonard would leave—Edith Hemphill was having a difficult pregnancy and maybe could be talked into taking a rest period to be restored in Louise's care. And with all the horrid industrial activity, workers were bound to get injured—Lenny was a prime example—and they'd need to be nursed.

By the time Katie's letter had come, Leonard was balking about staying at the Larsens. When Wally brought it, the supposed invalid was wolfing down a stack of buckwheat cakes and molasses and a glass of milk. Louise had wisely realized that trying to scare him with infections to keep him settled wasn't her only tool.

He was, unnecessarily, still in pajamas, a pair of Howard's old ones.

Louise insisted that he needn't be dressed for a meal, thinking this might help him to picture himself as a patient.

Wally sat at the table, slid the letter to him.

"Go on. It's from your honeypie."

He set down his fork, peered at the envelope.

"She's not my *honeypie*, Wally."

"Well, ain't you mighty fickle."

He shrugged.

Louise said, "If you'd rather wait until later . . ."

Wally said, "If she ain't his honeypie, then what she says could be news for everybody, right?" She grinned at him.

He opened the letter, a single page apparently. His eyes widened. "She's in the El Paso County jail!"

"What happened?" asked Louise. He palmed up to sign hold on, spent a few moments reading, folded the letter, slid it back into the envelope. He sighed. "Well, she says that when she landed there, they were on the lookout for her. She says her dad's coming on the train from Los Angeles to bail her out and take her back there if they let him."

"What else?" asked Wally.

He blushed. Louise said lightly, "Now, Wally, let the boy have a little privacy."

"With all the trouble that girl put us through, we pretty much have a claim to about everything there is to do with her."

Leonard said, "She wasn't a bit of trouble for me. Not one single bit, Wally."

Louise poked Wally's shoulder with a forefinger. "Didn't you tell me yesterday that the airplane ride was the most exciting thing ever happen to you?"

"Like to scared me to death," Wally grumbled.

Soon as Leonard had cleared his plate, Wally said, "I best be getting back. Left our new help in charge, and no telling what kind of mess I'll find."

"Who you got?" asked Leonard.

"The Petersen twins and a pal of theirs. They're way too young to have a lick of sense, but I reckon that's how we roped them into it. Only a crazy person or an idjit would wanna run a café in times like these. I let Otis talk me into serving breakfast, and now he's poking me about dinner."

"It'd be nice to have someplace to go for dinner," Louise mused. She was picturing candles, white linen tablecloths, an elderly Italian waiter, a violinist.

"Well, don't hold your breath. I'm about to tear my hair out as it is."

When she rose from the table, Leonard did, too. "Miz Larsen, I need to get back to my own place. I'm sure deep in your debt for all your good care and concern, but . . ."

"Oh, dear, Leonard! Are you sure you're up to it?"

"I reckon it was hearing we're offering breakfast these days."

Louise turned on her. "When did you ever *not* make him breakfast, Wally?"

"Aw, y'all, don't fuss. I just need to be . . . on my own a bit, figure things out."

After Leonard had gone, Louise sat drinking coffee and brooding. Itchy with dissatisfaction, like her skin could hardly contain her. When Howard came in, she was on the verge of digging out her secret stash of cigarettes and lighting one right in her own kitchen.

"I saw Lenny leaving with them." He sounded neither sad nor glad.

"He's had enough of *my* nursing, I guess."

"Oh, now sweetheart." He stood beside her and gently pat her shoulder. "You did him a world of good, no doubt about it."

She laid her forehead on the table and burst into sobs. He kept patting her shoulder the way you might a horse about to bolt. "There, there, sweetheart." That her crying always scared him a little never failed to both annoy and gratify her. When she wound down, he slipped into a chair at the table.

"You really think so?"

"Well, sure! You saw how healthy he looks, like a new man."

"It's easier to fix them when they're young and strong." Except, she considered, when they've had their brains bombarded silly or that hardy young flesh is riven by shrapnel.

"True to a point," said Howard.

"Was it okay for him to be here? I mean, okay for you?"

After a moment, he nodded. "Yeah. He and I got to chat some. If he'd stayed any longer, I'd have dug out my old chess set. He's a good lad. And it was good to think we were helping."

How gratifying that "we" was!

"Yes, I can't tell you how much pleasure it was to use what little knowledge I have, Howard. I know you missed me when I was at the hospital, and I'm sorry I wasn't here to help make things run smooth. But it did make me think—I mean, having Lenny here. When I was at Wally's yesterday I saw Edith Hemphill's sister—you know, Edna? the one with the birthmark on her cheek?—anyway, she said that Edith was having a hard time with the new one she's got in the oven and the doctor over in Loving told her that if she didn't stay in bed more she was liable to, you know, have some *medical disaster* befall her, and she'd heard, Edna that is, about Lenny recuperating here and she wondered if we couldn't put her up a little while just to keep her quiet and strong and her unborn baby safe from harm." She paused, took a breath. "I told her I'd talk to you about it."

"Hmm," said Howard.

"You remember Edith was the one gave us that incubator?"

"Hmm, yeah."

She kept quiet. She ached for that cigarette. She damn sure wasn't going to beg him. Such a small thing to ask for!

"Was she planning to pay, like at a doctor's office or a hospital? Or were you planning on just being neighborly?"

"I hadn't gotten that far," she said, feeling sullen. "I just told you I said I'd talk to you about it."

Howard stared at the ceiling. "Well, I don't see anything in particular wrong with the idea. I mean, so long as this doesn't become a house of charity." The phrasing maybe alluded to quibbling they'd had about the "influence" those Catholics supposedly had on her. "I guess having a bit of pin money would be a good thing for you."

Like a hobby, she thought. "I wouldn't dream of charging people—I mean Edith—any more than she thought she could easily pay, Howard. It just wouldn't be . . . neighborly."

"Yes, yes, you're right."

For an instant, her hidden elation urged her to build on this small success by mentioning the prospect of new workers here needing treatment, but she checked the impulse. When and if Edith had come and gone, then they'd see.

"Other thing is," Howard said. "I've always felt blessed to have a mate who pitches in like an equal. I'm thankful for it, sweetheart, truly I am. I don't know of anybody who's a harder worker. I couldn't begin to run this place without your help. I knew that right from the start back at Fort Sheridan. You're the kind of person who doesn't know how to say no to people, and I've always admired seeing how much you're willing to help your friends and people around you."

She knew Howard could be perfectly sincere in saying this as well as calculating how the effect of it on her might be useful to him. She reached over to squeeze his forearm and smile her thanks. Waited.

"I worry sometimes you'll work yourself sick. Can you promise me that taking on an extra burden—like Lenny or Edith—won't get to be too much for you? I just don't want to see you overdo things."

She suspected he meant that he didn't want her to apportion out her labor in any way that shorted her ordinary chores. She'd been careful about that the past three days, leaving no room for complaint. He would see those duties as first priority, of course, and it wasn't unreasonable to ask that—but it irritated her, anyway.

"Yes, of course! This farm is mine too, Howard. I'm your wife, first and foremost."

"That's all I ask!" he bent to peck her cheek. He appeared to be on the verge of bolting for the barn, so she set her hand on his forearm.

"How have I seemed to you?"

He looked puzzled. "How . . .?"

"I mean, since I came back from Carlsbad."

"Huh!" His brow furrowed; he squinted. "Now that you mention it, I'd say charged up, Sweetheart. Just charged up. I think you needed that vacation—"

"I wasn't on a vacation! I was—"

"Oh, no, sure, I meant distraction, maybe. No, that's not right, either. Change of pace? Change of place? I know you weren't sitting on your duff, Louise—didn't I just tell you how I know how hard you always work at everything? I just meant when you got back, I could tell being over there had been good for your spirits. It made me happy to see you that way."

She smiled. "Thank you."

Later they both took to the marital bed with expectations. Louise felt not only charitable but also "charged up," as he would say, needy in an indefinable way that looked to pleasure with Howard as a possible source of satisfaction, even if temporary. They knew each other; they could read the otherwise invisible signs of mutual desire. Louise felt that the experience of the past several days and her absence had jolted him from his fixation about Izzy. She guessed that his bountiful good mood came from feeling that he'd been generous with her, and so was feeling pretty darned pleased with himself. To have him concede to her heart's desire—well, men didn't seem to realize this, but that was . . . stimulating, far more so than flexing their muscles.

Ten minutes after he'd blown out the lantern, she excused herself to go the washroom. It was part of their ritual. She had no need to light a lantern. She moved quietly in the dark to the oak washstand and slid open the top drawer, reached into the back until her fingers found a small wooden box. She drew it out, set it on the top of the washstand, lifted the lid. Even if you weren't a nurse, you'd know you're supposed to wash your hands before handling it. She felt pent up, emotional, hurried, eager to get to it, and then get it over. Dealing with the device always took the edge off any urgency.

She turned on the bathtub tap, scrubbed her hands, and dried them.

Next, she retrieved a bottle of mineral oil from the drawer. She opened it, dribbled some onto her fingers, then lifted out her diaphragm. She dabbed the rim with the oil. She'd been told Vaseline would degrade the material. It was getting old, anyway, and possibly it would fail her sooner or later.

Despite how she'd done this many times and thanked her lucky stars she lived in an era when such contrivances were available, she balked now. After a moment, she sat back on the rim of the tub, as usual, lifted her nightgown, as usual, parted her knees, as usual, the diaphragm in her left hand, the circle pinched to a bow. Sometimes she'd add drops of vinegar in the cup for added safety, but now it seemed far too much trouble, and the procedure was draining off her *charged-up* sensations.

To hell with it, she thought. She stuffed the thing back in its box, put the box away, and shut the drawer.

5

MABEL WAS IN HER SCHOOLROOM PACKING HER TEACHING materials when George Purvis dropped off Katie's letter, a week after Leonard had received his. Katie had written it while on the train to Los Angeles with her father. She apologized for not writing sooner— she'd been in the middle of a whirlwind like those "dust devils" Mabel had shown her. She asked Mabel to say "howdy" to Leonard and Mrs. Larsen and her husband, and of course to Otis and Mrs. Jackson. *I owe you all so much.*

Yes, yes, yes, okay. The impersonality of it was, well, disappointing. Then Katie related how she came to be out of jail and on the train. Mabel understood that it would be her charge to pass along this news. She sighed. Yes, she wanted to know. She could see already that the thread led to a good end—otherwise, Katie wouldn't be on the train. Mabel was relieved she was out of danger, anyway.

Katie told her father the whole story about Curly and her mom, how Curly had dangled the possibility of making her his partner on the Beech-Nut tour, and how he'd *taken* her then betrayed her. *But please don't tell people this part!* (Well, it was nice to be the confidante!) Her dad was *hopping mad as Big H Big E double hockey sticks!* Mabel smiled and the girl's face floated into memory. Her dad called her mom and Curly both and told them that he knew every single detail about their sordid stuff and that if his daughter wasn't out of jail in twenty-four hours the police up there were going to get an earful about how a particular grown man did what he did to an innocent girl, and if they didn't get on the horn toot sweet and call the El Paso County District Attorney and tell him that they didn't want charges filed and that they'd *given permission* to take that aircraft, and if they had any doubts about getting that done *yesterday*, her dad was going to have sex crime charges brought against Curly and parental neglect against her mom, and that he was just about to go talk to the Beech-Nut folks, too. *Boy, howdy, you can bet that lit a fire under them!*

The nicest thing is, she wrote, he'd stopped drinking.

This was wonderful news, really. When you got down to it, though, even if Sheriff Browne had caught Katie, this might be the outcome, and so Mabel's "aiding and betting," as Wally put it, was superfluous. Who would've bailed out Mabel if the sheriff charged her as an accomplice? He too was "hopping mad as Big H Big E double hockey sticks" when he drove up moments after Katie had taken off from the road and had left Wally and Mabel standing in the dust raised by the propeller. *Why, Sheriff, we were just taking a stroll when that airplane just came out of nowhere and set right down here on the road, and then before we could even think twice, why then it took right off again!*

The letter's following paragraphs contained more news but nothing to do with Mabel personally. What had she expected? Katie's tone wasn't cold—it was breezy, happy go lucky, full of relief for her personal circumstance. But Mabel's thoughts about Katie had grown warmer by the day. She'd looked forward to being pen pals. She'd ignored Katie's legal problems and imagined going to visit Katie, maybe in California. These new details of her escape made that possible, though nothing in the letter invited it, so far.

My bed seems cold. That was to have been the first sentence of her own letter soon as she had an address to send it to.

Mabel sighed and turned back to the page. She'd never seen Katie's handwriting, and she judged it a bit childish and slap-dash, though readable. She'd written in pencil on paper torn from a Big Chief tablet. The awkward cursive and the cheap student paper made Mabel's heart ache, though she couldn't have said why.

Katie and her dad had wonderful plans, she wrote. They were taking time off to be together again and fly his Waco down to Cabo San Lucas, in Mexico, where he liked to fish. He was hoping to find commercial pilot work soon, and he said she could partner with him soon as she took the test, but for her it would probably be a snap! She was so excited about it!

So—the sword of the law was not poised over Katie's neck. She was blissfully free to relish the present and dream of a rosy future. She was wrapped up in her*self* in a way that was hurtful. Mabel and everyone in Noname would quickly evaporate from Katie's memory—there'd been no *please write and let me know how everybody is doing.* No fixed address, apparently, not even on the envelope, though surely that dad gets his mail somewhere. A painful oversight, surely not deliberate, merely the thoughtlessness of a person in thrall to her enthusiasm about a new life.

But then, at last, below her signature, an added note, separated as if intended only for Mabel: *I miss you a lot. I never thought I'd miss somebody Id only known for a couple of days, but I do really miss you. I think if we had a chance we could of been the dearest of friends! More slumber parties!!* Punctuated by a drawn heart colored in by, Mabel guessed, red nail polish.

Trembling, she set the letter down. Closed her eyes. Drew a breath. *Oh, Katie dear! You have no idea.*

As they were flying back from Carlsbad and were approaching Noname, Mabel kept a keen eye out for the red towel nailed to the ridgetop. As they passed over the Owl, they all spotted it, and Katie flew back north to the low-water crossing and landed. Mabel and

Wally crawled out of the front cockpit; Wally went down the wing to the ground before her, but Mabel stopped at the rim of the rear cockpit. Katie didn't plan to get out. With her goggles over her eyes and her helmet covering her hair, she was unidentifiable except for those freckled cheeks and mulberry-colored lips. Mabel leaned into the cockpit. Katie turned her face up toward her. A thought bubbled out of Mabel's mouth—*I love you!*—but the engine's throaty gurgle and the prop wash whisked the words away. She lurched forward and kissed Katie half on her mouth and half on her cheek. "Be safe!" she yelled.

They could see the rooster tail of the sheriff's approaching car as they stood in the road enveloped by the aircraft's dusty wake.

Wally said, "Your tears are making mud on your cheeks."

She folded the pages, put them in the envelope, opened the desk drawer, set the letter in it, closed the drawer. She rose slowly and went back to work, distracted.

Five minutes later, Arabella Bohanan came through the building's side door, the sounds of truck traffic on the street billowing in around her as she closed it.

"Good morning, Arabella."

"Good morning, Mabel."

Without waiting for an invitation, Arabella seated herself in a student's desk just before the teacher's desk, and Mabel reseated herself behind it.

"I just wanted you to know we've found a replacement, albeit temporary."

"Oh, how wonderful! I'm so relieved! You know I hated the idea of leaving you all in the lurch."

Arabella twisted her lips into a sour kiss. "Well, truthfully, Mabel, you couldn't have hated it all that much."

"I thought it was better now than after the term begins."

"I wish you'd reconsider."

After a moment, Mabel said, "Will she be from here?"

"He. No. A Mister Wilbarger."

"Oh, well, that will be a good change for the children."

"He can't come for a few weeks. He's in Abilene. Marianne Weaver will be coming next week to fill in for him."

"Oh, that's nice! Marianne will be good. Tell her that she can come by any time next couple of days, and I can go over our materials with her."

Mabel felt they were both struggling to be civil. Arabella had been deeply offended when Mabel had told her she was leaving. A matter of personal loyalty, it seemed. She told Mabel she'd been counting on Mabel's support in getting control of the chaos that had descended upon them. Within a week's time, four new shacks had been knocked up on the street for fly-by-night enterprises of the sort that boom towns seem to propagate like toadstools, and the sheriff had had to deputize a cousin to set up shop in one to keep the riffraff from turning the whole place upside down. Lacking a jail, he'd pounded two long steel posts deep in the ground fifty feet apart then stretched a chain between them, to which he padlocked his miscreants like dangles on a charm bracelet until they could be transported to Loving.

She had kept asking Mabel why.

Mabel had given evasive answers. Whatever motive she had was not Arabella's business, but also Mabel herself couldn't sort it out. It had something to do with Katie, or, rather with Katie's coming, or, rather, with having discovered a need she didn't fully understand, and her instincts told her that it wouldn't be fulfilled here. She could argue a lack of amenities and culture, or she could lie and say family matters demanded her presence back home. But she couldn't tell the truth because that remained murky, unnamed.

And now, Arabella appeared on the brink of asking again—Did we do something? Can we make any change that will keep you?

Mabel said, "I just got a letter from our aviatrix."

"Oh! I certainly hope you can share something of it!"

This was a dig. Mabel ignored it. "Of course. She wants us all to know how things are turning out." She told Arabella that Katie had singled out Arabella's fund raising to be the single most important help she got here. Mabel explained that Katie'd taken the airplane during a family squabble and that the family had arranged for her to be released from the El Paso County jail without charges, that she was now with her father in a new enterprise.

"Well, I'm so happy to hear that she seems to be thriving." Mabel noted the sarcasm. "I have to tell you I am still a bit sore that she lied to me. And here I'd gone so far out of my way to get all my friends together to hear her talk about what she hoped to do in that national race and all! It made me feel awfully foolish to learn later that most everything she told us was just pure hogwash. And I'd worked my fingers to the bone twenty-fours straight to arrange for that reception!" Arabella shook her head. "We were just hoodwinked. More than one person has complained to me about it, and they resent having been asked to donate knowing what they know now. If I knew where to find her, I just might demand that she pay back every single penny, I mean every red cent."

Mabel sighed. "Yes, that was wrong. No doubt about it."

Arabella waited as if to hear Mabel defend Katie, maybe wanting an argument that would give her an excuse to exercise her indignation at greater length and volume, but Mabel didn't take the bait.

"Well, I will tell Marianne Weaver that you're expecting her so that you can give her an orientation." Arabella rose, and Mabel took her cue and followed. They walked to the door, where, before opening it, Arabella said, "Surely you have no objection to giving Marianne that part of your monthly wage that you've already received but that you won't be here to work for. It would be two weeks' salary."

"None whatsoever."

6

"SAY, FELLA, WHAT THE SAM HILL ARE YOU DOING IN MY house!?"

The man was perched on the edge of Leonard's cot, unlacing a boot when Leonard lifted the door flap to his tipi and stepped inside.

"Aw, heck," groaned the fellow. "I'm just all sapped."

Leonard guessed him to be about his own age, blue denim overalls, a ragged old newsboy cap, shocks of blonde hair sticking out from under the bill. One eye looked swollen, red as rare beef.

"Well, that's my bed you're sitting on, too. You planning to nap on it?"

"That be okay with you? I can't find no place around here to stay."

"Where you reckon I'll sleep?"

"I only need it a few ares every afternoon 'cause I'm working all the damn time. How much you take to rent it?"

"I ain't renting out my own damn bed."

The fellow sighed, relaced the boot, rose, retrieved a bundle belted by a hank of hemp rope. He was a scrawny specimen, blow on him big he'd topple over.

"You got any notion where a man might go to lay his head?"

"Sorry. Reckon you're a whole lot more than a day late and a dollar short."

The fellow shrugged, nimbly stepped over the tipi's threshold, disappeared. Leonard felt a tad sorrier for him than his manner had shown but only a little. His native human sympathies had been sorely strained the last week since returning from the Larsens. On first setting foot inside his lodge since the day he'd gone to work for the driller, it was obvious somebody had made themselves at home. His sleeping bag was lying on the floor, books from his shelf likewise. A quick inventory showed to his relief that nothing had been taken—his crystal set seemed unmolested.

But a couple nights later while he was listening to WBAP, two drunk galoots barged in looking for "a squaw." And the next day in came a mother with two small children wanting to show them "some injuns." Obviously, some people presumed that this Comanche buffalo-skin lodge was a museum display, or, even if not, they presumed they had the right to poke their nose into a Comanche's house without an invitation. He'd written PRIVATE RESIDENCE on a chunk of cardboard tacked it to a stake and planted it beside the entrance. It had failed to deter the weary roustabout, however.

Leonard was exhausted, too. He was slinging his body about night and day, working not only for his uncle George—whose business now boomed—but also for several contractors and for Otis and Wally. Otis had hired a crew to add a big dining room onto the existing downstairs, and Leonard had worked as a framing carpenter and drove Otis's truck to the rail depot in Seagraves for lumber and hardware. Wally kept encouraging him to go into business as a contractor, not just be somebody's peon, this was his chance to build a future. Right time and place.

But it was only the right place and right time for that kind of work, and he didn't want to spend a lifetime at it.

He told her he did like being busy—it "keeps my mind off things," he said, "things" being primarily his lack of a mate. The sentences in Katie's letter that made him blush while reading it in front of Louise and Wally—they'd deeply wounded his spirits. It distressed and puzzled him that he couldn't inspire a reciprocal passion in a woman. Katie said, *You are probly the sweetest boy I ever met, your somebody a girl could trust to always do the right thing by her, the kind of boy most girls would look for to spend a life time with, I just know youll be a great dad too and I count myself really lucky to have had a chance to get to know you and I wont ever forget you.*

So, he thought, that's why you could never love me?

The whole thing about men and women was just plain crazy!

And then—to get kicked when he was down—he'd been eating a baloney sandwich in Wally's kitchen when she said, "I was just talking to Vera Gimble, and she said she heard that Mabel wasn't coming back to school. Did she say anything about that to you?"

"No! Really? You think it's true?"

Wally shrugged. "Dunno. She hasn't been herself lately, I do know that."

She's not alone, thought Leonard. "Gawd! I sure hope that's not true!"

Stunned, he spent the afternoon only half-dazed as he unloaded lumber from Otis's truck and hand-sawed studs. Why hadn't Mabel told him, told them? That she'd not said anything meant, maybe, that it was only a wild rumor. Everything here was so topsy-turvy anything could be false one minute and true the next or vice versa. He longed to seek her out to get this rumor confirmed or denied, but it would be embarrassing to ask and have it confirmed only to feel he'd been left out of the decision, as if not only his opinion didn't matter but also the effect of her decision on him didn't, either.

Just another bitter pill to swallow.

Meanwhile, at the Seagraves terminal, he'd spied a magazine on the desk of the freight agent. It was titled *Radio News*. He'd had a notion that such periodicals likely existed but had never seen one. This issue was from January 1927, and when he asked about it, the agent shrugged and said another fellow brought them by from time to time.

"Would you take a nickel for it?"

The agent chuckled and said sure, and when Leonard passed the coin and took the magazine, his hands were trembling.

The agent smirked. "Gee whiz, sonny, it ain't like it's a bunch of French postcards."

"Is to me."

The magazine was a treasure trove about electronics, advertisements for Cunningham radio tubes and Crosley radios and Tower speakers, and dozens of companies and products he'd never heard of; information about how to build your own three-tube universal shortwave receiver, an advertisement for a radio training course that promised "to pay for itself" by getting you into the radio business—*if you're earning less than $50 a week, clip the coupon for* FREE BOOK!! *Profusely illustrated, it tells all about the radio profession, thousands of openings* . . .

He wasn't a sap—he knew a come-on when he saw it. But still it was thrilling to think of these prospects.

The bulk of the 127 pages consisted of articles on history, technical things, plans, graphs, photographs of promising new devices ("What's New in Radio?"), articles on visible radio waves and broadcasting the weather, a list of all stations broadcasting in the United States—so many wonderful topics such as "Some Facts About Condensers," all written by experts and illustrated with schemata and photographs. "Radio News of the Month"— *The French government has just put into force a requirement that all commercial planes carrying ten passengers must be equipped with radiotelegraphic equipment . . .*

Getting all the way through this marvel word by word might take him weeks, he guessed, and he knew a lot of it he wouldn't understand. And that smarted.

This was only one month's issue! A year's subscription of twelve issues was $2.50. Soon as he could, he'd send off for one.

One night just after WBAP had signed off, he lit his kerosene lamp and turned to the magazine. He started a baffling article titled "The Carborundum Superheterodyne Receiver: An Ultra-Sensitive Long-Distance Circuit Using a Crystal Second Detector," then he heard Mabel call from outside his tipi.

"Lenny, are you there?"

He went to the flap and pushed it to the side.

"Hey, Mabel." It was extremely peculiar for her to walk in the dark this late with roughnecks roaming the settlement. Though she'd never been inside, he said, "Come on in."

They stood in the tipi's tall space. She looked about. "You know, I always wondered what the inside of this thing was like."

He shrugged. He felt both resentment and shame, and maybe irritated at her for his own embarrassment now that she'd proven to be so disloyal.

"*I* like it."

She spotted the magazine on his cot.

"Did I interrupt you? What are you reading? You know that Louise and Wally and I and some others often trade magazines with one another, you might be—"

"Not something y'all would care for, I reckon. *Radio News* is what it's called."

"Oh. No, I suppose not, unless it's about singing stars."

"It ain't." He let that nasal offender hang in the air unapologetically.

When she didn't correct him, he said, "Well, I'll give you a tour. That's my dresser." He pointed to it. "That's my desk. You already saw my bed." The thought rushed up to show off his crystal radio set, but he slapped it silly for rearing its head. "That there chair I got from Frank Bower's wife. She was gonna toss it out."

"May I sit in it, please?"

She was being especially polite in a way that was supposed to rebuke his bad manners, he guessed. But hellfire, it was eleven o'clock at night, and he hadn't asked her to show up, had he?

"Yeah, sure."

She eased into the chair, and he backed into his desk and shoved his hips onto it.

"I've got something I need to talk to you about."

"Boy, I *bet* you have!"

His outburst startled her. She sighed. "Well, I guess you've heard already. Lenny, you are the very first person I've talked to personally, I swear. But you know I had to tell Arabella because she had to replace me."

"I just figured you didn't care."

"No, no. Of course not! I do care. Very much," she said quietly.

Her softness and the idea that she'd come to him first threatened to break down his protective wall. A stinging sensation pushed up behind his eyes.

"I thought because you didn't talk to me that maybe it was just junk people were making up."

"No, it's true."

"But *why?*" He hated to sound whiney. "And where? I mean I thought you liked it here."

"I did. I have. I *do.*"

"So?"

"I never meant to stay forever. I was only going to stay one year because it was such a novelty, such a challenge. Then you know one year just became another and then another, and I realized that I could just watch my whole life slip away bit by bit without, you know, taking control of it."

"Is there a fellow somewhere?"

"Oh, God no, Lenny!"

"Do you *have* to?"

She looked away, recrossed her legs. "I need to."

"Where are you planning to go?"

She shrugged. "California, I guess."

"You *guess?!*"

"I mean some place I've never seen but always heard about. A bigger world than here." She smiled wanly. "You know, where there's electricity."

"Electricity."

"That's just a . . . synecdoche, I mean an example, you know, of what a more civilized place would have. Indoor plumbing."

"People been walking this Earth a long time without it."

She sighed. "Lenny, I don't want to argue about this." She seemed to scrutinize his face, and he tried to make it a mask of cool indifference. Apparently failed, because she said, "I know this hurts."

"I'm not all gaga over you no more. Any more."

She smiled. He let his heels bump against the drawers of the desk. "Take me with you."

Her mouth parted slightly, and she looked away.

"Lenny, you've been such a good friend—"

He shoved off the desk and stood. "Aw, now don't give me that speech again! I just said I'm not thinking of you that way. I don't mean that I'd want to be with you out there. Just hitch a ride, Mabel. I got savings, I can share the expense and the driving, and if anything goes wrong with that Lizzie, then I'll be there. Flat tire. Whatever. And you're just a woman alone out there on that road—you know you've got to cross the Mojave Desert, right?"

"Lenny, I . . ."

"When we get there, I promise I'll get out of that car and you won't ever set eyes on me again!"

"Oh, Lenny! Don't talk like that! That wouldn't be why . . ."

"What, then?"

"You have a life here. Wally thinks she's your mother and Otis's been as good as a father to you. I know he doesn't always show it, but I know your uncle George would miss you."

"So you think nobody's going to miss *you*?" He felt his voice rising, his blood beginning to rush into his skull. "So you're saying you wouldn't want me to go with you because it would be better for me to stay here?"

"I guess so," she murmured.

"Well, you wanna talk about *electricity*?"

He stepped to the cot, snatched up the magazine, riffled through the pages, raised it to read. "Listen here: The neutralized T. R. F. stage is of standard design, a split plate coil and balancing condenser being used for neutralization. A rheostat is included in the filament circuit to afford a check on regeneration and self-oscillation of the first tube . . .'" He slapped the magazine against his thigh. "Did you understand that?"

"No, not at all."

"Does it bother you that you don't?"

"Well, not really. I wouldn't expect—"

"Well, I don't understand it, either! And it bothers me one whole HELL of a lot! Pardon my French."

She nodded.

"If I ever want to understand something like that I need to be somewhere besides here. I don't plan to dig ditches and swing a hammer the rest of my life. And you know that. And if you really have my best interests at heart, you're gonna think twice about leaving me here."

7

OTIS TOLD WALLY HE HAD SOMETHING TO SHOW HER, SO after the breakfast rush, they left the girls and Delphy to prepare for the lunch mob. The new dining room was near completion, and since Wally had promised the twins a "promotion" after it had opened, they were eager to assure Wally that they could handle the responsibility. Wally had found herself coming to terms with their burgeoning business. She'd always been reluctant to be ambitious mostly because she felt a need to control every little thing, but she'd discovered that being in *command* had its pleasures, too, so she was assembling a staff big enough to release her from the grunt work.

Before they left in Otis's truck—not the old GMC but a '27 Ford pickup he'd traded up for—Wally had picked up the mail at George Purvis's store. She was sorting through it as they pulled into the street behind a string of trucks.

"How come you're not telling me where we're off to?" The mail was mostly invoices, bills. "You whisking me away on a dream vacation?"

Otis chuckled. "Now, if I was, where would that be? I got no idea of what you'd call one of those."

"Hmm. Well, maybe back to Pensacola, Florida. Went out deep-sea fishing one time. Caught a swordfish!"

Otis laughed. "How was it you did that?"

"Fellow was courting me."

"So this is a love story?"

"Well, might've been if he hadn't tried to steal all my money."

The day had started fairly cool, typical of an early October morning on the high plains, but as the sun was out, the rays flooded the cab and warmed her cheek as she flipped through the envelopes. There'd been a little zing of anxiety to not know their destination, but she settled into accepting it as an adventure.

"Hey, here's a letter from Lenny!" She waved the envelope.

"Read it out."

As she unsheathed the letter from the envelope, she noted that they'd gone past the turnoff to the Larsens, where she'd thought maybe they were headed.

"He says, '*Hi, folks! I'm awfully sorry it has taken me so darn long to let you know how and where I am but I've been busy as all get-out, I swear! Right now I'm living in Fresno California in a boarding house with a bunch of other galoots and bachelors and some downright no-goods if you want to know the truth. The landlady serves meals down in the dining room and they call it family style but it must be the worst-mannered family in the world, no kidding! And it just means they plop that food out there on the table and let all of us start scrambling for it, and if you don't get there right off the bat you might find yourself gnawing your shoe soles for comfort. They got a thing called 'boarding house reach' which is where some fellow next to you climbs into your lap to get at the bowl of taters on your other side when he ought to just say Pass the taters,* please*! I swear, Wally, I do terribly horribly miss your kitchen and your cooking and of course your own sweet self!'*

She broke off. "Aw, that boy! I miss him something awful!"

Otis took a hand off the wheel to dig into an overalls pocket for a handkerchief, passed it to her. They'd just turned off the Carlsbad road and were headed east toward the distant mesa on a sandy two-rut lane. The holes and pits in it jostled her and made it hard to read. "He says he's working all the time. *'This place has all kinds of fruits and vegetables and a whole lot of grapes that they use to make raisins. They are so happy about their raisins that they have a whole festival for them, parade with a band and cute girls high-kicking. Right now I'm working days at a place that cans tomatoes. I used to like them. But my big news is that I'm taking classes at the college here in electrical engineering at night! I have to study hard and do a lot of reading, so as you can imagine between working all day in the cannery and going to class, that doesn't leave a lot of hours free. But I'm happy as a clam, I swear, even though I am dog-tired most of the time. (Okay, I know Mabel would say I can't be a clam and a dog both!) Anyway, what happened was I went to Los Angeles with Mabel but that place was just too darned big and I met this fellow on the bus who told me about this town and the college. Anyway, the teachers are really interesting. One of them is talking about . . ."* Wally studied the word a moment. "Ruh-DAR?"

"What?" Otis asked.

"Maybe it's ray-dar. *'talking about radar. It's like radio waves going out and bouncing off of things and coming back to report in where it found that thing, you could say. Really neat stuff at school! Well, I better quite yakking and get some shut-eye. You all please write back to me c/o this address*

because I won't likely move unless I get too scared I'm gonna starve to
death or wind up charged with assault and battery over a last piece of pie!'

Wally could picture him at a boardinghouse table and felt a twinge of pity but also knew he was exaggerating and could likely hold his own. She'd heard from Louise that Mabel was teaching school and living with another schoolteacher she'd met. The two of them took little trips together on the roommate's motorcycle, of all things. Mabel was a more lusty-spirited person than most people gave her credit for, Wally thought.

The uncultivated fields beside the road showed hillocks of reddish sand topped by Spanish dagger and scrub oak, and the path dipped up and down over dry creek beds. As much as she was tempted to ask where they were going, she'd pretend indifference to provoke him into telling her first. The new truck was dandy, the bench seat comfy, the windows cranked up and down with ease, the motor noise quiet. Horn worked, too. Riding like a queen, you might say, sitting up pretty in something this shiny. Their profits were rising steadily, but she wondered if he'd used Bo's loan to buy the vehicle.

They went up a rise, and when they topped it, a house popped into view. Were they visiting somebody? Her eyes weren't so great beyond lariat-length, so it wasn't until he pulled into the yard that she saw it was vacant. Maybe hadn't had paint since the last century. Two windows looking onto the porch had no glass.

"Where the heck are we?" This came despite herself.

He got out and walked toward the porch. She sighed, opened the door, and stepped down. It was breezy out here, a bit nippy, and she pulled the wings of her sweater closer. He stood on the porch looking out over the fields. A big mesquite thicket grew up close. A rust-colored Hereford standing inside it was pooping a big brown stream while it grazed.

"All right, buster. I've had about enough of that buttoned lip."

He laughed. "You remember old Ray Showalter?"

"Horse kicked his head in?"

"This used to be his place."

"Ain't much to brag about so far."

"A hunnerd acres, some fenced. A well with a mill out back."

"So?" Her suspicions were tingling in her nerve ends.

"Let's take a look inside."

The instant he passed inside she knew what the deal was. No black man was going to just waltz into a white man's house empty or not without permission, and the owner of this wreck was stone cold dead.

Or he might go in there if it was his own.

She kept her trap shut and trailed along through the four rooms. The first room had a fireplace and an upturned cap on the mantle that held a bird's nest. An old calendar pinned to the wall, a beat-up sofa, old newspapers strewn about on the linoleum. The second room had a metal bed frame with peeling paint and a straight chair, the third was a kind of kitchen with cabinet doors ajar and shelves empty but for a saucer with a candle stub stuck to it, two old cane-bottom chairs with butt-sprung seats. There was a washroom with, surprisingly, a tub, filled with two orange crates and an empty motor oil can on its side.

"Old Ray wasn't much on keeping house."

"I reckon it was nice enough at one time. Could be again."

"All right, Otis. I ain't nobody's fool. You used that money you got from Bo to buy this place, didn't you?"

He grinned, but she didn't soften. "What—you planning on hitching me to a damn plow?"

"No, no, no, nothing like that! I ain't a farmer. Here, sit down a minute."

She took one cane-bottom chair, feeling repelled by the dust, he the other.

"I just don't think it's right that somebody who works as hard as you do ought to live in an attic. You deserve a house, a real house. And I want to give you one and live in it with you. I know right now this old place looks like the Devil's own abode, but you know how handy I am, and I can make it into a palace. I swear, Wally, when I'm through with it you'll be the happiest woman in the county."

"It needs about everything."

"True."

"What are you planning on doing with them hunnerd acres?"

"Most we can lease out for grazing. Or you might wanna have a new house on some other part—we'll go take a look. Plenty of room for more than one house."

"You reckon there's oil under it?"

"I don't know." He studied her face. "And I don't plan to find out."

That elicited a tiny dry smile. He did indeed understand who he was talking to. "That's good to know."

"Here's what I'm thinking. I—"

"How come you didn't say diddly squat about doing this? You know how upset I was when I had to hear from Arabella about getting that money from Bo? And you just kept saying it was a surprise. I see it was. Indeed, it was. How come you did that without word one about it, Otis? What if I don't give a hoot about this house or this land and tell you that you can just come live in your own damn palace by your own damn self?"

"Hon, I can sell it easy as I bought it. I got it before that oil well blew in so I reckon now it's worth twice what I paid."

"That don't answer my other question."

Otis sighed, planted his elbows on his thighs, and cupped his face between his palms. "I know, I know. That was plain wrong. But I guess I had a dream of us having a place like this together, away from everything, and I was afraid you'd bust the bubble before I'd had a chance to blow into it. I'm sorry, I really am. And like I said, you just say the word, and it's gone."

She mulled in irritation a moment. She had the upper hand, she knew, but wasn't sure whether to play it. Aside from her resentment of not being consulted, in truth, the prospect of getting out of that damn stuffy attic tugged at her. Having a *home*. Wouldn't have to clomp down the stairs when a yahoo banged on the cafe door. She took in a deep breath, caught a whiff of something foul.

"I think a critter died under the floorboards."

"You're probably right. Let's go to the porch."

They sat on the top stairstep. Wally surveyed the vista—rolling grassland, scrub cedar, mesquite, a big sky full of various weather, a low ridge in the distance giving the horizon visual interest.

"Not a bad view."

"Quiet. That's what I like." After a moment, Otis added, "There's something else."

"Uh-oh!" She gave him a twisted grin.

From his coat pocket he pulled out a little blue box and passed it over. She opened it.

"Aw, Otis. You silly thing! Is that a real diamond?"

"Hope to heck it is. Go ahead and put it on."

She slipped the ring on then waggled her fingers. "This mean you're marrying me?"

"Hope to."

She thought a moment. "Is this a bribe for playing along with your nonsense or a reward?"

"Well, I hope it's a show of how much you mean to me, hon."

"Why now?"

"Aw, I reckon it's because everything seems to be getting so hectic and complicated and noisy that I think we can be more of a team this way and keep it all off our backs. Us against the world."

"Does that mean I *always* get a say in what's to be done about things?"

He chuckled. "Sad but true."

Despite her inexplicable need to resist, she smiled. "You are a dog, Otis Jefferson."

"Is that your way of saying yes?"

She bumped his hip with her own, then looped her arm through his elbow and laid her cheek on his shoulder.

"I want a wedding, a real wedding. We can have it in our new dining room."

"Fine with me."

"I wish Lenny and Mabel were still here. They'll miss it."

"Me, too." After a moment, he said, "But I think there's one person for sure we oughta invite."

"Who's that?"

"Sheriff Browne."

Wally burst into laughter. "Oh, *hell* yes!"

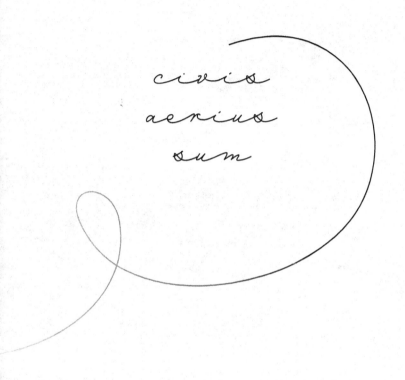

civis
aerius
sum

AT GALVESTON'S SCHOLES FIELD, SHE WENT THROUGH THE hanger door marked *Texas Air Transport Only*. Men at the table looked up then went back to their poker game. The air was blue with cigar smoke, and light streaming through high windows made a sinuous dazzling cloud of it. The mechanic, Bert, had his back to her. Mayo was across from him, but she was relieved that Rory was there, too.

She moved up behind Bert. Their table was the lid of an oil drum. Bert was perched low atop an upturned bucket, so she could see his cards. Five-card stud. He had a pair of 9s in hand, and two useless up-cards on the table. She was antsy but knew not to interrupt.

"Good morning, glory," said Rory when the hand had gone to Mayo. "You about to lift off?"

"In a bit."

Because she kept standing mute like a dummy, it gave Mayo the window to say, "What's he want?"

"Dad wants to know anybody got notes on the flight path to Love?"

"Where's his?"

"Uh . . . got wet."

Mayo said, "He oughta be able to sleepwalk it by now."

Bert, who'd gotten crosswise with her dad a time or two, said, "Maybe he was sleepwalking when he flew it before."

They laughed. He meant drunk.

"You were along, right?" Mayo tapped his cigar against the drum lid, and the ash nub tumbled to the concrete. "Didn't you pay any mind?"

She kept looking at Rory. She'd hoped to catch him alone. He was watching the cards fan in a fluttery blur as he shuffled. She'd always liked him, but his friendly manner reminded her too much of Curly, so she'd kept her distance. She hesitated to ask again—another lie would double her dad's embarrassment.

"Well," she said, "I reckon we'll reckon it."

"That's the spirit," said Mayo.

She strode toward the door, and Rory called to her back, "In my locker, Katie."

Mayo said, "But don't be taking anything's not yours."

They all laughed.

"Very funny."

A door led from the lounge into a long dark hallway that gave onto a room with a dozen metal wall lockers, a wooden bench running between as at a gymnasium, a shower room with two heads, two urinals, and a toilet in a stall. She avoided using this toilet but was thankful when she had to for the enclosure. Invariably, it seemed, when she was on the pot a pilot sauntered in to whizz not a foot away from the thin ply panel.

She hesitated on the threshold.

"Anybody here?"

She moved into the silence. White adhesive tape with Rory Book-out inscribed in brown with maybe a Crayola. She opened the unlocked door. A wristwatch, tie tack, and cufflinks were loose in the bottom. Of course, she wouldn't take anything not hers! She was tired of the joke. Her dad in his cups bragged about his little girl flying solo from Memphis to El Paso—and they had filled in the rest. She was "the girl who stole that Travel Air and flew it solo cross country." And wrecked it. They teased her about the theft, but they'd all wrecked an airplane or two, and her fugitive flight established her bona fides. They still ribbed her about being a "woman driver," but knew she was licensed now.

She needed to reframe their picture of her. She needed to shed the reputation of a person who'd take an airplane without permission on an impulse and without the experience needed to safely fly it. The days of slap-dash, swash-buckling aviators was slipping away, and if she wanted a future as a *paid pilot*, she'd have to impress somebody that she had a good head on her shoulders. And double for being female. No commercial airmail carrier had a female pilot on contract. Officially she was only her dad's sidekick assistant in some undefined service. Her dad couldn't log her in as a pilot, though she suspected the ground crews and many pilots knew the truth.

Rory's black book the size of an accountant's ledger leaned against the locker's inner wall. She carried it back into the lounge. The men were gone. At a battered roll-top desk she leafed through the pages for notes on CAM #21. She ignored the details between Scholes and the Houston airfield—short hop over Galveston Bay, then follow ships up the channel past Morgan's Point, over the bridge to Baytown until you reached the Port of Houston's Turning Basin. Then it's Buffalo Bayou and the channel west until you see two dirt runways and hangers.

From the field there, Waco stood 163 airmiles to the northwest. She used the back side of an old invoice to copy his notes. Yes, she had flown the route before but as a kind of stowaway lying on mail sacks in the dark cubby fashioned out of the airplane's forward cockpit, and that was the brunt of Mayo's embarrassing wisecrack.

Rory had knitted a flight path using local roads and the Southern Pacific rail lines, noting the towns threaded like beads in sequence—Hockley, Waller, Prairie View, Navasota, Bryan, Hearne—with landmarks (*Hearne water tower has name, at Navasota Brazos Riv runs se-nw on left, Southr'n Pacfc rail hub in Hockley*). Compass bearing 319.79° (NW). She'd stopped an incoming pilot to check the wind and the weather upstate—5 to 10 mph out of the SW as usual, with clear sailing under high cirrus to Waco, so she estimated two hours in the air to Rich Field.

Another eighty-seven miles north from there to Love. Unfortunately, she couldn't make out his notes on that leg clearly as he'd apparently spilled coffee on them. She wrote a thank-you to Rory on another scrap, slipped it into the logbook, and returned the ledger to his locker.

It was going on nine o'clock when she strode out of the hanger carrying a parachute slung over her shoulder. Her dad refused to wear one. Ironically, she used it out of deference to the rules of the company whose other rules she blatantly flouted. Out on the airstrip, theirs was the only aircraft in sight, parked perpendicular to the path with the prop overhanging the strip, *Texas Air Transport US Mail No. 21* in flowing yellow script on its gleaming dark green fuselage. The company maintained a fleet of Pitcairn PA-5 Mailwings, and the others were out at various points of the service area: San Antonio, Austin, Brownsville, Fort Worth, Dallas, Waco, Houston, Galveston, and Beaumont. The airplanes were new, produced and manufactured specifically for airmail duty, and had no space for a passenger. She appreciated the off-again, on-again chance to pilot it, depending on her dad, though done on the sly and at risk to his job.

When she'd left the airplane earlier, her dad was sitting on the port side tire, smoking and rubbing his temples. Now nowhere to be seen. She sighed. So exasperating. And to think he hoped to move up to TAT's coming passenger service out of Fort Worth's Meachum to Chicago, hoped to fly the six-passenger Fokker Superuniversals with the enclosed cockpit. *Crew of two!* he'd say and grin, as if he actually believed TAT would put her in the co-pilot seat of that airplane. Or any other. And then he'd talk about how they needed a more settled life, so he might get hired as an instructor for TAT's flying schools in San Antonio or Dallas.

All well and good, Dad, but where are you *right now*? She'd had a devil of a time getting him here this morning. He woke her up at 6 a.m. coming in, fell onto the cot they'd rented at the front desk, and an hour later she'd risen and shaken him roughly, roused him enough for him to dress, went downstairs to the hotel's kitchen and brought back coffee.

He'd fallen asleep in the taxi on the way to Scholes.

Something knocked against the side of the fuselage. She hopped onto the trailing edge of the lower wing and stepped to the rim of the mail bin. Down in the dimness, he was sprawled atop dark gray canvas mail sacks, so while she was gone, they'd brought it. He was rubbing his face with his palms and yawning.

"Are you awake?" She meant *Are you fit to fly?*

"Yeah," he groaned. He leaned up on his elbows.

"We're due in Houston shortly."

"Aw, damnation. I feel like Death warmed over." Apparently holding himself half-upright took too great an effort, so he collapsed and pitched his head back into the bags.

"Where'd you go last night?"

"Aw, Jack Briggs knew somebody has a cottage at Crystal Beach. We were gonna fish."

"What happened."

"Aw, you know. Got to thinking."

What she figured. "And so you got to drinking."

"About the size of it."

She hated this excuse: *Just thinking about your mom and it got me down.* Once she'd snapped back—*Other way around, Dad. Why do you think she left?*

When he seemed to be falling asleep, she leaned into the bin, grabbed his ankle, and yanked on it.

"Hey! I will take us to Rich, but you've got to fly the leg into Love because there's too many company people there."

"Deal."

"Open or closed?"

His vague wave and squint showed the light annoyed him. She tugged the heavy waxed canvas over the mail bin's mouth and used the cover's snaps to secure it. When she rode there, she liked to have it open—she could rise up on her knees, hang her arms over the gunwale with her chin propped on stacked wrists, and watch the countryside pass by. The sky bloomed before and above the craft with its marvelous cloudish array, while below, towns and settlements with their mysteriously unknown citizenry would ease from fore to aft as if on a leisurely conveyor belt. From her aerial perspective, they appeared more or less the same, but she'd learned otherwise—almost always when a tiny cluster of dwellings slid into view she remembered the first sight of Noname and could imagine that down there lived a Mabel and a Leonard who could be a friend, an Otis and Wally an aunt or uncle, or that fellow with the happy but smelly dog and his wife who seemed to have a maternal streak that, like a moving sunbeam, had shone briefly on Katie. Then, she'd feel anew the yearning and envy for the connection she imagined they felt for one another. The memory was bittersweet and the thoughts too melancholy to suit her, really, since she believed herself to be, as she always said, a half-full kind of person. Or wanted to be. If she studied her life too closely, she wound up listing too many "have-no's," so it was better not to.

She needed to be settled, helmeted, in the cockpit before they sent somebody out to prop the airplane—not that whoever it was wouldn't realize that she was there and not her dad, as this was an open secret. But it was better practice to be as inconspicuous as possible. She slipped into the parachute and hoisted herself up using the built-in steps on the flank of the fuselage, lowered herself into the pilot's seat.

Hunkered down, having to wait, she sighed, drifted into a blue mood. Always a double-edged thing, these opportunities, and she sometimes felt guilty for the eagerness that swelled up in her to pilot the craft when her dad wasn't up to it. He could snooze down there in the bin right through a squall, though, confident in her ability even though the bin had no restraints for humans, and if you needed to be strapped down while the airplane pitched and bucked and yawed, you had to burrow under the roped-down sacks.

She wished her dad . . .

Well, if wishes were horses . . .

Despite her best intentions, the blue funk chased her down. Have no family, really. Sure, there's her dad, but when he was like this, he might as well be married to his problem and father to his problem, his family was nothing but his problem, and she always felt lonely and helpless and yet responsible. People ask where are you from, and she has no from. Or to—except for a boardinghouse on Gaston in Dallas where she and her dad live in separate rooms and you hardly ever know from one day to the next who'll show up at the dinner table, more likely than not the person you were hoping wouldn't. A boy named Billy Owens had a room across from hers for a while, worked in the big Sears & Roebuck warehouse on Lamar cruising the aisles on roller-skates filling orders, and he was fun to talk to, but he wanted to kiss more than talk and went back home to East Texas, anyway . . . However much those yahoos in the pilot's lounge might respect her skills, she feared she wasn't going to be a bona fide pilot anytime soon, and she might as well go to secretarial school like those Foster sisters down the hall and spend all day bent over a typewriter, and another girl who lived there worked in a mattress factory in Deep Ellum, planted at a sewing machine and said one time, without being asked, I can get you on if you like.

She sighed.

Boo hoo.

Poor Katie.

Bert walked out from the hanger and gave her a big phony wave and a grin as he strode past the wings to the nose. They got the engine running, he pulled the wheel chocks, she looked into the sky at both ends of the strip to make sure it was clear, revved and pulled the aircraft into line.

She held the brakes and goosed the engine, watching the tach. The radial-piston power soared up through the seat and into her spine, shoulders, and she released the brakes and shoved the throttle full open. She half-checked her air speed, scanned the oil temp and oil pressure fuel level dials, the time, the compass, but more of her awareness sank in toward her own body. Her dad and all the old-timers—Curly included—always said don't fly by the instruments all the time, fly by your butt, your back, your arms, you gotta feel the craft in your soles, your calves, your thighs, your haunches, you listen to the wind singing or whining in the wires, you gotta wear the damn thing like a big suit, like your body is half-aluminum and wood sticks and linen and your airplane has your blood in the lines, your flesh in the wings, like you're a big ole actual bird—that's the way we flew, the way you learn to fly.

So, she looked ahead but pitched her awareness down into her gut, where the machine felt loggy, heavy, earth-bound, straining forward with complaint, like a fat boy aroused out of dream-sleep and instantly put to work on a coal-barge towline on a canal *ugh ugh ugh ooo ooo ooo*, struggling to summon and condense its own weight. Then the second wind, the sprint, the airplane rolling and roaring faster down the strip like a race car, that speed quickening her pulse, the machine outpacing its own drowsy mechanical resistance, bouncing a bit on the outrigger landing struts, the wings flexing and testing the airflow, tentatively, gingerly, bringing the wheels up an inch or two then down, gathering its mechanical confidence, its readiness. And for Katie these were the relished and useful moments, so exhilarating and healing—it seemed each forward foot, each upward inch, stiff-armed away her troubles as they clutched at her, knocked off those have-no's one by one, the weight of the craft freeing from gravity, her weight with it, her sadness with it, the sky ahead beckoning.

This was her ritual practice, this way of healing, and at the instant the airplane escaped the grip of the turf when as she eased back the stick to lift the nose, she spoke a phrase like a mantra. She'd seen it on a name plate in a hangar at Love and asked the fellow sitting at the desk what it meant. He said it was Latin, gave her the translation, and the phrase lit her up like standing in the glare of landing lights. Oh, Jeepers! she said. That's so wonderful! I oughta get that tattooed on my arm!

Civis Aerius Sum, she murmured now as bright yellow wings flung up their tips to embrace a welcoming sky. *Civis Aerius Sum.*

I am a citizen of the air.

AFTERWORD

LIKE MANY AMERICANS, I GREW UP THINKING AMELIA EARHART was the only notable woman pilot in the twentieth century, her fame solidified by her doomed effort at flying around the globe and the mystery of its end. My protagonist, Katie Burke, is quick to let her people know that she is only one among many. (By one count, by 1930, two hundred women had earned a license.) My idea of her singular fame was underscored by this connection: growing up in a small town in New Mexico (Hobbs), I once heard that Earhart made a forced landing in 1928 on the only street—scarcely more than a dirt path—in what was then only a village of a dozen buildings.

Her emergency landing must've caused quite a stir, I thought.

Testing the tale decades later, I learned that in September 1928, she set out to make her first solo cross-continental flight from East to West in an open-cockpit biplane. She made many stops, one in Hobbs. As one biographer has it (*East to the Dawn* by Susan Butler), "The townspeople helped her fold up the wings of the little Avian and move it to a safe place for the night (an overhelpful cowboy managed to put his foot through a wing; a piece of tablecloth was glued down over it), fed her at the Owl Cafe, found her some gasoline, and gave her a bed. The next morning, she took off down Main Street."

She had motor trouble and had to set down in Toyah, Texas, was then towed to Pecos, Texas, where she spent a few days waiting for her engine to be repaired.

While my story is obviously based loosely on that flight, I was quickly led into reading about the aviatrixes of the 1910s and 1920s. Some were more colorful than Earhart (Pancho Barnes, for example), maybe better pilots, certainly equally worthy of attention. (As a side note, I'd add that it wasn't until 1934 that a female pilot, Helen Richey, was licensed to fly the mail from Washington, DC, to Detroit piloting a Ford Trimotor.)

I didn't want to write a thinly disguised fictionalization of Earhart's exploits but rather wanted to use the events for my own purposes as a novelist. I was as interested in the inhabitants of the town as I was in the pilot who set down among them.